## ALL'S FAIR IN LOVE AND WAR. . . .

*Maude Teasdale Cavendish,* a twenty-nine year old divorcée, was eager to be an independent career woman and see her byline on the front page of the *San Francisco Globe.*

*George Teasdale,* Maude's younger brother. An expert Boy Scout, he saw spies under every monocle.

*Sophie Von Gluck,* the temptress spy. A mistress of disguise, her patriotic zeal was something to be reckoned with.

*Baron Gustav Wechsler,* impoverished gentry with his own hopes for Germany's future. He knew Sophie's tricks better than any man alive.

*Louise Arbor,* unschooled in politics, but Phi Beta Kappa in the arts of flirtation and romance.

*Professor Arbor,* the only American scientist who could manufacture helium for the enemy, though against his will.

D1054987

# YOUNG
# MRS. CAVENDISH
# AND
# THE KAISER'S MEN

## K. K. Beck

IVY BOOKS • NEW YORK

Ivy Books
Published by Ballantine Books
Copyright © 1987 by K.K. Beck

Library of Congress Catalog Card Number: 87-15314

ISBN 0-8041-0370-4

This edition published by arrangement with Walker and Company.

All the characters and events portrayed in this story are fictitious.

Manufactured in the United States of America

First Ballantine Books Edition: April 1989

To Ernest, who found the story.

# PROLOGUE

**K**ARL Joachim Kohler had been wandering in the desert for some time before he began to ask himself where he was going, and indeed, where he had been. The sun was low on the horizon and the vast sky was taking on a deep blue cast—bluer than any sky he had ever seen at home. Something about the slant of the rays and the shadows of the tall saguaro cactuses gave him the impression it was morning.

He stopped and looked behind him. There was a line of footprints in the sand. It was packed down hard, but he could make out a trail, a trail that seemed to waver and zigzag. It was when he saw those footprints that he became alarmed. These weren't the footsteps of a sane man.

He looked down at himself and was startled to see he was wearing a thin cotton nightshirt and his feet were bare. They were also cut. On his head, he wore a black homburg hat.

Of course! That was it. He had decided to leave. He had decided to take his hat and go. He remembered now, the little square adobe room, the narrow bed, the fever. The fever had broken during the night. He had awoken bathed in sweat, the thin fabric of the nightshirt clinging to him. Somehow he had got it into his mind that he must go

1

home. Back to Hamburg. Back to the cool, quiet house on the lake. And he had taken his hat and set out. It had been absurdly easy. The guard was asleep. And he had simply spread the barbed wires apart and slipped between them. He looked down at his small, plump hands. They were cut across the palm. As soon as he saw the wounds he remembered the barbed wire biting into them. The memory made them hurt again.

He must have been mad. It wasn't just the fever. It was madness, brought on by months in this terrible place. And his nerves had always been delicate. "The price you must pay for your fine intellect," his mother had always told him.

He must get back to the camp. He couldn't survive out here. He looked up at the sun and saw black spots before his eyes. But they weren't spots, he realized, they were birds, great black birds making circles in the sky. They were vultures, waiting for him to die. Hideous birds with glossy black feathers and naked red necks for more efficient scavenging. He had seen a picture of them in a book as a boy.

How long ago that seemed, sitting on the slick horsehair sofa in his mother's parlor, his legs straight out because they were too short to bend at the edge of the sofa, a book propped in his lap. The parlor had been so cozy, with a fire in the fireplace and rain falling outside the leaded diamond panes of the window. He remembered so vividly the wallpaper in that room, yellow, with bunches of flowers in baskets and ribbons on the handles of the baskets.

He would never see that wallpaper again, he supposed. Or any other, or any living person. But no, he was being morbid again. A little rest was what he needed and then he would set out again, and when his work was finished he'd sail home and it would all be a nightmare from the past.

Right now it was easy just to slip into unconsciousness for a moment. Right now, the sun didn't seem so cruel. It was rather pleasant, actually. He removed his hat, set it next to him, and relaxed on the scorching sand. He let his mind drift back to that yellow wallpaper in the parlor.

2

\*    \*    \*

About an hour later, three men on horseback came up to the figure in the white nightshirt, the black homburg hat set precisely at its side.

As they came closer, a few vultures who were hopping quietly some yards away moved off, still curious but less brave.

The leader of the men dismounted. He was tall and dark, with curly black hair shining with sweat coming out from under the brim of his sombrero. But his eyes, framed by dark lashes, were a smoky blue. He knelt down by Karl Joachim Kohler and emptied a canteen full of water on his face. "Dr. Kohler?" he shouted.

The doctor's eyes opened, and his round pink face became animated. He clutched the hand that held the canteen. "You won't bury me here?" he said. "You mustn't bury me here, Herr Gottlieb." And then his head fell back again, and a rasping noise came from his throat.

A little later, when they decided Dr. Kohler was indeed dead, Gottlieb gave an order to the other men in Spanish. They dug a shallow grave in the sand, taking turns with a short shovel that had been attached to one of the saddles. Then they lowered the body and the homburg hat into the grave, crossed themselves, and covered him over.

# CHAPTER

# 1

**M**AUDE Teasdale Cavendish tucked her pencil behind her ear and read over to herself the last paragraphs of what she had written. Maude was tall and rather athletic looking, twenty-nine years old, with abundant hair pinned in a simple chignon. She had an attractive, though not a beautiful, face, with a rather merry expression. Her grey-green eyes were almond shaped and set at a slant. Her mouth had a curve of amusement to it. Her short, straight nose and slightly cleft chin gave her a look of determination.

She read slightly under her breath and very fast. "Mrs. Albert Dalrymple looked regal in mauve peau-de-soie with a simple dog collar of pearls. Her daughter, Miss Gladys Dalrymple, looking very jeune-fille in white organdy with sweet, simple bunches of violets at her waist, chose not to join the party of young people who repaired to the parlor for turkey trots and maxixes to a Victrola playing the latest ragtime music. That contingent of the younger smart set was led by Louise Arbor, who, since her cotillion debut last season, has made a name for herself as one of society's most vivacious debutantes.

"Miss Arbor was stunning in a dashing gown from Poiret, a long tunic of pleated chiffon trimmed with wide bands of green beads, and two enchanting green silk slippers with Turkish toes peeping out from beneath the hem. Incidentally, readers, Louise Arbor created a small sensation by motoring unaccompanied to the festive gathering all the way from Palo Alto, without her chauffeur, and indeed, without any companion at all. Her father, Doctor Arbor, Stanford's distinguished professor as well as a member of the prominent Arbor family, does not go out much in society, his scientific work taking a good deal of his time. Gone, we suppose, are the days when young women were expected to be chaperoned everywhere, although there are still very few modern young ladies whose command of the motor car can give them quite as much range as Miss Arbor. The entire party found it highly amusing when she doffed her motoring duster and gauze veil to reveal her elegant evening dress beneath.''

There. That had to be enough. She was sure the readers would be pleased to hear about Louise Arbor rattling all over the peninsula by herself.

Maude took the pages over to Mr. McLaren, city editor of the San Francisco *Globe*. Mr. McLaren scanned the pages without reading them—he never read the society news—and said, ''Is that all?''

''Believe me,'' she said firmly, ''I've wrung every last detail out of the event.''

''The ladies want more details,'' he said frowning. ''Lots of details. Did you run through all the clothes?''

''Of course.''

''And you've got a few spicy bits in there?''

''Well, hardly what you'd call spicy,'' said Maude. ''Just a little hint that debutante Louise Arbor is fast and reckless.''

''Good,'' said McLaren, lighting a cigar. ''Good work, Cavendish. Keep it up.''

''You know,'' said Maude, staring straight into his cigar smoke without blinking, ''you'll never know what a good reporter I can be until you get me off the society page.''

''Now, Cavendish,'' said McLaren testily, ''let's not get up on your high horse about that again. You're very valuable to the *Globe* right where you are. You know the ins and outs of this social stuff—seem to get yourself invited to all the important goings-on—and you've got just the right note in your writing. Refined, but every now and then just a little trace of acid. It's good. We like it."

"Mr. McLaren, I want a chance to do some real reporting."

McLaren rose and with a sweeping hand indicated the littered collection of desks that made up the city room. Hunched over telephones, bent over copy, strolling among the desks, smoking cigarettes, and exchanging jokes, was a small army of men in somber suits, some in shirtsleeves, some, like Mr. McLaren himself, wearing their hats. "Take a look at that," he said. "Looks like a pool hall, doesn't it?"

"I suppose it does," said Maude. "Can't say as I've spent much time in pool halls."

"That's just what I'm getting at," said McLaren impatiently. "You're a lady, for Christ's——" He stopped himself. "—for heaven's sake." Still somewhat agitated he sat back down and scanned her copy once more. "This fast debutante you were telling me about sounds promising. Let's get some more about her. What did you say her name was?"

"Louise Arbor."

"Pretty?"

"Very."

He smiled. "Good. Keep an eye on her. With any luck she'll get herself involved in some juicy scandal."

"You've changed the subject," said Maude.

"The subject is closed, Cavendish. You're good at this social business and besides, you're a lady."

Maude glared at him, reached over, and removed his soft felt hat from his head, depositing it with a flourish in his wastepaper basket. "Well, you can't have it both ways," she said. "If I'm too much of a lady to be a regular reporter, then the least you can do is remove your hat when you speak to me."

She turned on her heel and left him, listening with fury to his hearty laugh and the ring of the bell on his desk to summon the copy boy to fetch her story.

* * *

When Sophie Von Gluck arrived at the railroad station in the Swiss town, she sent her maid on ahead with her jewel case, arranged for a porter to bring her steamer trunk to the Grand Hotel, and took a taxi directly to the rendezvous point. Şhe hated Switzerland. It was so clean and crisp and dull and cold. She was glad she was wearing the purple traveling suit with its heavy sable collar and cuffs and the matching toque hat. Still, her hands in thin kidskin gloves were frozen, and she thrust them into the muff she wore around her neck on a black velvet cord. She saw her misty breath in the taxi.

Sophie was nervous. She had very bad news. Everything had been going so well, and then, as her train crossed the Swiss border, she had received the word. The admiral wouldn't know yet. Sophie's organization was so tight that only she knew the latest details. The admiral had arranged it that way. And, old wise fox that he was, he had been right. So many of Germany's regular operations in America had been uncovered. Sophie's network, however, remained intact. And it would only be a short time more before the main event was complete and her work was finished.

Sophie was brunette, almost Italian looking, which had helped her career—the career the world knew about, that is. She possessed a rich mezzo-soprano voice, and while it wasn't strong enough to fill the biggest houses, it had an emotional intensity that moved audiences to tears. She could act with that voice. Sophie was also very beautiful. Some sopranos, less beautiful, didn't want her on stage with them. Still, Sophie had enough engagements to keep her traveling around the world without arousing the least suspicion. No one expected an opera singer to be intelligent, least of all a beautiful woman opera singer.

Sometimes Sophie wondered why she enjoyed the secret life so much. It had started rather casually, before the war, because she was a lover of an Englishman of interest to the German government. She was approached in London by a man from the German embassy there, and he made an appeal to her patriotism. The Englishman was beginning to bore her, so she accepted the assignment.

It turned out she had an aptitude for the work. It was assumed by Sophie's contacts in the Secret Service that patriotism was what kept her going; of course, the financial rewards were considerable also. Sophie knew, though, the real truth. For her, the life of a secret agent was the greatest role she could ever play. And her ability to act this role was something that would outlast her voice. There were no bravas, but that was part of the excitement. Only a handful of people knew just how convincing an actress Sophie could be.

It was safe to meet the admiral rather openly because everyone thought she was his mistress. When they met in society she gave him knowing looks for the benefit of others and the admiral's wife's manner to her was always frosty, and suspicious. When Sophie and the admiral were alone together their meetings, though actually brusque and businesslike, were made somehow more piquant by the subterfuge. The admiral was in late middle age. Still handsome, his manner always precluded flirtation. He lived for his work and took great delight in imaginative plotting. He was a gambler who seldom lost.

Sophie brushed past the reception desk and climbed the worn wooden steps to his room. This hotel was small but respectable—just the spot for a tryst. Sophie cared nothing about her reputation. It suited her purposes to be careless.

She found the admiral before the fire in a low-ceilinged room with a view of the Alps, comfortable chairs, and a puffy eiderdown coverlet.

Sophie sat down, pulled off her gloves, and came straight to the point. "Kohler is dead," she said in her low musical voice. A few melting snowdrops glistened among the silky hairs of the sable collar.

"Dead? How?" The admiral stood up, startled, and poked the fire.

"What does it matter, really? The fact is he was ill, was taken with a fever, and staggered delirious into the desert. He was always high-strung. He wasn't the right man for the job."

"He was the best man in his field. One of the best, anyway. What will this do to our timetable?" He sat down again.

"It's a very grave setback indeed. We must be prepared to act soon. The Mexican frontier is as hot as we can hope for. Already the Villistas have raided American settlements. There have even been some Americans killed. And still Wilson refuses to act!" She sighed.

"We must find a replacement for Kohler soon," the admiral said. "And get him in place immediately."

"There is someone near the site," said Sophie slowly. "An American."

"And do you think he'd be amenable? It's very risky."

Sophie smiled slowly. "He's a lonely widower. Perhaps I could convince him."

"I'm very sure you could. But time is of the essence. I'm afraid we must resort to cruder methods."

Sophie looked slightly miffed, but she said: "Very well. I can get you a complete report on him. I'll prepare it immediately. He's one of the leaders in the field. And he lives near San Francisco. Dr. Arbor. He doesn't go about much in society, but his daughter does, and he's from one of the best families. We can certainly gain entrée somehow. Next month I'll be singing Carmen in San Francisco. And the steamship line is still above suspicion."

"The steamship line is the *only* thing left after that idiot Franz Bopp blundered so badly. We gave Ambassador Von Bernsdorf one hundred and fifty million American dollars to spend and he uses fools, bunglers, and amateurs to do his work. It's an outrage. The whole organization along America's West Coast is exposed! A propaganda coup for our enemies."

Sophie nodded. "I can tell you, San Francisco is fascinated with the case."

"But perhaps it's not such a bad thing," said the admiral thoughtfully. "The Americans are a simple people, without subtlety. Now they will be sure that, since they've uncovered the sabotage and Bopp's work with the Hindoos, they've discovered everything. While Kessler Shipping is unsuspected—you can use them still? You're sure?"

"Absolutely." She nodded. "My agent is in place. And he's had no connection with this other business."

"Fine. Get me a report on this Dr. Arbor. We'll have to use the steamship line organization to get him where we want him. Can they arrange for any rough work? I mean . . ." His voice trailed off delicately.

"Some of the Hindoos, members of the Ghadar party—young, simple fanatics who can be used to our purpose—they're available. They are eager to work with us if we help them tweak the tail of the British lion."

"Excellent. Now tell me about the rest of it. Our supplies are arriving unmolested?"

"Like clockwork. Some things have come in from the Mexican side, but the terrain there is so rough and the political situation so unstable that most of it is arriving by rail from San Francisco. All labeled as supplies for the Aztec Mining Company. It's working well. Our agent in the steamship company has been most punctilious."

"We'll have to get Dr. Kohler's replacement there before you arrive. I'll send instructions to Mexico City and arrange for a courier to take them to San Francisco. Nothing must stop us now. This is just the push the Mexicans need to understand where their interests lie. Now, shall we take some chocolate? It will warm you. You look cold."

She nodded, and he rose and rang the bell.

"The Kaiser is most anxious, most anxious, that the United States stay out of this war. And the two of us are about to grant his wish." He smiled. "Thrilling, isn't it?"

"Let's not get too smug," said Sophie. "Our scheme is a very daring one."

"All the more reason it will work," said the admiral. "It is only the most daring schemes that work."

# CHAPTER
## 2

**M**AUDE came home cross and tired. Her attempt to get a real story to work on had met with total disaster, and a visit afterwards to her dressmaker had been even worse. Madame Cecile, a sour-faced Belgian woman, undeniably clever with her needle, had said flat out that the blue gown wasn't ready. After much cajoling, Maude had asked to see the dress and discovered that only the hem and a ruffle at the sleeves remained to be sewn. She finally got Madame Cecile to promise to deliver it that evening in time for Mrs. Lacoste's dinner party.

It was a lovely gown, robin's egg blue, cut very simply, rather daringly decolleté but with demure ruffles at the shoulder.

Maude wanted to look attractive tonight, especially, because she knew Nicky would be there, and she always wanted Nicky to see her looking at her best. Not many hostesses would have invited Maude to a gathering where she would encounter the husband she had divorced two years before, but Mrs. Lacoste was rather raffish and bohemian. Why Maude wanted Nicky to see her looking attractive when she had been so glad to shed him as a husband was something she didn't dwell on for too long. Her feelings for Nicky were still stormy, although, she decided, the dominant note was pride.

11

Mrs. Lacoste had also promised an Austrian baron—a friend or something of Franz Kessler, that tedious little man who always went on about opera and who ran that apparently very successful shipping concern. No doubt Frau Kessler would be there too, a fierce woman with a face like a hatchet, who pursed her lips unpleasantly whenever she met Maude. No doubt she was scandalized at having to socialize with a divorced woman. The Kesslers were really very common. It was only Herr Kessler's musical interests, and the fortune he'd made in shipping that had made his entrée to society possible.

Maude took a cable car up the hill and walked a few more blocks to the small, neat house on Russian Hill. Her fourteen-year-old brother George was in the small, book-lined study when she arrived, working on his scrapbook.

"Hello," he said, wielding a pot of library paste and a brush. "Take a look, Maude, I've got some new things for the book."

"Oh, please, George," said Maude, sinking into a small chair. "Don't ask me to look at it now. I've got a horrible headache and I have to go out tonight."

"Working at night again. They don't pay you enough at the *Globe*," said George.

"Yes, but they let me sleep to eleven. Listen, dear, I'm going to lie down for half an hour. Madame Cecile is coming around with a dress, so fetch me then, will you? I've told Clara to fix you something simple tonight."

"That's fine," said George. "I'll just eat in the kitchen."

George was such a sweet boy, she thought. He never seemed to mind those simple dinners in the kitchen. Of course, he was so preoccupied with his projects. She watched him paste a clipping meticulously into his book, his thick spectacles sliding slightly down his nose. He was gangly and long-limbed, with a shock of red hair. The kind of hair Maude had had at fourteen. Now hers had turned to a light reddish brown.

"We don't owe Madame Cecile any money, do we?" he said now, looking up at her with concern.

"Don't worry about it," said Maude. "She gives me a

rate because I tell people about her. I've sent quite a few ladies her way. Why else do you think I put up with her?''

"I'm going to get a job as soon as I finish school," said George, "and then you can quit the old *Globe*."

"George, I *like* the *Globe*. And besides, you're very smart. I want you to go to college. Mama and Papa would never forgive me if they knew I hadn't made sure you went to college."

"We'll be in the war, anyway," said George with a shrug. "I'll be a soldier."

"George, don't even talk about that," said Maude sharply. "Mr. Wilson will keep us out of this war. As he should. Why on earth do you want to be a soldier?"

"The Germans want to take over the world," said George. "We've got to stop them."

"Isn't it enough that I've lost Mama and Papa? Do you want me to lose you, too? I won't listen to this kind of talk."

Maude got up from her chair. George followed her out of the room with his scrapbook. "Look at this," he said. "It's all here. They've found more German spies. We're surrounded by them."

Maude glanced at his book, a collection of clippings about German sabotage and violations of American neutrality.

The headline revealed the latest in the German–Hindoo plots that federal authorities were investigating. Apparently, German Consul General Bopp was suspected of plotting with East Indian nationals to send arms for an Indian uprising against the British.

"Don't you see?" said George. "The German Empire is everywhere. They're trying to start trouble on the Mexican border, so our troops will be busy there. They're trying to tie down British regiments in the British Empire. How can you be so blind?"

"Please, George, you mustn't get yourself so agitated. And don't let's talk about it now. I want to lie down."

"All right. I'm sorry. But I think my Scout troop should start working against this German menace. I'm thinking of bringing it up with our troop leader."

"Oh, for goodness sake, George. I thought the Scouts were supposed to be learning nature crafts or something." She frowned at him. "Have you done your homework?" Without waiting for an answer, she went into the kitchen and spoke to Clara. "I've had a perfectly awful day," she told her. "Could you bring me a cup of tea?"

"Of course, Mrs. Cavendish. A nice cup of tea will be just what you need. Going out again this evening?"

"I'm afraid so. I've got to write about a party for the *Globe*."

Clara never seemed to understand that going to parties was part of Maude's work. "Well, if you want to, I suppose you should. Poor little fellow," she said, referring to George, "I've made him a nice stew with the bit of lamb left over from Sunday, and some carrots and potatoes. And there's a nice custard too, in the icebox. That boy's ready for another growing spurt, he's eating like the dickens."

Maude trudged upstairs and loosened her corset. If only Mr. McLaren could see her point of view. It wasn't as if there hadn't been plenty of women reporters. Why, Nellie Bly had gone around the world years ago. And right here in San Francisco there had been women reporters. Try as she might, though, Maude could never bring herself to detest Mr. McLaren. At least he came right out and told her she'd never get to work on real stories. Maybe that was why she couldn't hate him, he was so straightforward.

And maybe because Nicky hadn't bothered to hide his infidelities, it was so hard to hate him. She sighed. She wanted Nicky to think she looked beautiful in Madame Cecile's blue gown. She wanted him to be sorry.

Gustav sat in his office—a small room off the main lobby of the Kessler steamship company on Market Street just a few blocks west of the *Globe* offices. He had his feet propped up comfortably on the wastebasket, and he peered at a ledger opened before him on the golden oak desk.

Here it was again. A reference to Ledger D. The sums were large. And they only went out. Except for one equally large sum that had gone in some time ago. And the interesting thing about that first sum—the two hundred thousand dollars—was that it had arrived from Switzerland.

Baron Gustav Wechsler was in his early thirties with a lean, almost ascetic face. He had soft-looking brown-grey eyes, with almost a dreamy quality to them. People seldom noticed that dreamy quality—their attention was caught by the most prominent feature in Gustav Wechsler's face, a thin white scar on the right cheek, from below the eye to the corner of his mouth. His hair was worn short, his well-shaped hands were carefully manicured, his shoes had a military polish.

From out of the corner of his eye he saw Herr Kessler coming towards his open office door. Gustav swung his legs down from the wastepaper basket and set his feet flat on the floor, straightening up in his chair.

"Ah, Herr Baron," said Herr Kessler. "I see you are hard at work. But you must have some amusement too. Frau Kessler and I are going to a little gathering this evening, and I hope you can come with us. My hostess will be thrilled to include you. These Americans, you will discover, Baron Weschler, are very excited by titles." He twinkled.

Baron Gustav Wechsler smiled blandly. He doubted seriously whether any American hostess could be more thrilled with a title than Herr Kessler seemed to be. It had been absurdly easy getting a job with the firm. The fact that he was an excellent bookkeeper seemed to be secondary. Now, if it were only as easy to gain his employer's complete confidence. In any case, this dinner party was a promising beginning.

"How kind, Herr Kessler," Gustav said stiffly. "As you know, I am new to San Francisco and I'd be delighted to know some of the people here."

"A very nice city, a nice city. You will like it. This dinner party," added Herr Kessler confidentially, "will be very pleasant, I am sure. Our hostess is one of the leading cultural lights of the city. She has a passion for art and music and gathers around her some interesting people. Not absolutely the top drawer, you understand, but very nice people. I understand there is some musical entertainment planned. That is no doubt why I am invited. Mrs. Lacoste knows that I am a great patron of the opera.''

"Well, I look forward to it very much," said Gustav.

"Excellent. Excellent. I'm sure the ladies will all be intrigued. An Austrian baron. Most of the nobility they meet are Italians.''

"Well, no doubt a minor noble who must work for a living will be of less interest to them,'' said Gustav.

Herr Kessler waved a dimpled hand in the air impatiently. "Think nothing of that, dear fellow. Nothing at all. Here, there is a great deal of suspicion of men who are not involved in some business or other. You will find, in fact, that all the men are so busy making money that the cultural life of the place is completely in the hands of the ladies.''

"And charming ladies they seem to be.''

"Ah? You like these American girls? Some of them are very handsome, it is true, but I tell you, dear Baron, it is a comfort to me that when I came to this country I had already married. My dear Lisl is an old-fashioned woman. Take my advice, when you find a baroness, make sure that she is womanly and sweet, like my dear Lisl.''

Gustav thought Frau Kessler anything but womanly and sweet. She and her husband made an odd pair. Franz was round, plump, pink, and cherubic, with silvery curls. His wife, her dark hair scraped into a severe knot on top of her head had fierce eyebrows and a strong, square jaw. She was corseted like a battleship. All Gustav's attempts to charm the woman had met with frosty reserve. Unlike her husband, she had no particular fascination with his title. Gustav had resolved to give her a wide berth. She wasn't particularly intelligent, he had decided, but she might well be shrewd, and he didn't want his true purpose to be revealed to her husband by her.

In her dressing room in a large stone house in the hills above Palo Alto, Louise Arbor was dressing. Her maid had just done up the row of buttons on the wonderful new dress Madame Cecile had made for her. It was lovely, a little low in the front, perhaps, and certainly low in the back. "A little rice powder on my back, Marie," she said to her maid, turning around and inspecting herself in the glass. "I really have a lovely back, don't I, Marie?" she said dreamily.

"Yes, Miss, you do," murmured her maid, but Louise wasn't really listening. "The silver slippers, I think," she said. Mrs. Lacoste's party might be terribly dreary, but sometimes there were some rather racy people there. Maybe there would be some exciting new man. She had really better hurry if she meant to get to the city on time. Papa had been horrid about the article in the *Globe* that that old cat Maude Teasdale Cavendish had written, and had insisted she go with the chauffeur. Brandon never drove more than twenty-five miles an hour. And why had Papa even read the *Globe*? He was ususally buried away in that laboratory of his and never read any newspaper at all, least of all the semi-sensational *Globe*. Probably, Mrs. Cooper, the housekeeper, showed it to him. It was just awful, no one wanted her to have a good time. Louise Arbor made a vow that she would manage, at whatever cost, to have a good time.

She sent Marie out of the room. No reason to let anyone know she was using rouge. Just a little. It made her eyes sparkle. They were lovely blue eyes, with thick dark lashes. Louise had soft, fine, almost-blonde brown hair piled up around a merry, catlike little face with a neat chin and short retroussé nose. Looking at herself in the mirror with satisfaction, she decided she was absolutely adorable. And Madame Cecile's robin's-egg blue gown with the ruffles at the shoulder was absolutely perfect.

# CHAPTER
# 3

B Y the time the taxi arrived to take her to Mrs. Lacoste's dinner party on Nob Hill, Maude's headache was worse. Madame Cecile had taken forever with the gown, and finally Maude had telephoned her. Madame Cecile declared that it was impossible to bring the gown by that evening. Maude thought for a moment of wearing something else—perhaps the rose chiffon—but then she became angry. And besides, Nicky had seen her in that rose chiffon a dozen times.

"I'm sorry to have to remind you," she said icily, "that I have brought a great deal of custom your way. I should like to be able to continue to recommend you without reservation."

The wire was silent for a moment, and then Maude heard a sigh. "Very well," Madame Cecile had said, and indeed the gown arrived at Maude's house just in the nick of time. She said good-bye to George, who was eating his stew at the oilcloth-covered table in the kitchen, a book propped up in front of him—some lurid Phillips Oppenheim novel about spies. George flung himself into things so. For a while it had been chess and he'd been nagging her constantly to watch him work out chess moves. Now, this German menace business seemed to be at its peak. She hoped it would abate soon. It seemed an unwholesome preoccupation.

The dress did fit like a dream, however. There was that consolation. She wore only a simple strand of pearls with it—the pearls she had taken in her apron pocket ten years ago on that day in April of 1906 when she and George had set out through the smoke and rubble—refugees from the fire that destroyed most of San Francisco after the earthquake.

Mrs. Lacoste lived in an Italianate house on Nob Hill that commanded a view of the bright blue bay and the golden hills of Marin across the water. It was a formal structure, with clipped gardens in front and some fine statuary—a row of marble gods and goddesses lined up against a clipped yew hedge.

"Mrs. Teasdale Cavendish," said the butler as she came in. Mrs. Lacoste, a small, birdlike woman, disengaged herself from a few guests and came to greet her. "Oh, my dear Mrs. Cavendish. Welcome." She waved at a footman who was bearing a tray of small stemmed glasses. Mrs. Lacoste was very up-to-date and always served cocktails. "I told you before," she breathed into Maude's ear, "that Mr. Cavendish would be here. But I felt sure you wouldn't mind." The woman's bright, brittle eyes inspected Maude for a reaction, and seemed disappointed to find only a smile and a slight shrug. Mrs. Lacoste tried at all costs to make her parties *interesting*, and Maude thought that inviting the two of them to such an intimate gathering—there were to be only twenty-five or thirty people at dinner—had been an effort to add spice to the evening.

"And there are some other young people here, too. Louise Arbor, for instance. I read all about her in your column in tonight's paper," Mrs. Lacoste said conspiratorially. Then her eyes went to Maude and slid up and down her slim form. "Oh," she said. "Oh, my."

"What is it?" said Maude, looking down at her gown, wondering if Madame Cecile had done something unspeakable that Maude herself hadn't noticed.

"Oh, dear," said Mrs. Lacoste, putting a hand to the side of her face and loking flustered.

"Whatever is it?" said Maude impatiently. "Is there something wrong?"

"Oh, my, no," said her hostess. "That is. Well, your dress is very lovely. And most attractive on you. Most attractive." She took Maude by the hand. "Come and meet the others."

Maude acknowledged the Kesslers and made a mental note for her paper of Mrs. Kessler's unbecoming green gown, which seemed cut as if to emphasize her sturdy form. Mr. Kessler was effusive as usual, bowing over her hand while his wife looked on in disapproval.

"And we would like to present Baron Gustav Wechsler," said Herr Kessler, his mouth lingering lovingly over the title. "He is associated with my firm," he explained. "Mrs. Cavendish."

Maude turned to greet a tall man with intelligent gray eyes. He took her hand, and with a click of his heels that Maude found too Prussian for words he bowed correctly over it, his fingers barely brushing the glacé kid glove. When he straightened up she noticed that he had a monocle on a black silk cord around his neck. He screwed it into place, giving her form an appraising look that made her slightly uncomfortable. But perhaps his appraisal was for her dress rather than for her figure. He seemed to sense he'd been rather bold, and coughed delicately, casting his eyes immediately over to some pictures on the opposite wall. "Our hostess has advanced views on art," he said with a tinge of disapproval. His voice was warm and rich, with an accent that gave evidence of a good English education.

A moment later Maude heard laughter, and when she looked up she saw why both her hostess and the baron had seemed so interested in her gown and so apparently embarrassed. Louise Arbor was wearing Maude's dress. That horrible Madame Cecile had sold Louise Arbor the same gown. And on the debutante's arm was Nicky, laughing, too, and looking very handsome at his sparkling best.

"My dress," murmured Maude.

"And your husband, too," said Mrs. Kessler.

"Not really," said Maude coolly. "Not anymore. I am divorced," she said to the baron. He seemed to find that rather intriguing. "And that isn't really my dress, either. It just happens to be identical to mine."

Louise Arbor stopped and stared at Maude. Maude smiled and went toward her, and just a beat later Louise picked up her cue and met Maude halfway.

"You look lovely, Miss Arbor," said Maude cheerfully, wondering which woman the dress flattered more. Louise Arbor was beautiful. Maude was often described as handsome.

"And so do you," said Louise, laughing merrily. "And what shall we do with that dressmaker? I'd like to boil her in oil."

"Perhaps we'll be able to think of the appropriate torture at dinner," said Maude. "Meanwhile, we must both pretend we are terrific sports about the whole business."

She thought this did the job sufficiently, and turned to her former husband.

"Hello, Nicky," she said, giving him a sidelong glance.

"You're looking fit, Maude," he said with his usual wolfish grin. If only Nicky didn't always seem so confident. "I must say you ladies are being a little severe with your dressmaker, aren't you? Seems to me she's seen to it that you both look ravishing. I'll ask Mrs. Lacoste if I can take you both in to dinner. Like twins. One on each arm. Wouldn't that be fun?"

"No, it wouldn't," said Maude, taking a sip of her cocktail for the first time. It was dreadfully sweet. "It'll be easier for you, Nicky, if you learn to stick to one female at a time."

Louise Arbor giggled, apparently intrigued by such a racy line of talk. "I think it's very modern and clever of you two to be so civilized," she gushed. "After your divorce and everything. It's so much more fun, isn't it?"

Maude gave her a withering glance, but Nicky said, "My sentiments exactly," and eyed Maude in the way she remembered only too well. She felt the stirrings of attraction to him and tried to suppress a smile.

Dinner was announced, and Baron Wechsler offered Maude his arm. No doubt he thinks I'm fast, she thought—a divorced woman, and one who chats with her former husband without turning a hair, lacking any of the finer feminine sensibilities. So far, the evening had been horrible. She smiled rather frostily at the baron and saw with slight horror a thin white line on his cheek that she hadn't noticed earlier. She realized that he had stood stiffly in three-quarter profile when he had met her.

Aware of her reaction, he touched his cheek lightly with the tips of his fingers. "A rather barbaric custom of ours, I'm afraid. A relic of student days."

"But I thought you were *proud* of dueling scars," she said. "You Germans."

"I am an Austrian," he corrected. "Yes, they are a badge of honor." His earlier moment of discomfort seemed to vanish and his face took on a haughty aspect.

The baron was, she discovered, her dinner partner as well. He should be good for a line or two of copy, she thought. Not only did he have a title, he looked the part. Monocle, dueling scar, heel-clicking—the whole business. She smiled, thinking that George would have suspected him immediately of being a German spy.

Their conversation at the table remained correct and general. The baron was full of Teutonic reserve.

He talked very pleasantly of practically nothing at all, murmuring about the natural beauty of California and the charm of San Francisco. Across the table, Nicky smiled at her and toasted her. The baron's conversation became a background murmur as she returned Nicky's look. Oh, why did he have to be so handsome? He was blond and fit-looking, with bright blue eyes, an open, friendly sort of face but with a gleam of sensuality to it. He was the typical sportier type of club man, not terribly intellectual in appearance, but with a healthy vitality. And Maude remembered only too well how healthy and vital he was, how full of energy. In the early days of their marriage, she had longed for him when he was away, she had hurried to meet him at the door, she had kissed him in front of the servants, he had helped her brush out her hair after an evening out. And there had been that time after the yacht club ball, after their marriage had ended. Like a fool she'd gone with him to his car, shuddered with delight at his caresses, racked with fear that their absence might be discovered. It must never happen again, she told herself then, but now she was weakening and Nicky seemed to sense it.

"I'm sorry. I must be boring you awfully," said the baron at her side, glancing over at Nicky and then back at her.

Maude blushed and looked down at her plate. "Not at all."

"Perhaps you are disconcerted by the presence of Mr. Cavendish," said the baron softly. She turned to him, her face colored now with anger at his impertinence, but his expression was surprisingly kind. "Please forgive me, Mrs. Cavendish. I cannot help but feel that a lady of your apparent sensibility would never have accepted an invitation had she known—that is to say . . ."

"Oh, but I did know, Baron Wechsler. I did know. And I am afraid that my profession requires that I must do things a lady of delicate sensibilities could never bear to do."

"Your profession? You have a profession?" His eyebrows shot up in amazement and he fumbled for his monocle. "How astonishing."

"I am a journalist," she said. "Perhaps you are unused to American women. You see, Baron, here ladies *do* things. All sorts of things. And we will do many more things once we are given the opportunity. Perhaps I should say once we take the opportunity, for I fear very little will be given us."

"So you are a suffragist, Mrs. Cavendish."

"Women will win the vote, Baron. It is a natural progression of democracy. We are a fair country and women will win justice."

23

Maude stopped herself and took a sip of her wine. Normally she kept her more flamboyant opinions in check. If she became known as a fiery woman's-rights advocate, entrée to better houses might be denied her. She let her features soften. "Do I shock you?" she said.

"No. I find your views facinating," he replied. "And further, from what I have seen of your country so far, I am half inclined to believe that you ladies will get what you want. The results I cannot begin to guess at."

"When women vote," said Maude, "there may be fewer wars. Perhaps that doesn't sound attractive to you?"

"No one wants war, Mrs. Cavendish. No one ever wants war."

"No? There is a great deal of blood being spilled all over Europe tonight. And no one wants war."

"When one's country calls, however," said the baron, "one's duty is clear. It is a call ladies have never been required to answer and I hope, even if you get what you want, that they never shall."

"But the mothers," began Maude, now hopelessly embroiled in a conversation she didn't want, and with a man from the Central Powers too, "the mothers are asked to give their sons."

"I understand we are to have some music after dinner," he said blandly, with a deadly serious look meant to squelch her line of conversation.

"Perhaps you prefer not to discuss politics with ladies," she said icily. The evening couldn't get worse. She was practically arguing with this man, and she wasn't quite sure how it had happened.

"I am unused to it," he admitted. "It could be rather piquant, I am sure." Mrs. Lacoste rang a little bell to turn the table, the baron gave Maude a dry little smile and a nod, and Maude turned to talk to the man on her left—one of Mrs. Lacoste's more artistic young men, a discovery of hers from Carmel's artists' colony, who had, Maude knew, sold their hostess a great many dreary-looking glazed ceramic pots that were dotted about the place, adding a ludicrous peasanty touch to the decor.

After dinner, while Maude longed to go home, they all sat on little gilt chairs while a large woman in black velvet (completely out of season) sang lieder of Schumann and Schubert to Mrs. Kessler's leaden piano accompaniment.

At a break in the entertainment, Maude gave in to the temptation to duck out through the partly open French doors to the terrace. Why had she come to Mrs. Lacoste's? This was hardly one of society's more glittering events. The *Globe* could manage quite well without the description of an evening of rather strained cultural uplifting. Had she come to see Nicky?

She sighed and leaned on the stone railing that separated the terrace from the manicured green lawn. Beyond was the bay, dark and inky. A fog played among the Marin headlands, and here in the garden heavy with the scent of jasmine, a cool, damp mist obscured her surroundings and gave her a strange, muffled feeling of comfort. She would leave as soon as decently possible. She had enough for her column. The baron was certainly worth a line or two, and Mr. McLaren had said to keep an eye on Louise Arbor. But how could she describe Louise's dress without also benefiting Madame Cecile? First thing in the morning she would call Madame Cecile and *demand* an explanation. No doubt Louise Arbor would too.

A human shape came up to her in the fog. It was a second before she recognized Nicky.

"Hello, Maude," he said easily.

"Oh. It's you."

"What's the matter, old girl? Meeting someone else out here?"

"Don't be ridiculous. Come on, Nicky, let's not start scrapping. I'm too tired."

"All work and no play, eh? Cheer up. Want a cigarette?"

"Oh, I shouldn't, Nicky," she glanced over her shoulder at the yellow squares of light, the French doors through the mist. "But I'd love one."

He snapped open his silver cigarette case, standing close to her, smiling down at her. The case was empty.

"I'm sorry, Maude. I'll go and get some. I think I saw a

25

big alabaster cigarette box somewhere." He started to leave, then he said softly, "You'll stay right there, won't you?"

"Yes, if you come right back."

What *was* she doing here, waiting for Nicky to pay her some attention? After the way he'd treated her? After the way he'd had his lawyers handle the meager settlement? Nicky Cavendish had made her very miserable. How could she be so weak? It had been a dreadful mistake to come.

The fog grew thicker now, and it was getting damp. At first it had felt cool and refreshing. Now it was clammy, and Maude gave a little shudder.

"Oh, there you are," she said rather impatiently as Nicky returned. But it wasn't Nicky at all—it was Baron Wechsler, in the act of lighting a cigarette of his own.

"Oh, but you're not . . ." she began.

"No," he replied, sounding amused. "Evidently I'm not so fortunate, Mrs. Cavendish. Naturally, I shall go back in the house. I'm sorry."

Oh, honestly! Nothing worse could happen to me today, she thought to herself. This was the limit. The baron saw how I looked at Nicky. Now he'll tell that horrible Mrs. Kessler, no doubt, that I'm in love with my former husband. My reputation is precarious as it is. What a silly fool I am. Well, the consolation is that after everything today—Mr. McLaren and the dratted dress and Nicky and Baron Wechsler and my wretched headache—nothing more can happen.

Just then Maude heard a sort of thrashing sound in the neatly-trimmed boxwood shrubbery alongside the terrace.

Startled, she turned and looked in the direction of the noise, one hand resting lightly on the stone rail, her head erect, her eyes wide. Before her stood two very dark men with luxuriant moustaches and glossy, blue-black hair. A second later she felt a cloth held against her nose and mouth and she was overpowered by a sickly-sweet smell. She gasped for breath and took the substance deeper into her lungs. Her body crumpled, and with a rustle of silk she fell against one of her assailants. He took her roughly in his arms and, after his companion had clambered over the rail, the first man pushed Maude's limp body hastily over to him. She was thrown unceremoniously over one shoulder, and the two assailants made their way quickly across the lawn.

Nicky Cavendish, who had stopped to flirt with Louise Arbor while on his errand to Mrs. Lacoste's alabaster cigarette box, stepped out onto the terrace just in time to see Maude being carried away. At first he peered incredulously into the fog. Yes, it certainly appeared Maude was being abducted. Then he began to shout and, dropping his cigarette case, he bounded over the rail and set off in pursuit. His call brought others outside, but by the time they'd arrived Maude and the two dark men were gone, and Nicky was flailing about in the boxwood hedge shouting her name.

A second later Mrs. Lacoste's guests, all standing at the stone rail of the terrace like an awestruck audience, heard the sound of an automobile engine and a spattering of gravel. Evidently Maude had been bundled into a waiting car.

Mrs. Lacoste began to scream, the butler went to the hall phone box to call the police, and Baron Gustav Wechsler ran across the lawn and through some bushes to where Nicky stood gaping in the gravel drive. "They just took her," Nicky said. "Two little dark men. They looked like Mexicans, but darker."

"We must follow them," said Gustav. "Have you a machine?"

"Yes, yes, of course."

"Well, come along then." Gustav took Nicky by the arm to the side of the house where cars were lined up in a row.

Nicky waved aside his chauffeur and took the wheel himself. Baron Wechsler cranked the car and then hopped in.

"They can't have had too much of a head start," said Nicky. He careened out of Mrs. Lacoste's circular drive. They took off towards Van Ness. "Hold on to 'something.'' Nicky accelerated and the car bounced down Green Street. ''There. That's their car, I think, a black limousine. Queer sort of business. Wonder what old Maude is mixed up in.''

By several more blocks, Nicky had considerably shortened the distance between his own white runabout and the fleeing black car. ''That must be they,'' said the baron excitedly. ''They're driving awfully fast.''

''Not as fast as I can,'' said Nicky, his even, white teeth flashing in a confident smile. He was only a block away now as their quarry reached the base of Nob Hill and prepared to turn right on Van Ness. The baron lurched forward as Nicky executed a quick maneuver to avoid a horse-drawn dray, and he heard a nervous whinny through the partially open window and saw one of the big draft horses, usually solemn beasts, toss its head and flash a frightened eye.

There was little traffic on Van Ness at this hour, but a few klaxons sounded as Nicky overtook other motor cars.

''You've almost got them now,'' said Gustav.

''I'll try to pull ahead and cut them off,'' said Nicky.

Soon he was a nose away from the black car, but the other driver must have had the gas pedal pressed against the floor, for Nicky couldn't seem to pass. Soon, however, Nicky Cavendish drew up alongside, the other car at his right. The baron stared into the car and saw its driver, his dark brown face tight with concentration as he hunched over the wheel.

''Why, they're not Mexicans,'' he said. ''I believe they're Hindoos.''

''I can't seem to pass the fellow. Damn.''

''Get as close as you can, then. Crowd him.''

Nicky obliged, and a moment later the baron had clambered out onto the running board. ''Get closer and I can get onto their car,'' he shouted over the noise of the engines. Both cars were going at a good clip, perhaps twenty-five miles an hour. The baron had one hand on the door handle of Nicky's car, and he reached over with one patent-leather-clad foot for the running board of the other car. He had an impression of two dark faces inside, and in the rear seat a crumple of blue silk.

"Watch it," shouted Nicky. He was coming up on a wagon loaded with furniture. There was no way it could get out of his way. He swerved away from the black limousine just as the baron managed to pull himself across to its running board.

While Nicky went around the furniture van, trying to come up again alongside the black car, Gustav beat his fist against the glass by the driver's seat, clinging with the other hand to the door handle.

Ahead of them as they approached Golden Gate Avenue, an old gentleman in a frock coat and a top hat stepped nonchalantly out in front of the black car. The car braked with a squealing sound and Gustav lost his footing, but he clung to the handle of the door, his arms outstretched, his feet on the ground. In one more second, he knew, the car would take off again, and with great effort he pulled himself erect. He was about to leap back on the car's running board when the old gentleman in the frock coat came and pulled him off the car.

"My God, sir, did that machine strike you?" he demanded indignantly.

"No, no," shouted Gustav, shrugging off the man. "It's all right." He tried to regain his position but the man in the frock coat was dusting off the baron's evening clothes. While Gustav tried to disentangle himself from his would-be savior, the car took off. The gentleman in the frock coat shook a gold-knobbed stick at the car and shouted, "Bandits! Assassins!"

Gustav ran a hand through his hair and sighed.

"I can see you're a gentleman," said the old man. "Please come and have a little something at my club. What a shock it must have been, sir. Why, they almost killed me, too. And to think, as they were about to strike me down, they had already knocked you over. Some very unsavory types involved in motoring these days. Dreadful. Should be strung up from lamp posts."

Further down the road, Nicky was still in pursuit, vaguely

aware that Gustav had disappeared. At Market Street the black car turned right and Nicky followed closely, still keeping his quarry in his sights. But when the black car cut closely in front of a streetcar and made a left turn into the crowded neighborhood south of the slot, Nicky couldn't follow. The streetcar was coming down on him.

"Oh, what the hell," he said, "maybe I can make it." He pulled the car sharply to the left and was rewarded a moment later with a horrible sound of crunching metal. The car was carried several yards sideways. Smoke rose from under the crushed hood, an irate conductor came leaping off the streetcar, his hands outstretched as if he was about to strangle Nicky, and the engine gave a final shudder and went silent.

# CHAPTER
# 4

**M**AUDE woke in a tiny room. She was lying on a bit of worn, dirty Turkish carpet, a cloth was tied tightly around her mouth, and coarse rope bit into the flesh of her wrists and ankles where they were securely tied. The last thing she could remember was standing on the terrace at Mrs. Lacoste's, waiting for Nicky. And staring into the two dark faces. And then there'd been that sweet, sickly smell. Chloroform. It must have been. She'd been chloroformed and taken away by those two men. But why?

*Knowing why isn't the first order of business,* she said to herself. I must escape. She crawled across the floor over to the door and pulled herself awkwardly to her feet. Turning with her back to the door, she fumbled with her fingers at the doorknob. Locked, of course. She hobbled over to the window. It was rather high, and with her hands tied behind her she couldn't reach the curtain to draw it back and see where she was. One thing she could tell, however. A rosy gleam of light from behind the fabric seemed to indicate that it was dawn.

Was she to be held for ransom? Who would pay? The only one with any money was Nicky. Or could it be white slavers? She shuddered for a moment at the thought, then decided it couldn't be. White slavers didn't come and snatch society ladies from Nob Hill terraces. Perhaps these men were mad.

Maude, exhausted from the effort of crawling about the room and furious at being bound and gagged, fell against the wall. There was a greasy, yellowish paper on the walls, and normally the thought of leaning against anything so filthy would have appalled her. The general squalor of the place wasn't important, now, though. She just wanted out.

It was painful being bound and gagged. The rope bit into her flesh, her body was hunched in an uncomfortable position so that her back ached. Worse of all was the gag. There seemed to be a piece of cloth tied across her mouth, but worse, there was some sort of wadded cloth inside her mouth practically choking her.

Experimentally she tried to make a noise with her voice. A muffled rasp was the best she could manage. Whoever these people were, they seemed rather too expert in these things.

Maude wanted something to happen. What was the point of waiting here in this state? She made her way awkwardly, like a crab scuttling along the shore, over to the door of the room and fell against it. She repeated the gesture, thumping out a tattoo on the door that became more and more insistent. What the result of this would be, Maude had no idea. Right now all she wanted was some kind of result. Anything—even something dangerous—was preferable to the helplessness of being bound, gagged, and alone.

She heard footsteps outside her door. She kept up the thumping. Perhaps, who knows, she would be rescued and the whole thing would be over.

There was the sound of a key in the lock and her heart sank. Whoever had the key to this door meant her no good.

She tried to move away from the door, but tied as she was, she wasn't fast eough. The door opened inward and cracked her smartly across the forehead. She cried out, but the only sound was the horrible muffled rasp.

A pair of hands grabbed her shoulders and propped her into a sitting position. The hands belonged to one of the men who'd taken her away from Mrs. Lacoste's. He was a good-looking man and, she thought now, perhaps an Arab. No, he was too dark for an Arab. He was probably an East Indian. He wore a rather scruffy black suit with a cheap celluloid collar and cuffs, and his face, with a curved, aquiline nose and high cheekbones with deep hollows beneath them, looked like polished, dark wood. He had a thick moustache, and his blue-black hair was parted on one side and worn rather long, falling in glossy waves.

He stood before her nonchalantly, hands in pockets, looking very pleased with himself. "I'm so sorry," he said in a chirpy accent, obviously East Indian but with an overlay of cultivated British English. "I hope you are not too uncomfortable. It won't be for long, I promise you. Not if all goes according to plan."

She made rasping sounds with her throat, and her eyes widened and stared as if she were trying to communicate her horror with the only part of her that wasn't immobilized.

"I will send someone with your breakfast," he continued, as if capturing women and tying them and gagging them and shutting them up in greasy little rooms was part of his normal routine. "Just remember one thing. We are very steadfast in our aims, and nothing will sway us from that purpose. You are simply a part of our plan. Your father is, anyway. And the sooner you and he do as we wish, the sooner this will be all over. We have very little need of you."

He left the room, whistling cheerfully. Maude had the distinct impression he enjoyed seeing her bound and helpless. The lock clicked shut again, and she fell down on the floor, her blue silk gown rustling around her. For a moment she let sheer hopelessness wash over her. She felt bleak and empty and alone.

What had the man been talking about? What was his purpose? And what was all this about her father? Maude's father, and her mother too, had died in the devastating earthquake of April 6, 1906, when a heavy beam in their house had fallen on the bed in which they slept.

It sounded more and more as if this man was some sort of bandit, holding her for ransom. Perhaps he thought anyone in evening dress on Nob Hill would be a fine victim for this sort of thing. But he hadn't asked her her name. It was as if he thought he knew who she was. But of course, he didn't. He spoke as if her father were alive.

Again she heard the key in the lock. She pulled herself back up and sat alert. A small, dark woman came in. She wore a white sari—some plain muslin—tucked and draped around her, and there was a red caste mark on her forehead. She carried a tray with some steaming dishes on it, smelling spicy and foreign. At the sight of Maude she drew her breath inward sharply and took a step backward, but then she seemed to screw up her courage and came forward. She knelt and set down the tray and then loosened Maude's gag. Coughing and sputtering, her jaw and throat aching, Maude felt a surge of relief to have that cloth stuffed into her mouth gone. Next came the knots that bound her hands, which the little woman undid dexterously. Maude massaged her wrists to get the blood back into them. The rope had left a red mark, almost like a rash.

Maude caught the Indian woman looking with horror at the red marks. It was clear she didn't really approve of whatever scheme these men were involved in.

"Why am I being held?" demanded Maude.

The woman shook her head back and forth and talked in some language Maude had never heard before.

"Can you speak English?" said Maude. "English?"

The woman shook her head and looked apologetic and confused for a moment. Then she handed Maude her tray. Food was the last thing on Maude's mind, but she ate it slowly—a strange collection of rice and vegetables and a cup of strong tea. As she ate, she watched the little brown woman, who sat on her heels over by the door looking at her, the line of violet-grey pigment under her dark eyes giving her an even more melancholy aspect.

Well, Maude thought, at least they are feeding me. That's a good sign. If they planned to kill me they wouldn't bother to feed me. Still, she ate as slowly as possible. Somehow the presence of the little brown woman was comforting. The woman seemed to bear her no ill will. Perhaps, like the Japanese and Chinese, she had been sent from India as a mail-order bride.

Maude had just finished eating the last crumbs when the man came into the room again. He motioned to the woman, who scuttled away bearing her tray. "Now, Miss," he said, "I'll tell you that we are not concerned with you, but with your father. He will be interested to know we have you. And, to make sure he's sufficiently worried, we'll wait a little longer before we contact him."

Maude opened her mouth to say her father was dead, but she closed it again and remained silent. Obviously they had confused her with someone else. If she told them she was the wrong person they might do something desperate. Whoever they thought they had, she was apparently more valuable to them alive than dead. Besides, the beginning of a plan was taking shape in her head.

There was nothing for it but to whimper a little for this man's benefit, not that Maude didn't feel like whimpering anyway. She sobbed softly, and the man, who seemed embarrassed, though just a moment before he'd been gloating, tied her hands and feet again. She shuddered at the intimacy of it all, watching his strong, dark hands tie the knots expertly. She tried to hold her wrists in such a way that there would be some slack in the rope, but he jerked it so violently that she was bound as tightly as ever.

When he had left, she propped herself up against a wall. It surprised her that she felt so sleepy. Surely her fear would keep her awake. But she knew nothing would happen until her next meal. And she'd been told her "father" would be left dangling for a while. So there would be another meal. Maybe many more. She tried to put that thought out of her mind.

Her lids heavy, she wondered about poor George. He'd be worried. He would have called the police by now. But could they find her? Had anyone seen her abducted? She dragged her mind back to the terrace at Mrs. Lacoste's. Oh, yes! The baron. What was his name? Good-looking and Teutonic. He'd been there. Or had he turned and gone? She'd been so embarrassed to be discovered there waiting for a private moment with Nicky. The evening had been dreadful from the beginning. Ever since Mrs. Lacoste had looked with alarm at her new blue dress—the one Louise Arbor was wearing.

Her eyes flew open. That must be it! Louise Arbor. They thought they had Louise Arbor. She had a father. And one who could pay a ransom. But how did they know about her blue dress? Had they trailed her from Palo Alto? Or had someone pointed her out to them while she was on the terrace?

Perhaps it would be wise to tell them they had the wrong woman. But would they let her go, then? Or would they discover there was no one willing to pay a price for her, and dump her unceremoniously in the bay?

All in all, Maude thought, the best thing to do would be to try and escape. The police might never find her. If only she knew what lay beyond the locked door and that little window with its stained curtains. She nudged her way over to the wall that faced the street.

She listened hard. Outside there were children playing. And she thought she heard a streetcar. It was clear she was still in the city. Crawling over to the door proved less informative. There was a strong smell of cooking—like the food she'd eaten—and soft voices in a foreign language. Maude fell asleep against the door.

George was pale and shaken. He sat gloomily in the living room. In front of him was a tray of food he had barely touched. Opposite him his former brother-in-law, Nicky Cavendish, was sprawled in a wing chair.

"I'm sure we'll hear something soon. Buck up, George." Nicky reached over and gave the boy's shoulder a squeeze.

"It's this stupid job with the *Globe*," said George. "If

she hadn't been at that stupid party this wouldn't have happened.''

"Well, I'm sure the police will find her," said Nicky. unconvincingly.

"The police? Well, maybe," said George. "I don't know. They asked me a funny question this morning, though. They asked me if I thought she'd pull a stunt like this so as to be able to write about it in the *Globe*. Made me wonder if they even believed she'd been kidnapped."

"She was seized in front of a whole group of witnesses. Pretty respectable ones, too." Nicky helped himself to one of George's sandwiches. Clara hadn't offered him anything. " 'Course it could have been rigged. McLaren at the *Globe* has been known to pull a stunt or two in his time." Nicky laughed. "If he did, I'm going to get him to pay for my car. It's a total ruin."

George turned to Nicky with tears in his eyes. "She'd never do anything like that without telling me. She'd know I'd be worried."

Clara came into the room and looked down at the plate of sandwiches, and then up at George. "Eat something," she said. "It'll do you good. There's a gentleman at the door to see you," she added, handing George a visiting card.

"Baron Gustav Wechsler," said George aloud. "Who's that?"

"Oh, he's the fellow I was telling you about. The one who helped me try and save Maude. Send him in."

Clara frowned at Nicky. She said pointedly to George, "Shall I send him in, George?"

"All right," he said listlessly.

George rose when the baron came in, introduced himself, and shook hands. He looked at his visitor solemnly from behind his spectacles. "You're a German," he said.

"An Austrian," said Gustav. "And you are Mrs. Cavendish's brother." He turned his face away a fraction. The boy was staring at his scar. "This is Nicky Cavendish, my brother-in-law," said George. "But you met him last night."

"If Maude were here she'd say 'former' brother-in-law," said Nicky easily. He shook Baron Wechsler's hand. "Well, old sport, we gave it a shot but those funny little dark men were too fast for us."

"It's a shocking thing," said Gustav. "I came to say how concerned I was and to ask if there's anything I can do."

"Very kind of you," said Nicky expansively, "but we have everything in hand. Nothing to do but wait, right now."

Gustav frowned a little. The situation was peculiar indeed. Mrs. Cavendish seemed to be on intimate terms with the man she had divorced. It was extraordinary. The man was obviously making himself completely at home. Neither did he seem terribly distraught. But perhaps he was putting up a brave front.

The boy indicated a chair, and they all sat. He was an intellectual-looking boy—pale, perhaps with worry. But his face took on a look of animation for a moment. He leaned over to Gustav. "Say, how do you feel about the Austrian ambassador, Mr. Dumba, getting kicked out of Washington for being a spy? Pretty scandalous, isn't it? My goodness, an awful lot of your people seem to be spies, don't they?"

When Maude woke, the light from the curtains seemed much weaker. It must be almost evening. Outside she heard a telephone ring. This was interesting. How strange that such a hovel should possess a telephone. It meant they would learn instantly that Maude wasn't who they thought she was. She heard new voices now. Speaking English. There seemed to be several of them, all with that Indian accent. But there was another voice, lower and harder to catch. It had an accent, too. But it wasn't an Indian one. Where had she heard an accent like that recently? The baron. It was a German accent. She strained to hear more, but there was no more, and then she heard a door slam closed, evidently an outside door, and lots of feet seemed to be leaving. This was heartening.

A short while later she heard church bells. Heavy clanging bells. They were, she thought, though she may have been imagining it, the bells at Mission Dolores. She was somewhere south of the slot. It was a poor neighborhood, and crowded. If only she could get herself out of the house itself she felt sure she'd be safe. There would be people about.

About twenty minutes later she heard the key in the lock again, and the woman came in with a tray. She smiled shyly at Maude. How could anybody smile at someone trussed up like a chicken! The woman must be wanting.

Maude scanned the tray for a knife. Perhaps she could keep one and use it later to saw the ropes that bound her. She also noticed that the woman didn't lock the door behind her. When she knelt in front of Maude to untie her hands, and then loosened that horrible gag, Maude decided to act.

Swiftly, she pulled the woman down and covered her mouth with the soggy bit of cloth that had been thrust into her own mouth. All she saw were two brown, frightened eyes looking up at her. The woman began to squirm, but she was a tiny thing, no bigger than a child. Still, she seemed full of energy. Maude pulled her down to the floor and cracked her head smartly on the radiator. It made a tinny sound, but it was no different from the peculiar sounds the radiator had been emitting all on its own.

The woman wasn't knocked out but she stopped struggling. Maude secured the gag around her face—she had learned something of this art from her captors—and then tied the woman's wrists with the rope that had bound her. Deftly she undid her own ankles, rubbed them for a second and examined the marks they had made, deep indentations in the flesh under her silk stockings. Before she tied the woman's ankles she removed her sari. There were surprisingly many yards of the flimsy stuff. It was awkward work, and she ripped the materials as she went, but she kept at it until her prisoner was completely naked. Seeing her naked, Maude realized she looked no more than fifteen.

The woman seemed to be offering no resistance. She was plainly terrified. To keep her that way, Maude gave her a smart slap across the face. She hated to do it, but she found some satisfaction in the act as her pent-up rage found its outlet.

She ripped off her own dress, the row of covered blue buttons popping, and stepped out of it. Now she was wearing a corset and stockings and a silk embroidered corset cover. Quickly she wrapped the sari material around her. She wished she'd noticed exactly how it was fastened. In the end she managed somehow. There was a skirtlike part which was shockingly short, for the woman was tiny, and Maude's slippers and stockings looked ludicrous poking out from beneath the hem. She wound the additional yards around her torso, leaving a length to cover her head like a nun's coif, as the woman had worn it.

She took up the tray and hunched over so as to make herself as small as possible. Carefully balancing it, her breath came in pants as she stepped outside the door. She found herself in a narrow, uncarpeted hall lined with doors. At the end of the hall sat a man behind a newspaper. He flicked the newspaper aside for just a second and she hunched over the tray. Her untouched meal smelled pungent, and a plume of steam came from the teapot, a cheap brass affair.

The newspaper moved back into place, and Maude peered out from behind the gauzy covering of the sari. In order to go down the stairs she had to pass in front of the man. He sat there in a straight-backed chair, apparently taking no notice.

She inched her way down the hall, trying to hurry, as she thought a too slow gait would make him suspicious. As she passed him, her heart beating wildly, her back strained from the unnatural stoop she felt she must maintain to carry off the deception, he spoke to her. She didn't know what he said in the strange language, but she felt certain he had asked her a question. She passed him, not daring to turn around, and gave a sort of noncommittal grunt.

She wrapped one hand around the handle of the teapot just as she heard the quick rustle of his newspaper and the noise of the wooden chair scraping on the bare floor. She dropped the tray with a clatter and ran down the steps, turning as she did so to see him step on the tray and slide down the broken crockery. He scrambled to his feet, a long patch of curry-colored food on his shirt front. She was about six steps in front of him, and the stairs, mercifully, led to what looked like a door to the street. The door had a large oval panel of glass obscured by a heavy lace curtain. That oval of light was a beacon to her, and she ran towards it, still clutching the teapot, feeling its hot spatters on her arms.

At the door she managed to reach the knob just as she felt his hand pulling on a length of material that had somehow come untucked. She turned quickly and poured the scalding tea on his hand, then threw the rest in his face. He screamed, and she tugged the door inward. He tried to shut it, one hand on the door, the other on his face. Maude ducked low and scurried under his arm, but he pulled the door shut on her, squeezing her hard. She bit into his hand and heard him scream as her teeth sank as deep into his flesh as she could grind them. Now he let go and she managed to get outside. He fell against the glass, shattering it and probably cutting himself, but she didn't stop to look.

She ran along the street screaming, trailing the ludicrous garment behind her, looking, she felt sure, like a madwoman. The Indian was behind her. She heard his feet pounding along the pavement. Passersby looked on curiously, and finally they must have stopped him, for she was able to run and keep running, without hearing those pounding feet, never daring to look behind her. She wasn't sure where she was, but soon she found herself on Mission Street. She tried to hail a taxi, but two of them passed her by. She kept moving and finally, when a third taxi came along, she stood in front of it, forcing the driver to stop.

"Well, aren't you a vision?" the driver said, eyeing her exposed calves and general disheveled appearance. She tried to tuck the ends of the sari back in place. "One of these new-style barefoot dancers or something? Or maybe just a loony. San Francisco hasn't had a real good loony since Emperor Norton died.'' He pushed his cap back on his head and grinned.

"Take me to the San Francisco *Globe* offices," she said imperiously.

"Sure. And who's going to pay me?"

Her bag, she realized with a start, had been left at Mrs. Lacoste's house.

"See here, my man, I'm a reporter for the *Globe*. On a special assignment. I've been abducted by white-slavers and I've just escaped from their clutches. The *Globe* will take care of your fare."

"Aw, get in, lady. I'm on my way to pick up a fare at the Palace. I'm a gambling man, but I don't think the *Globe*'ll pay me a plug nickel. Hop in. Just don't call me 'my man' and we'll get along fine."

"Follow me," she said when they arrived at the *Globe*'s Market Street offices. She sailed into the city room. Typewriters ceased, conversations stopped, and the entire city room stood up and stared. "Someone pay this gentleman fifty cents," she said. "And give him a nice tip, too. And tell McLaren I've got a sensational story. He'll want to put out an extra."

# CHAPTER
# 5

"**T**HIS better be good" murmured an old and jaded reporter. "Cavendish missed her deadline, and she won't be the first newspaperman to stage an elaborate excuse."

"She'd be the first one to show her legs like that," said Clarence Fogerty, a rewrite man with a red face and thinning red hair.

"What's the matter, Fogerty?" snapped Maude, "haven't you ever been to a leg show? Where's McLaren?" All of a sudden her appearance didn't bother her. She felt rather giddy and euphoric. She had a terrific story.

Mr. McLaren had emerged from his office. "What's going on?" he demanded. "It's quiet out here. Did somebody see a ghost or something?"

He stopped and stared at Maude. "Good God, what's happened to you, Cavendish? Your kid brother's been looking for you. He's had the police down here."

"I'll tell you as soon as you pay this taxi driver," she replied. "He's got a fare waiting for him at the Palace."

McLaren fished in his pocket and came up with a silver dollar. "Step into my office, Cavendish. I don't know why you're wrapped in a sheet with your legs sticking out like a schoolboy's, but I want to know why you missed your deadline."

Maude collapsed in a chair in his office and started to tell her story. "Wait. Stop," he said, holding up a hand like a traffic policeman. He went to the door of his office and shouted, "Fogerty, get in here. I want this in shorthand."

Maude dictated her story, dwelling on the moments of terror, describing the mysterious Hindoos, explaining that they apparently expected ransom and that the real target was Louise Arbor, "prominent debutante and vivacious society beauty."

When she'd finished, exhausted and pleased, she said, "Think I could have a cup of coffee, Mr. McLaren? I've been through a lot."

"My God, yes," said McLaren, ringing the bell on his desk. "Now Maude, for God's sake go home and rest. I'll send a doctor around to look in on you, compliments of the *Globe*."

"Oh, my goodness," said Maude. "George." She grabbed the phone from her boss's desk and called home.

"Maude!" cried George. "Thank God you're safe. Nicky's been here all night. We called the police and everything. Nicky, she's safe, she's safe," he called out.

"George, listen, I'm coming home now. Get Nicky out of there. I want to rest and be alone. Tell him to go away."

"But Maude, he tried to rescue you. He told me all about it. He wrecked his machine."

"What? Tell it all to me." A copy boy handed her a cup of coffee, and she sipped it as George gave her a concise account of Nicky's chase. Maude fed it to Fogerty, who took it all down in his fluid shorthand. When that part of the story was done she felt ready to go home.

Mr. McLaren was bellowing into the phone to stop the presses, and Fogerty was rushing off to transcribe the story.

Maude wanted very much to go home, now, and rest, but she had one more thing to do. She placed a telephone call to Louise Arbor.

Louise was at home. "Oh! Mrs. Cavendish?" she said.

"My goodness, you disappeared last night. We were all so startled. It was absolutely thrilling. But I guess you're all right now."

"Yes, I'm all right," said Maude. "Thrilling" indeed. How would *she* have liked to have been bound and gagged and manhandled?

"Miss Arbor, I've managed to escape but I must tell you I think there is a good chance my captors were after you. In fact I'm going to say so in my story in the *Globe*. You see, we were wearing the same dress last night. And the people who held me seemed to think I had a father who they would be contacting. Well, I haven't a father. He died. So I think they were after you."

"Why?" said Louise.

"I'm not sure," said Maude.

"Oh, it's too much to believe," said Louise. "Papa would be furious. He hates me being in the papers."

"Miss Arbor, we're talking about more than publicity, here," said Maude. "You may be in danger. Please take every precaution."

"Well, if they took you by mistake and you say they meant to take me in the paper," said Louise, "they probably won't dare try anything. I'm almost jealous, Mrs. Cavendish. Nothing exciting ever happens to me."

"Just *be careful*," said Maude.

When Maude returned to her Russian Hill house, George rushed to greet her. A *Globe* photographer recorded their embrace on the front porch. A moment later Nicky emerged from the house, a tearful Clara behind him. Maude turned to the photographer. "That's it," she said. "I don't want any with *him*." She pointed at Nicky.

"We've been worried, old girl," said Nicky. "Couldn't imagine what happened to you."

"I'll tell you some other time, Nicky, all right? Right now I'd like to rest." She took George's hand. "Isn't it grand?" she said. "I just gave the *Globe* a real story. You'll see my byline on the front page, for a change. This'll make McLaren sit up and take notice." Suddenly she frowned. "Why aren't you in school?"

"Don't be silly, Maude," said George, putting his hands in his pockets. "How could I go to school when I was so worried about you?"

"Of course. I'm not really thinking. Maybe you'd better go now. No. Don't do that. Go down to the *Globe* offices, will you, and rush right home with a paper when the 'extra' edition comes out? I'll write a note to your teacher."

"Okay. I'll leave in a little while. As soon as you tell me everything. You know, Nicky was awfully worried about you."

"Come on, Maude. Let's all go inside and hear about it," said Nicky, steadfastly ignoring her cold glare. "After all, I wrecked my machine trying to save you. That German baron tried to help, too," he added.

"That Hun came around today," said George darkly. "Said he was worried about you. I bet he's a German spy. He's got a dueling scar and a monocle and everything."

"Well, for heaven's sake, let me get out of these rags," said Maude, exasperated. "And maybe I could have a bite to eat."

"Fine, fine," said Nicky, taking command as usual. "Clara, fetch Mrs. Cavendish something, will you? And maybe some coffee for me while you're at it. We'll be in the parlor."

Clara ignored him and raised her eyebrows questioningly at Maude, who replied with a resigned nod.

Seething, Maude traipsed upstairs and shed the gauzy white cotton garment. Suddenly she felt very dirty and wanted a bath. Well, why shouldn't she have one? Everyone would just have to wait. She went into the bathroom and started the water running. A nice hot bath would be sheer heaven.

She was just about to step into it when she heard the doorbell ring, and a second later Clara came upstairs. "The police, Mrs. Cavendish. They want to talk to you."

"Tell them I'll see them in twenty minutes," Maude answered, putting one foot into the luxurious warm water.

"They were most insistent," she replied. "Said they must see you immediately."

Maude sighed and withdrew her foot. She decided she didn't need to dress—she certainly wasn't going to wear her corset—so she put on a loose tea gown and bedroom slippers, made a few adjustments to her coiffure, pushing in an errant hairpin or two, and trooped downstairs.

In the parlor Nicky was holding forth with two detectives, solid-looking men in dark suits. George was helping himself to the little sandwiches Clara had provided and gazing at the detectives with admiration. "Mrs. Cavendish was snatched away right from beneath our noses," Nicky was saying. "So I hopped right in the car and went after 'em."

"Very distressing, I'm sure," said one of the men, "to have your wife seized like that. Extraordinary."

"Yes," said Nicky, "I thought so." He seemed to be enjoying himself hugely, and his manner indicated he was talking about an interesting hunting or fishing expedition rather than an abduction.

"Mr. Cavendish," said Maude sternly from the doorway, "is my *former* husband."

"I see," said the second detective, giving his partner a meaningful look. It was clear the detectives did not approve.

"We've heard all about your escape from McLaren down at the *Globe*," the first man said. "And of course we'll investigate it. But we want to warn you that if this is some kind of publicity stunt for the *Globe*—I mean it wouldn't be the first time. Just a word of caution. Giving false information to the police is against the law."

"My sister would never do that," George said. "And neither would I," he added. "I took an oath," he said, "when I became a Scout, and my word is my bond."

There was a knock at the door, and a moment later Clara came in. "The doctor's here, ma'am," she said. "The one the *Globe* sent."

"I'm perfectly all right," Maude protested, but a second later a distinguished-looking gentleman in a frock coat came in and rushed to her side.

"This is the patient? Nervous exhaustion, no doubt. I've heard about your ordeal, Mrs. Cavendish. Right to bed with you, right to bed. You ladies must never forget that your delicate constitution and more complex nervous structure cannot be taxed too greatly. Right to bed and I'll give you a sleeping draught.''

"I would love to sleep. I haven't had much. But I don't think I need a draught of anything,'' said Maude.

"We were hoping Mrs. Cavendish could lead us back to the place where she was held,'' said one of the detectives. He flipped up the lapel of his coat and revealed, to George's delight, a shiny star.

"Out of the question,'' said the doctor.

"It was on Church Street. Near the Mission,'' said Maude. "But I'm not sure I could get you to the exact house. I ran out of there so fast, and I didn't stop for blocks. But I'd be glad to go back and take a look.''

"Out of the question,'' repeated the doctor. "Medically unwise.''

"Did I hear the housekeeper say the *Globe* sent you?'' said one of the detectives cynically.

"That's right,'' said Maude.

"I'd hate to think this was part of a scheme to keep us from tumbling to the fact that it's a stunt to beef up the circulation down at the *Globe*.''

"Oh, I'm so tired and you're all badgering me so and I spent a wretched night tied up and gagged with a filthy piece of cloth stuffed in my mouth and this horrible dark man came in and gloated at me and then I had to run all over town dressed in those filthy rags with my legs exposed practically up to the knee,'' (the doctor gasped at this revelation) "and the taxi man thought I was a lunatic and then Nicky's here acting like he's still my husband and I simply can't bear any more.''

Maude stopped talking for a moment and looked at the men's faces looking back at her, all of them thinking she was hysterical, which she was, and with good reason, too, she felt. She wanted to cry, and then she decided why not? Why shouldn't she? And she burst into tears and buried her face in a cushion on the sofa.

"Now look what you've done!'' said the doctor severely. He motioned to Clara. "Help me get her into bed."

"You've upset my wife," said Nicky to the detectives gruffly.

"I'm *not* your wife," wailed Maude as Clara led her upstairs.

"Guess I'll mosey on down to the *Globe* and wait for that extra," said George evenly. "You coming, Nicky?"

A few hours later Maude woke, in her nightdress with her hair unpinned and streaming over the pillow, feeling rather refreshed. There was a fierce knocking at her bedroom door.

"Maude, Maude, wake up," said George.

"Come in."

He came in flourishing the *Globe* with a huge "Extra" banner across the top.

"Hooray, hooray. My story. Let me see." She pushed up the lace-trimmed sleeves of her nightdress and seized the paper.

The headline was huge. It fairly screamed: "*Globe*'s Society Reporter Held by Hindoo Bandits." The subhead read: "Maude Teasdale Cavendish Snatched from Terrace of Nob Hill Mansion. A Thrilling Automobile Chase Across the City Ends in a Smash. A Daring and Clever Escape by our Reporter."

The next line, however, sent her soaring spirits crashing back down to earth. It read: "by Clarence P. Fogerty."

# CHAPTER
## 6

Tommy Cutter and his cousin Will sat on the buckboard of a heavy dray cart, two skinny horses pulling and straining in their traces before them. Tommy had the reins. Will kept looking behind them in satisfaction at their load, a wooden crate that, though it was small, was heavy enough to make the horses really struggle and to sink the wheels of the dray deep into the dust of the road.

"You sure it'll work?" said Tommy. He was teasing. Will was always so nervous.

"It'll work," said Will. "It'll work, all right. This'll be the most exciting plane anyone's ever seen in San Diego County, in the whole state of California, maybe in the whole country. And you're going to fly it."

Tommy had wanted to fly it for a long time. It had been tantalizing to see the progress they'd made on the plane—the skeletal structure of steel taking shape, then the shiny silver body. He'd sat in the cockpit, a luxurious leather seat, and felt the controls in his hands, closed his eyes, and imagined the plane in the air. If it worked the way Cousin Will said it would, it would be a pretty exciting ride.

"You sure we haven't gone too far?" said Tommy now. "You sure the engine will fit in with everything you've done so far?"

"I just couldn't wait," said Will. "Every dime we got I wanted to put it into that plane right away so it wouldn't go anywhere else."

"Yeah," laughed Tommy. "Like to my landlady. Or the greengrocer's." Tommy was six feet tall, with broad shoulders, a handsome, intelligent face, dark hazel eyes, a nose that would have been like the nose on the Arrow collar man if it hadn't been broken twice, and a humorous mouth. His cousin looked like him in coloring and general appearance, but his expression was more introspective and he wore thick-lensed spectacles. Will, the elder by six years, also had a hairline that had begun to recede.

"Anyway," said Will, dismissing these mundane matters without comment, "the specifications from the manufacturer were pretty precise. I think we can just drop this engine in there and we'll have a hell of a plane. One of the first with steel struts. It'll make the others around look like something a caveman came up with."

"Now," said Tommy, "after I have the thrill of flying it, the real work begins. Selling her."

"We'll sell her, all right." Will rubbed his hands. "Read the papers this morning? Things are plenty hot on the Mexican border. I can't think of a better plane for keeping an eye on Pancho Villa. The army'll snap it up."

"We still haven't heard from them. Let's send another wire," said Tommy.

"Don't want to seem too pushy, do we?" said Will.

"Hell, yes, we want to seem pushy. That's the only way we'll get what we want. If there isn't a reply by this week, we'll wire them again. This time we'll tell them the plane's all ready. It should be ready this week. They'd be crazy not to investigate this plane."

"You know," Tommy went on, looking critically at the skinny haunches of the two horses in front of them, "the old pirate that hired us this wagon should be cited for cruelty. These animals can scarcely pull us. It's pathetic."

Will shrugged. "Well, their only alternative is probably the glue factory. Look at it that way."

"You always look at things that way," said Tommy.

"What I can't understand is how someone as gloomy as you can be so optimistic about selling this plane."

Will looked at him earnestly through the thick spectacles. "This plane," he said simply, "is going to be marvelous. There's no question about that. None at all."

When they finally reached the stable on the outskirts of town, now converted into their workshop, with a grassy stretch of landing strip nearby, the horses were practically dropping in their traces. Tommy had taken a slow pace and he'd stopped and watered them twice. The poor beasts, their heads low, dragged through the gate.

"We'll let them rest up before we take them back," said Tommy. "And we'll give 'em a little alfalfa, too. That old crook who keeps them doesn't seem to feed them. It's a disgrace."

"Touching—your concern for the horses," said Will. "Horses are on their way out. The only examples will be in zoos. Everything will be motorized. It'll be a great day. There'll be motor equipages strong enough to carry heavy loads like this. Cars will be more than rich men's toys."

"Maybe so," said Tommy, unfastening the horses and leading them slowly by their bridles to an old water trough, "but I'd rather deal with one of these." He stroked one of the horses and felt its lathered neck. "Better walk 'em a little before they get colicky."

"I don't understand why you aren't interested in cars, being a pilot and all."

"That's much different," said Tommy. "Up there you're on your own. No one but you and your machine. Down here, well, there are things to hit. And people who'll get in your way. Never mind automobiles, Will, just let me fly."

Will stood squinting at the crate on the back of the wagon. "I think we can ease it to the edge, then use a lever or something . . ."

A bicycle bell interrupted his thought. A Western Union boy made a dusty stop in front of them. "Mr. Cutter?" he said. Tommy and Will both nodded. The boy handed them a telegram and touched his uniform cap. Tommy reached into his pocket. He'd spent his last nickel on hiring the wagon. "Sorry, kid," he said. "Fresh out of change." The boy scowled. "But come back in a week. If it's okay with your mother, I'll give you a ride in an aeroplane."

The kid grinned. "Gee, thanks." He hesitated. "Mother doesn't need to know anything about it," he added. Saluting snappily, he climbed back on his bike and negotiated the way down the drive with his hands in his pockets. He was whistling "Come Josephine in my flying machine."

Will had opened the wire. His face blossomed into a wide smile and he handed over the flimsy bit of paper.

"WANT TO EXAMINE YOUR MACHINE AT ONCE. PLEASE DELIVER IT TO OUR BASE AT EL PASO, TEXAS. POST HASTE. WE WILL BE EXAMINING SEVERAL MACHINES AND MUST DECIDE SOON AS WE ARE INTERESTED IN IMMEDIATE PROCUREMENT. LIEUTENANT JEREMIAH PAYSON, UNITED STATES ARMY."

Tommy gave Will a hug. And the two men waltzed clumsily around the dusty yard for a minute or two. Then Tommy threw his cap into the air. "Hallelujah," he said. "They want to see her."


"And furthermore," said Maude, pounding her gloved fist on Mr. McLaren's untidy yellow oak desk, "I suppose you hired that old horse-doctor or whatever he was, to sedate me in case I found out you gave the byline on my story to that broken-down old rewrite man, Clarence P. Fogerty. What does the 'P' stand for, by the way? Pickled? Which is what Clarence Fogerty so often is?"

"Fogerty was a good man, before he hit the bottle." McLaren was solemn. "I guess it's no secret that we had to pull him off his beat. Couldn't walk by a saloon without stepping in for a nip. But Maude, he's got a wife and five children. He needed a break. A story like this might give him the self-respect he needs to get back on track again."

Maude's eyes narrowed. "Frankly, Mr. Fogerty's self-respect or lack thereof couldn't interest me less. This was my big break. And you took it away from me. You know, Mr. McLaren, if I'd had the remotest suspicion you would have done anything so low, why, I would have just taken that story to the *Chronicle*. Or the *Call*, or the *Examiner*. They'd have been glad to get it. But no. I was loyal to the *Globe*. And this is my reward.''

She sank into the chair. "I can't believe you've done this.''

"Are you feeling faint? Maybe there are some smelling salts around here.''

"No! I'm not feeling faint. I'm feeling furious.''

"Well, you must be having some kind of spell, or you wouldn't be talking about giving that story to someone else. The *Globe* is in a fight for its life. You wouldn't forget that now, would you, Maude?''

"If there's any more to the story, and I'm willing to bet there is, I'm going to get it. I want you to take me off the society beat while I pursue a few angles.''

McLaren looked down at his desk and pulled at his collar. "Can't do it, Maude.''

"Why not?''

"You're too valuable. Can't spare you.''

"Don't be ridiculous,'' snapped Maude. "There are a dozen people who could do what I do.'' She paused. "Maybe not so well, I'll grant you that. And of course I do have a certain entrée to society.'

"That's it. That's just it. The *Globe* needs you to keep on doing what you do so well. And besides—''

"Besides what?''

"I told Fogerty he could follow up on it.''

"Oh, you did, did you?'' Maude rose again and tried to control her trembling. In a moment she might just seize Mr. McLaren's horrible old felt hat and stamp on it. "Well, I wish him luck, because I'm going to be following it up myself. And if I get anything, you can't have it. Not unless I get a byline. And a raise,'' she added as an afterthought. "And unless you let me write about something other than clothes, parties, and the same old dull people who've been giving the same old dull parties since the Gold Rush.''

"Don't you threaten me, young lady,'' said McLaren, growing red in the face now.

Maude was delighted. Mr. McLaren had never got red in the face when he was talking to her before, and he did it regularly with all the men.

"If I don't get fifteen inches of that society stuff a day, I'll fire you. Throw you out in the street. Don't think I won't. I've done it before. An editor can't be too soft-hearted. I didn't get where I am today by being softhearted."

"That's right," Maude said coolly. "I see what a stern line you took with Fogerty. You really laid down the law with him, didn't you? How many times did you have to brush the sawdust off his suit and pour him into a taxicab before you gave him an inside job? And how long did you keep him around here massacring everyone's copy until you gave him the hottest scoop this town has had all year? You were tough with that dipsomaniac, weren't you?"

Mr. McLaren's mouth fell gently open, and Maude stopped. It was amazing, she thought to herself. Here she was shouting at Mr. McLaren just like the other reporters did all the time, and she wasn't a bit afraid. In fact, she felt rather good. A second later, however, she realized Mr. McLaren's gaping mouth and slightly glazed-over eyes weren't because of anything she'd said to him. Behind her, standing in the doorway to McLaren's office, stood Clarence Fogerty. Maude had no idea how much he'd overheard.

"Nice to see you, Mrs. Cavendish," he said with a leer. "Glad you're up and about. After your ordeal and all. Shouldn't you be resting?"

Maude tossed her head a little, murmured something about having to cover a ladies' tea and swept past him.

"How'm I going to follow this story, boss?" Fogerty said. "The Louise Arbor angle's a dead end, and the police aren't very interested. They seem to think it's all a circulation stunt."

"Hmm," said McLaren, running a hand over his jaw. "It's simple, Fogerty. Just follow Cavendish."

George Teasdale was rather nervous as he set out towards the ferry building at the foot of Market. First of all, the *Globe* offices were on Market Street, and he worried that through some horrible quirk of fate his sister might see him and naturally wonder why he wasn't in school. He walked on the opposite side of the street, away from the *Globe* building, and pulled down his cap as he went past at a brisk pace.

Later, as he boarded a ferry for Berkeley, he began to worry about truant officers. At fourteen, of course, George could be out of school and holding a job, but George looked young for his age, as everyone was always so fond of telling him, and he felt guilty about playing hooky, even in such a good cause.

It was absolutely vital, he told himself, as he leaned on the rail and watched the swooping of seagulls in the blue sky above the bay, that he follow up on all the leads. He had to take care of Maude, and he'd been certain that the police weren't taking her abduction seriously. Poor Maude. She'd cried and cried when they didn't give her the byline on that story. The only thing for it was to solve the mystery himself and let her know about it so she could tell old Mr. McLaren what was what.

Besides, for all he knew, this was another German plot. After all, hadn't that Austrian baron showed up and taken a keen interest in the whole thing? George hadn't trusted the man one bit. He was right there, on the scene, when Maude had been taken away. And then he'd nosed around the house. And when George had made a few remarks about the Austro-Hungarian ambassador, Mr. Dumba, who'd been kicked out of the United States for spying, well, the man had looked decidedly uncomfortable and cut him off. There was no doubt where the mysterious foreigner's sympathies lay.

In Berkeley, George took a streetcar to the University of California, and after some preliminary inquiries, managed to find the department of Oriental languages, as good a place to begin as any. A rather grim-faced woman sat there, battering away at a typewriter. He told her that he needed to consult an expert in Hindoo affairs. "It's for a Scout project," he added offhandedly, hoping the woman wouldn't ask him just what kind of a project it might be.

"Well," said the woman dubiously, "Professor Cartwright is probably as knowledgeable a man as you'll find on the Pacific Coast, but I don't know if he'll have the time . . . and in any case, he's not in now. He's at home with a bad cold. I'll be glad to leave a message for him."

"Perhaps you could give me his address and I could write him," said George.

"You can write him care of this department," she said. George thanked her and left. He set out across the campus, asking a young man in tweeds where the college library was. At the library he asked for a city directory and found Professor Cartwright's address.

George didn't know when he could get away from school again. And a cold didn't sound too serious. The professor was probably having a cozy time tucked up in front of a fire and would be glad of a little company.

Whistling, George set off for Cartwright's house, a small, sturdy brick affair with a neat little garden around it, rather near the Claremont Hotel on a curved, tree-lined street.

"I'm George Teasdale," he said to the swarthy man in a turban who answered his knock. "Sorry I haven't got a card. I wanted to talk to the professor about Hindoos, like you."

"My man is a Sikh," said a portly man who appeared in the entrance hall in a flannel bathrobe, a scarf tied around his neck. He sounded irritable. "Not a Hindoo. It's shocking how little we Americans know of India. But I'm afraid I can't help you. I have a terrible cold." He sneezed vigorously. "There, you see. Now run along. You're too young to be one of my students, anyway. I can't imagine who you are."

The Sikh withdrew and George, who'd been somewhat intimidated by his presence, said, "I'm the brother of the girl who was kidnapped by the Hindoos. It was in the *Globe* yesterday. And the *Chronicle* this morning."

"Shocking business," said the professor. "All right. I'll talk to you for a moment. I've been rather curious about that whole affair. Wondered if it wasn't some British propaganda. You never know. Come along."

He led George into a smoky little parlor covered with Oriental rugs and full of brass objects and inlaid wood tables. The place was crammed with books, papers, and cushions. On the mantel stood a voluptuous stone goddess wrapped in snakes. George stared for a moment at her round breasts and naked limbs while the professor cleared off some books and papers from the sofa, and pushed aside a tray of dirty dishes.

George sat down. "I want to find out why my sister was taken away," he said simply. "And I thought I should start by finding out about Hindoos. Are there any criminal secret societies of Hindoos in our midst?"

"Of course not," said the professor. "What nonsense. There are groups of farsighted Indians—Hindoo, Sikh and Muslim—who are working for a free India. But they aren't criminals. They are patriots dedicated to throwing off the yoke of the British. They wouldn't be involved in anything like this at all. It's ridiculous."

"How interesting," said George. "You mean revolutionaries?"

"A perfectly honorable word," said the professor. "What were Patrick Henry and Thomas Paine, eh, answer me that? Revolutionists, young man, pure and simple."

"I see," said George solemnly. "I can't imagine Patrick Henry or Tom Paine kidnapping my sister."

"Of course not. The Free India movement wouldn't want to do anything like that."

"What *do* they do?" said George.

"Well, they work to take back their own country," said the professor. "To let the high flower of Oriental culture blossom uncorrupted by Western domination."

"But what do they do in this country?" persisted George.

"Education, mostly," said the professor. "That's all that need concern the American public right now. Here in Berkeley they have a fine newspaper. The *Ghadar*."

George asked the professor to spell it. He pronounced it so it sounded like "gutter." "Means mutiny," said the professor.

"How interesting," said George again, having found

that this phrase was all that was needed to get the professor to elucidate further. "I'd like to read it."

"It's in Urdu," said the professor. "Some editions are published in other languages. Fine group of men. Dedicated. The *Ghadar* was edited for some time by Har Dyal. Fascinating man, an Oxford graduate. A credit to his people. And when he left, a young man named Ram Chandra took over. Doing a fine job, too."

"Oh. Did this first man, this Har Dyal fellow, did he go back to India to mutiny?" said George.

"No. No. Too dangerous for him. The British wouldn't tolerate that. Young man, you have no idea how repressive the British Empire is. There's nothing they hate more than an educated, patriotic Indian. He went . . ." Professor Cartwright stopped himself. "Well, never mind. Just let me assure you that *Ghadar* couldn't be mixed up in anything like this."

"Where *did* this Har Dyal fellow go?" said George, having noticed the professor's reluctance to tell him.

"Well," said the professor rather defiantly, "I happen to know where he went." He blew his nose loudly. "These Indians are up against it, and they've got to realize that Britain's enemies are their friends. It's that simple. Two years ago, Har Dyal went to do some important work organizing the Indian Revolutionary Society. In Berlin."

Sophie Von Gluck wore a long velvet dressing gown with watered silk lapels, a rich, wine color with a silk cord. It was eleven o'clock, and Sophie didn't normally dress until luncheon. She received her guest in the sitting room of her suite at the Palace Hotel.

Herr Kessler had looked rather nonplussed to see her so attired, but after a flicker of surprise, his features composed themselves. He regarded her with his round, rather infantile face, now wearing a rather forced smile.

"Believe me, it will not happen again. Fortunately, very little damage has been done. My informants tell me the police do not even believe this Mrs. Cavendish. They think it was all a cheap effort to get publicity for the *Globe*."

"The whole thing has been handled disgracefully," said Sophie. "You have let us down badly."

"But, Fraulein, I assure you, the damage is negligible. Why, the girl couldn't even lead the police back to the house. It's made her story even more unbelievable."

"What do you know about this Maude Teasdale Cavendish?" Sophie frowned. "It's unfortunate that she is a journalist. Very unfortunate."

"Oh, she's not a real journalist," said Kessler, waving his plump hand airily. "She's a society reporter. She came from a respectable family and married well. Nicky Cavendish is a very rich man. But there was a divorce."

"Really?" The singer's finely arched brows rose. "Was she the injured party?"

"Naturally. Although the lady couldn't have been entirely blameless. In any case, since the divorce she has become a society reporter. I can't think why. I'm sure Mr. Cavendish gave her an excellent settlement. He's a gentleman. She is a willful woman, I think. Why else would she be gadding about as a reporter?"

"Let us hope she's only interested in society reporting. I still can't imagine how this stupid mistake was made."

Kessler sighed. "She has the same coloring as Miss Arbor. And she was wearing the same gown. I pointed out Miss Arbor to my men at the entrance. I had hoped she would be traveling alone by motorcar, as she is known to do. My agents were positioned in some shrubbery and their motor was around the corner. They were supposed to follow her and waylay her somewhere on the road home. But when Miss Cavendish went out alone onto the terrace . . ." He shrugged.

Sophie drummed her fingers on the arm of a chair. "I shall take charge of this personally," she said. "Her habit of motoring alone is very useful. Can you give me a few of these men?"

Kessler nodded. "I'm meeting with one of them tonight at the Heidelberg Cafe."

"Fine. Make sure they know that I am in charge. I plan to make the arrangements myself. My last performance is next week. By then she will be on her way. I suppose the private railway car is still at our disposal?''

"Yes, yes. It can go along with one of our regular shipments.''

"Well,'' said Sophie, "although you have bungled badly about the girl it appears that your work in getting materials to the site has been handled very efficiently.''

"Thank you, Fraulein. Believe me, I am desolated about this other business.''

"I think that while you have a good head for business, you don't have the stomach for what needs to be done in time of war,'' said Sophie, rising and pacing slowly across the room.

"These Hindoos,'' said Herr Kessler, his lower lip trembling, "are not entirely reliable.''

"I'll handle them,'' said Sophie. "They are fanatics. They should be easy to handle. I am more concerned about Mrs. Cavendish. We must keep an eye on her. If there's the slightest chance she will interfere with us, we must take measures to stop her. Can you arrange for me to meet her?''

Herr Kessler shrugged. "I suppose I could invite her to the supper after your last performance. Frau Kessler might not like it. . . .''

"This is more important than your wife's little whims,'' said Sophie. "I'll decide when I meet her if Mrs. Cavendish can pose a danger to us. It may seem like a little thing, but nothing must stop us now. We are about to change the course of history and to perform a very valuable service to the Fatherland.''

# CHAPTER
## 7

K<small>ESSLER</small> bustled into the office at noon, just as Gustav was preparing to go out for lunch. Where had he been? Kessler certainly spent enough time away from the office. At first, Gustav had thought it was likely that Herr Kessler was exactly what he appeared to be—a prosperous businessman, more American than German. But there were signs that Kessler Shipping was not exactly what it appeared to be. Certain references in the ledgers had aroused his suspicions. And there were his employer's strange absences.

Kessler always returned from these mysterious errands rather bright-eyed and pink-cheeked. At first Gustav had suspected a woman somewhere. But there was more than excitement in the man's face when he came back from a mysterious errand. There was a little fear there, too. Of course, that could be a genuine fear of Frau Kessler.

Gustav was always a little aloof with Herr Kessler, as befit his pose as an impoverished nobleman forced to taint himself with commerce. It seemed to intrigue the snobbish Kessler even more, and he was never too familiar with Gustav.

Today, however, Kessler shed his coat and hat—Gustav kept his office door open so he could observe all his comings and goings—and came in to talk to the baron.

"I have just been on a most delightful errand," said Kessler. "You know I am the president of the German Culture Club, and in that capacity I have called on Sophie Von Gluck at the Palace Hotel. A most charming woman."

Gustav looked up from his ledger. "Indeed?" he said. His heart raced. Sophie. Here in San Francisco. "Yes."

"Do you know her, Herr Baron?"

"I have heard her sing," he said evasively. "A fine voice."

"And a very good actress, too," said Kessler.

"Yes, a very good actress," said Gustav. Could Kessler see that his hands were trembling?

"She was wearing," said Herr Kohler conspiratorially, "a dressing gown. At eleven o'clock in the morning." He rubbed his hands together. "She received me in her dressing gown. Very intimate, don't you think?"

Gustav remembered only too well. How many times had he called on Sophie in her dressing gown, kissed her, and then with one hand in her hair, unfastened the sash and slid his hand beneath the silk or satin to touch her warm skin? The maid would scurry from the room, he would wrench the garment from Sophie's shoulders and kiss her all over before carrying her to her ridiculous bed, a huge, carved swan-bed like a boat.

"I wonder," said Kessler, "if she wore her corsets beneath it." He gave Gustav a man-of-the-world leer.

"Couldn't you tell?" said Gustav, placing his monocle in his eye and giving Kessler a fishy, aristocratic stare.

Kessler laughed appreciatively. "Well, Herr Baron, if the truth be known, I had the impression that the lady was uncorseted. Her body shifted rather deliciously beneath the fabric."

Sophie probably knew only too well how she was affecting this silly old man, thought Gustav disapprovingly. How like her to enjoy the effect she had on men. What in his youthful innocence he had mistaken for passion was really Sophie's passion for herself—for the excitement of a young student amazed and dazzled to find that such a beautiful and willing woman could be his.

"In fact," burbled Kessler, "I am going to hear her sing Carmen next week. Afterwards there will be a supper at my house. Perhaps you would be so good as to join us?"

Gustav went slightly pale. What should he do? He must refuse, of course. He must avoid anyone who knew him from his student days. His passionate political feelings, held so firmly in check, mustn't be aired now. One chance remark and he could be exposed.

"It's so difficult to get a suitable guest list at short notice," complained Kessler. "I didn't dare hope the lady would agree to grace our little supper."

What he left unsaid was that he wanted a baron to add panache to the evening, thought Gustav with a start. One thing he had learned was that the man was a terrific snob. Even if Gustav didn't attend, there was a good chance Kessler would drop his name in front of Sophie. And what would she do then? Would she mention that she had known Baron Wechsler—as a fierce Bohemian patriot with anti-German views? It was a risk he'd have to take. But quickly he changed his mind. It was better to be there in person. Then he might have some control over the situation.

George stood in front of the counter at Schulz's grocery and gazed at the glass jars full of candies. He'd already bought an apple, a slice of sausage, a large sour pickle and a crusty sourdough roll. A little something sweet would finish off his snack and get him through to dinner.

Behind the counter, Mrs. Schulz shifted her weight from one foot to the other while she waited for him to decide.

"A couple of licorice whips," said George.

She nodded, added them to the pile, and began wrapping the items.

"How's Herman doing?" said George suspiciously. Herman, a big, ham-handed youth of about twenty or so, hadn't been seen around the neighborhood lately. George kept an eye on any Germans of age for military service. He knew that the German government had violated American neutrality laws by arranging false documents for safe passage to Germany for men who wanted to serve the Kaiser. Captain Von Papen, the German military attaché who'd been kicked out of America for his acts of sabotage, was known to have been in charge of the efforts to get young German men home, and George wondered if the Germans were still up to their old tricks.

"Herman? He got a job," said Mrs. Schulz, taking out a pencil, licking it, and adding up George's purchases on the butcher paper of his package.

"Kind of wondered if he didn't run off and get himself in the war. You people being Germans and all," said George with a smile. "Oh, you packed the licorice whips. I thought I'd have them on the way home."

Mrs. Schulz sighed and undid the string, flinging the licorice whips on the counter and reassembling the package. "What are you talking about?" she said impatiently. "Of course Herman didn't join the German army. He was born here. He's an American."

"Just thought about it, seeing as he's gone and all," said George. "Herman seemed like he was ready for a good scrap. Thought he might want to help the old Fatherland."

Mr. Schulz came up behind his wife and glared at George. "Herman got a job. In a mine. Left two weeks ago. Will there be anything else?"

"In a mine?" George took his time, even though another customer was waiting. "Thought you needed him here in the store, you're so busy and all." He indicated the waiting customer.

"Yes. He got a job in a mine in Arizona."

"Oh, really?" George let the Schulzes know he didn't believe it for a minute. "But I read in the papers where all these German boys make their way home with false passports and serve the Kaiser in Europe."

Mr. Shultz gestured with a meat cleaver to a postcard pinned up on the wall behind him. "See there. Herman sent us a postcard. From Arizona. Picture of a cactus on it and everything."

"How interesting," said George. "Let me see that. Intresting country. Hot, though."

Mr. Schulz pulled the postcard off the wall and flung it on the counter. "Now step aside, please, and let the lady have her turn."

Sucking thoughtfully on his licorice whip, George examined the postcard. It had a picture of a cactus on it, all right. He flipped it over. He couldn't understand what it said. It was written in German. All he could make out was Mama and Papa and the signature, Herman. The card was postmarked Aztec, Arizona.

Of course it could be a plant. But it was a rather elaborate ruse to have someone send a postcard to the Schulz grocery from the desert. Maybe Herman *was* in Aztec, Arizona, working in a mine. Still, you never knew. It paid to keep an eye on things. Smiling, George pushed the postcard back across the counter. "Put it on our account, please," he said, and left the shop and climbed the two blocks up the hill to home.

Louise Arbor sat at the wheel of her white roadster. Her chauffeur cranked the car and stepped aside, and she maneuvered the big automobile out of the garage—an old converted stable—and into the circular gravel drive in front of the house. The gardener, she imagined, hated the spray of gravel she made as she went out the gates. He'd stood there frowning, leaning on his rake. She gave him a cheery wave.

She wore her riding clothes, as she was off to Woodside for a gallop with some frends. The weather looked a bit gloomy. It might rain any minute. But her car had a special windscreen wiper, and, if when she arrived in Woodside the weather was too poor to go riding, well, then, they'd all lounge in front of the fire and roast chestnuts or something. Meantime, there was the delirious, lovely trip in the car, away from those glum servants and the big, empty house. Father was lecturing today, and when he came home she knew he'd bolt dinner, as usual, and then go out to his little laboratory and fool with his precious experiments until late at night.

She picked up speed, taking the bumpy way through grassy fields and golden hills, a little greener now that it was winter. The roads cut through the valleys, and ahead of her lay sweeping vistas. It wasn't until Louise had learned to drive that she had been able to be so free, so unchaperoned, so absolutely alone, the only figure in the landscape.

Suddenly, as she turned a corner, the big black shape of another car loomed ahead of her, blocking the road. It was startling; she seldom met other cars on a weekday morning on the back roads of the Peninsula. She applied the brakes, but she was going so fast she knew she'd never stop in time. Who were these idiots? Apparently they had mechanical trouble. Or perhaps they'd run out of gasoline.

As she came closer she saw two men standing at the side of the road. They were very dark men, and she had a brief impression of rather shabby frock coats as she pulled the car to one side, bounced and stopped.

Her head smacked down hard on the windscreen and she was dizzy for a moment. She opened the door and saw that her automobile sat lodged in a ditch. Dried weeds and grasses veiled her view of the two men who came scurrying towards her. Their foreign appearance frightened her, but mostly she was annoyed that they had blocked the road, causing her to veer into this infernal ditch. She put a hand to her forehead, where she felt sure a bump would appear soon, and pushed open the door. Her jodhpur-clad legs tumbled out and she pulled herself up. But a moment later, her face froze in terror as she saw the two dark faces hovering above hers, felt strong arms on her shoulders. A damp handkerchief was pushed into her face, she inhaled sweet, overpowering fumes, struggled and scratched for a frantic minute, and then collapsed back into her car, her body splayed out, torso on the leather upholstery of the driver's seat, legs dangling across the running board and hanging limply in the ditch.

The two men carried her inert body to the dark saloon car and set her gently in the back seat, which was occupied. The occupant was the celebrated opera singer, Sophie Von Gluck, although her public would probably not have recognized her. Her usually elaborately coiffured hair was scraped into a sensible knot, and she wore the starched, white linen uniform, the short blue cloak, and the stiff cap of a nurse.

Sophie pulled the curtains at the opera windows closed, waited while the two men got into the front seat, rapped on the glass, and gave them a rather Teutonic gesture indicating they should go. Then she examined Louise Arbor, brushing her golden brown hair back from her face. Reaching into a leather satchel at her side, she produced a hypodermic needle. She squinted at it rather uncertainly—the procedure was new to her—and then, with a little moue of squeamishness, pushed up the sleeves of Louise's hacking jacket and the blouse underneath and plunged the needle into the pale skin of the inner arm.

Hours later the handsome, dark-haired nurse was seen helping a staggering, incoherent young woman into a private railway car. Here the patient was turned over to another nurse, a large woman with a German accent who gave the porter a dollar bill from her rather shabby black handbag. "A very delicate nerve case," she explained. "On no account must we be disturbed. We'll take our meals on trays, which I will fetch from the dining car." The patient was hustled onto a bed.

The porter looked alarmed at the pale, frightened face of the girl as the nurse injected her. Her eyes fluttered a little and she sank into unconsciousness. "Lunacy in the family," confided the nurse. "Sad case. But the desert air may well do her good. She needs a complete rest. And quiet. Any little thing might set her off."

Nervously, the porter backed out of the car.

"All right, George, let's be very logical about all this," said Maude. She and George had just made a batch of fudge, and they sat in the back parlor eating it by the flickering light of the fire. Fudge was the only thing either of them knew how to prepare, and Clara's night out usually meant a dinner of leftovers and a feast of fudge and coffee afterwards.

"Well," said George. "It's clear to me. Somehow, Maude, you got yourself mixed up with some German spies."

"Perhaps," said Maude, trying not to squelch George's enthusiasm, although she felt his preoccupation with spies lurking behind every lamp post tended to color his judgment.

"Well, I found out all about it, didn't I?" said George. "That professor spilled it, all right. I suppose the next thing we should do is somehow infiltrate the Indian gang."

"Don't be absurd," said Maude. "What are we supposed to do, go at our faces with a burnt cork?"

"No," said George. "That would make us too dark. Oil of walnuts or something, I think." He paused. "But you're right. It's a little far-fetched. After all, we don't speak Urdu."

"It seems to me," said Maude, "that the real key to it all lies somewhere with Louise Arbor. She must have been the one they were really after. Why else talk about 'my father?' And of course, we were wearing the same dress."

"You know, George, that awful Madame Cecile has already sent her bill around for that dress. And I've lost the dress. And anyway, she said it was an exclusive model and it obviously wasn't, much to my embarrassment and Miss Arbor's."

"Seems to me like you're well rid of the dress. It was hoodooed."

"Where do you pick up these slang expressions?" Maude asked, frowning.

"Well, you already talked to Louise Arbor and she's perfectly safe," said George, inspecting the fudge. "There're two pieces left. One for you and one for me."

"But will she continue to be safe?" said Maude. "She was so cavalier about it all. You know, I think I really should have talked to Professor Arbor himself. That Arbor girl is young and rather silly. You should have seen her giggling away at Mrs. Lacoste's at everything Nicky said."

"Nicky's like that," said George. "He makes people happy. Except you."

"Let's call Professor Arbor right now," said Maude, "and ask him if Louise is safe."

"All right," said George. "Why don't you do that and I'll run some water in the fudge pan."

Maude stood on tiptoe in the hall and cranked the handle of the telephone. When Maude had got the phone, the company had sent a very tall workman to install the instrument. "Hello, Central? I'd like to place a call to Palo Alto."

A few minutes later, when George rejoined her, she had Professor Arbor on the line. His butler had seemed reluctant to fetch him from his laboratory, but Maude had badgered him in her most grande-dame voice.

"Yes?" he said irritably.

"Professor Arbor, this is Maude Teasdale Cavendish speaking."

"Oh. Name sounds familiar. Oh yes, the reporter. You wrote something in the *Globe* about Louise when she drove down to that party alone. Well, we don't speak to journalists in this house. Good evening."

"Wait," said Maude.

"Madame," said Dr. Arbor, "I have work to do. If you want to write anything more about my gadabout daughter I'll have to talk to my lawyers. There's no call for you to put the girl's head full of notions by dragging her name all over the papers. Why, Louise's mother, the late Mrs. Arbor, would be very put out with me. She knew there was no reason for respectable people to provide entertainment for the hoi poloi in these newspaper columns."

"Dr. Arbor," said Maude across the crackling wire, "I'm calling about Louise's safety." Quickly she outlined her abduction, something of which Professor Arbor seemed completely unaware, and explained how the identical dresses the women had been wearing had made Maude wonder if Louise had been the intended victim.

"Good Lord," said the professor, now sounding genuinely alarmed. "Why wasn't I told of this? Why didn't the police warn me?"

"Where's Louise now?" said Maude.

"Eh? Now? Gone out, I guess. Goes out a good deal. Of course, it's dull around here for a young girl. I don't know where she is. Must ask the servants."

He rang off hastily.

"Well?" said George.

"I don't think Professor Arbor keeps track of his daughter's comings and goings very much," said Maude. "But he seems to care about her. He was awfully agitated. Hadn't heard about me and the Hindoos at all. Queer. I guess he doesn't even read the papers."

"Must be one of these absent-minded professors," said George. "I wonder why those Hindoo-Hun conspirators were so interested in him."

At his large house in Palo Alto, Professor Arbor, wearing a long white laboratory coat, raked his silver beard with a long hand. Then he mussed up his white hair, leaving it in startling peaks.

"Mrs. Cooper," he shouted, and he began to pace around the hall. "Where's Louise?"

The butler, an elegant Chinese gentleman, crept into the hall. "Miss Arbor is out," he said. "She went to luncheon and riding over in Woodside. She told us she didn't know when she'd return."

Mrs. Cooper, the housekeeper, joined them. "Of course," she said, pursing her lips with disapproval, "she has her own latchkey so that the servants can go to bed in case she comes in very late."

"She has her own latchkey? Is that proper?" said the professor.

The butler and the housekeeper exchanged a meaningful glance, but they didn't answer.

"Do you know where she is in Woodside?" said the professor. "Are they on the phone? Call them and tell them I must speak to her. I'll be in my laboratory."

Professor Arbor trudged back through the garden to his lab. It was a small guest house that had been fitted out with a long table, a pair of sinks, and shelves full of scientific equipment. He puttered about for a while, tidying up. A series of lab assistants, recruited from his chemistry classes at Stanford, had all been fired. The first batch of them hadn't been any good; they just weren't methodical enough. And the last one had developed a passion for Louise. It was with great reluctance that Dr. Arbor had sent him packing. He was the only fellow who put things back where they belonged, who could read Dr. Arbor's notes, and who didn't seem to mind being hollered at now and again.

When things were tidied up, Dr. Arbor went back into the house. What was the matter with those servants? Hadn't they reached that place over in Woodside yet?

"I'm so sorry," said Lee the butler. "Apparently there is some difficulty with the lines. I can't reach the residence in Woodside."

Dr. Arbor glowered.

The telephone rang.

Lee picked up the instrument and held the receiving horn to his ear. "Dr. Arbor's residence," he said into the mouthpiece. "One moment, please."

He handed the phone to his employer.

"We have your daughter," said a rich female voice. "Dr. Arbor, she will be safe if you follow our instructions completely. First of all, you must swear that you will tell absolutely no one of this communication. Miss Arbor's life is at stake."

Dr. Arbor grew pale, but he managed to wave away the servants. Then he listened for several minutes, nodding, and his eyes grew rounder and his brow broke out in a sweat. He leaned against the dark paneling of the hall and slumped to a chair, clutching the instrument in his hand, clapping the receiver to his ear. "Yes," he said softly, "I'll do anything you say."

# CHAPTER
# 8

T OMMY Cutter stood on the wing and gave a big wave to the crowd, flashed a smile—it was all part of the show, right down to the smile—swung behind the windscreen, and slid into the seat. There was a nice dramatic silence. The crowd, which a moment ago had been buzzing with conversation, stood and stared. Tommy liked that silence. It helped him forget about all the people and think about what really interested him—his new plane.

This was the plane that would make him rich. After this flight he'd be on his way to El Paso to show it to a certain farsighted lieutenant in the signal corps. And with American troops massed against the Mexican border, ready for a skirmish with Villa's guerrillas, there was no better time to make a fast sale and get Will and Tommy a swell government contract. But speed was of the essence. Tommy and his cousin Will weren't the only ones after that contract.

The craft was a single-engine, two-man biplane, quick and maneuverable and very forgiving. Despite the roughest handling, she'd perform. Even an inexperienced pilot would get a lot out of her. Her gas-welded, steel-tubed frame—Will's pride and joy—made her the latest in aeronautical engineering. They'd spared no expense. The aeroplane was covered with doped Irish linen, stretched tightly over

73

the framework and painted an elegant silver. The army would be simply crazy not to buy her and start looking for those elusive *bandidos* right away. And they'd probably order a few more. Everything they'd worked for was about to happen. All Tommy had to do was get her to El Paso.

He slid his goggles into place, zipped up his leather jacket, and started to hand-pump air pressure into the gas tank, making sure the ignition switch was in the off position and his air and gas intake valves were open. This crowd didn't know it, but this was more than just another exhibition, this was the last test flight of the new bird. "Okay, Will, spin her," he called out, and with his left hand he slowly turned down the air valve.

Will pushed his glasses further up the bridge of his nose and started to spin the propeller, slowly at first as he pushed against the compression of the engine. "Contact!" he shouted, as a little murmur went up from the crowd and Tommy flicked on the ignition. Will dived and the engine roared into life, setting the plane to rattling and vibrating.

He taxied for about five hundred feet and then he was almost airborne. Just then a little kid ran in front of the plane. Tommy saw the boy's cap fly off and heard him scream. He veered fast to the left, and the machine stayed stable. There wasn't a hint of a side slip. This was a terrific plane, all right. He pulled back on the stick and in a few moments he was airborne.

He made a few passes over the grassy field and then curved over the grounds of the San Diego Exposition. Below him lay the red tile roofs of the cluster of Spanish-style buildings. He dipped his wings in a salute and then swooped over the parking area. Tommy couldn't believe how many cars there were in one place. He'd even heard it cost money for the fairgoers to park their motorcars! What a world it was becoming. He took the plane up another couple of hundred feet until the motorcars beneath him looked like little squares of winking metal. Then, even though the fair management had told him they wanted him to keep his flight over the fairgrounds, he took off for the ocean, heading over the Pacific and executing a few spec-

tacular rolls over the water, bracing himself with his legs
to stay in the machine. He came back by way of the
Coronado Hotel, from the air a great cluster of roofs and
gables, with a sweep of beach in front. He came down a
little lower and watched with satisfaction as people on the
beaches pointed, everyone stock still with their faces turned
up at him.

Tommy felt a little guilty that he'd taken the plane out
away from the fairgrounds. He didn't want any dispute
about his fee. So when he went back he eased up on the
throttle and cruised nice and low over the fairgrounds,
giving everyone a good look at the machine. Then he
climbed back up into the blue and pushed the plane for all
it was worth. He figured he must be going over a hundred
miles an hour. That ought to give them their money's
worth. When he made it to the grassy field again, he
executed a few touch-and-gos—landing, rolling for a short
distance, gunning it and taking off again—so the silver
plane looked like a stone skipping over water.

When he finally brought the plane to a stop he saw the
crowd rushing out to him, little kids leading the way. He
spotted a few pretty girls in white dresses running along
like colts, holding onto their hats, and he gave them a
wave and a bow. Will pushed his way through the crowd
and tried to keep little boys from climbing on the plane.

"I got our money, Tommy," he called out.

"Enough to get me to El Paso and buy a few boxes of
cigars for those Army men?"

"That and a little more." Will was panting from the
effort of working his way through the crowd. "Wire me
when you get to Yuma. You've got plenty of fuel to get
you to Yuma. Got your road map?"

"I'll refuel in Yuma and push on to Tucson to spend the
night," said Tommy. "This plane can't rattle the get-up-
and-go out of me for hours."

Will came up and gave him a big hug. "This is it,
Tommy" he said. "The beginning."

"Sure you don't want to come?"

Will looked alarmed. "We already talked about it,

Tommy. You know how sick I get up in these things. Besides, you'll make better time without the extra weight.''

"Just kidding, Will, just kidding. You designed this beauty. The least I can do is fly her. Wish me luck.'' He gave the crowd a final wave, acknowledged their applause and cheers, and climbed back into the sky.

Would she recognize him? How many young students had there been? Somehow Gustav didn't think there'd been too many. Most of Sophie's lovers had probably been men who could do her some good.

Herr Kessler and his formidable wife, the latter done up in draped purple satin, stood receiving guests. The baron clicked his heels and bowed over Frau Kessler's hand. The important thing, he felt, was to find Sophie as soon as possible and see if she remembered him, and if she remembered his strong political views. If worse came to worst, perhaps he could jolly her out of telling anyone—namely Herr Kessler—about him. Gustav's stiff appearance, the monocle, the very correct evening clothes, the rather Prussian haircut—perhaps they would convince her that his passionate declarations about the necessity of a free Bohemia were only a youthful aberration.

He entered the salon and found himself in a rather vulgarly appointed room full of overstuffed red plush furniture with lots of tassles and fringes. There was a vast expanse of space here, filled with lots of little tables with lace scarves on them. Gustav's own home, in Mendocino County, was so different—spare and simple with the new style of California furniture, simple dark wood in a Mission pattern. How he wished he could be back there, watching the hops grow. He sighed and surveyed the room. At once he saw Maude Teasdale Cavendish, the reporter who'd been abducted. She looked charming, very fresh and wholesome. She was a pretty woman, and despite her generous curves, she seemed rather athletic. The corset she was obviously wearing under her white satin dress was apparently a concession to propriety only.

Forgetting his purpose, he went at once to her side.

"Mrs. Cavendish," he said, and she turned.

"Oh, Baron Wechsler. I must thank you. I understand you tried to save me," she said.

"Alas, I failed. You were compelled to save yourself, as it turned out. That you were resourceful enough to do so is indeed a tribute to modern American womanhood." He bowed and fixed his monocle in his eye. She enchanted him by smiling. She really had a lovely face when she smiled. All the defensiveness he'd seen in her before seemed to vanish for a moment. He briefly took note of the fact that life for a divorced woman in respectable society must be a hard thing.

"Oh, you remember our last conversation. About women's rights. How dreadful of me, Baron," she said. "I should have written you a note to thank you. I do apologize. I must plead nervous strain. It was a very frightening adventure. But I do thank you."

He shrugged. "As I say, I failed. But I had hopes that Mr. Cavendish would have been able to save you."

"I'm afraid I've learned long ago not to rely on my former husband," she said lightly.

"But tell me," he said rather urgently, "who in the world would do such a thing?"

Maude laughed. "My little brother thinks it was the work of German spies. He has a bee in his bonnet about German spies. In fact, he probably thought you were one when you called."

The monocle dropped from his eye and her eyes followed it as it swung on its black silk cord.

"But that's preposterous," he said.

"Well, I only mention it in case George was rude." She sighed. "He can be a trial sometimes. Thirteen is a difficult age, and I'm raising him myself. Sometimes I don't feel up to the task. Please accept my apologies for him."

"No apologies are needed," he replied, "but tell me, what made him think that you were abducted by German spies?"

She looked slightly guarded, he thought, but she said, "Well, the men who grabbed me were East Indians. Apparently there is some sort of understanding between Berlin and some revolutionists among the Hindoos.''

"That's true," he said solemnly, and then he added quickly, "That is, I believe I have heard of such a connection. Of course, these things are all a little obscure to me. I left the old country behind and I intend to become an American citizen.''

"You do?" She raised her eyebrows. "My readers will be interested to hear that. But it will make you less interesting to them.''

"Why should I be of any interest to your readers at all?" he said, frankly puzzled.

"Why, you're a baron, of course," she said. "Won't you have to give up your title?''

"I suppose so," he said, smiling. "But tell me, why should the Kaiser be interested in *you*, Mrs. Cavendish?''

"I don't think he is, really," she said. "I think it was all some sort of mistake.''

"A mistake. How intriguing," he said pensively. "Then I take it you are in no further danger?''

"Well, George thinks I might be if I pursue the case," she said. "But that's just because of his notion to see conspirators behind every lamp post.''

"Perhaps he is correct," said the baron. "I hope you will give his views some weight." Gustav looked genuinely alarmed now.

"George? He's a dear boy but very dramatic. He'd love to think there was some lovely conspiracy afoot. But I can't back off now. I'm a newspaperwoman.''

"Your brother doubtless feels some responsibility for you," said Gustav rather stiffly. "After all, you are quite alone in the world without the protection of—''

"A husband or father?" said Maude. "It's true. But a schoolboy is hardly expected to take care of me. Really, Baron, I'm a grown woman." She thrust out her chin and looked rather defiant. He reflected that she was a stubborn, troublesome woman. Still, this whole affair might be something of importance. "Anyway," she was saying, "if I give his views some weight, then I'll have to believe you are an Austrian spy. Oh," she interrupted herself. "Here is our guest of honor. Quite a social coup for your employer, I would say," she added rather cynically. Perhaps newspaper work had made her hard.

Sophie Van Gluck had come into the room. She was smaller than he remembered, but as beautiful as ever. She was wearing a tight scarlet dress with black trimming, very decolleté. Her breasts were lovely—like a young girl's. Her hair was piled up on her head and looked glossy and blue-black. Her face was a perfect oval—an intelligent forehead, beautifully shaped brows, dark eyes, and a voluptuous mouth that smiled out over the assembled company. It was definitely a planned entrance that she was making now. She waited until the room was quiet, and then a few "bravas" could be heard from the guests. She bowed prettily and placed a hand on her heart. It was really very affecting. Sophie was magnificent in her own way.

"Red peau-de-soie," muttered Maude Teasdale Cavendish at his side, "trimmed with jet; modified train." He realized she was memorizing the details for her column. "Daringly cut. Hmm."

When Sophie lifted her face to the company again, her eyes met Gustav's. There was no question. She recognized him instantly. There was shock on her face. How extraordinary. Why should she look shocked?

He was barely aware that Maude Teasdale Cavendish was watching him with interest. She had seen Sophie's expression, too. "Are you acquainted with Miss Von Gluck?" she said. He didn't answer.

He began to make his way across the room. Maude was at his side. "You must introduce me," she said.

"Must I?" he said impatiently. He knew he sounded rude.

"Well, it would be nice," said Maude testily. "My readers, you know."

Sophie came toward him and the baron bowed over her hand with a click of his heels. She was wearing some sort of musky scent. It was almost overpowering.

"So correct, Herr Baron," Sophie said softly in her delicious voice.

"You remembered," he said, straightening up and looking into her eyes. They were narrowed, giving her face a look of sensual cunning.

"Of course."

Maude, at his side, cleared her throat.

"I beg your pardon," he said coldly, turning to Maude and presenting her to Sophie. "Mrs. Cavendish."

"Oh!" said Sophie, her eyes growing wide with interest. "How interesting. I've heard about your abduction. You must tell me more about it. Who were the brigands who captured you?"

"I have no idea," said Maude. "But I intend to find out."

"Mrs. Cavendish is a newspaperwoman," explained Gustav.

"Yes, of course. But surely you're not going to try and track down those men yourself? Isn't that better left to the police?"

"It would make a marvelous story," said Maude. "I'm working very hard on it."

"But I understand you reported on social matters," said Sophie.

"Now I do," said Maude. Again Gustav noted the determined set of the young woman's chin. "But this adventure, horrifying as it was, may give me the opportunity to do other kinds of reporting. But tell us, Miss Von Gluck, a little about you. Are you enjoying our city?"

"A wonderful city," said Sophie with a warm smile. "And a wonderful public. I am happy when I sing for people who really love opera. It's truly inspiring."

"I see," said Maude, her mouth twitching slightly with amusement. Gustav guessed that Mrs. Cavendish had heard this sort of gushing comment before. No doubt it was just the sort of thing her readers adored.

Herr Kessler joined them. "Oh, I see you have met Mrs. Cavendish," he said to Sophie Von Gluck. "Excellent. And Baron Wechsler."

"Yes," said Sophie. "The Baron and I are old friends."

"Indeed?" Herr Kessler looked surprised. "I didn't know."

"Naturally," said Gustav, "I didn't want to presume. When you asked me if I knew Fraulein Von Gluck I thought it better to let the lady acknowledge the acquaintanceship."

"So," said Kessler, looking confused.

"And," continued Gustav, wishing he'd stop talking but seeming unable to, "I wasn't sure Fraulein Von Gluck would remember me. It was some time ago. I was a student."

"She remembered," said Maude quietly at his side. He turned and looked at the reporter sharply. She had that same irritating, ironic, amused look. She had guessed, from that first glance between them. This society reporting was no doubt very bad for the woman's character.

Sophie gave the train of her gown a twitch, and at the sound of the rustling fabric Gustav turned back to her. She tilted her head a little to one side. It was a summons. Gustav offered her his arm and they walked away from the others with little more than a nod.

"I can't believe it," Sophie said. "What are you doing here?"

"I'm a hop farmer, actually," said Gustav, "but right now I'm engaged in commerce as well. I'm keeping books. I need to save a little money to make improvements in my farm. And then I'm going to grow the best hops and make the best Bohemian-style beer imaginable. Far away from Bohemia."

"Far away from Bohemia? But you were so fierce about it. Wanted to help throw off the yoke of the Austro-Hungarian Empire." She was teasing him.

"Well, I was younger then," said Gustav. "I decided to get away from all that and start a new life here. My elder brother will inherit the old estate—and all the hop vines."

"I see."

"And you? Your career has blossomed. Everyone talks about you. You are a mad success."

"Of course I am," said Sophie. "I always knew I

would be.'' They took glasses of champagne from a passing servant.

*I suppose, now that you are so very grand, you no longer have time to dally with students in provincial towns,* thought Gustav bitterly. ''You must have been very bored in those days, being with a provincial company,'' he said. ''Forced to depend upon the companionship of impoverished students for amusement.''

She turned to face him directly. ''I thought you would be grateful later if I ended it the way I did,'' she said in a fierce, low tone, almost a whisper. ''But you see, Gustav, I have never forgotten you. No one has ever loved me as you did. Your love was like an aphrodisiac.''

Gustav looked nervously around. He hadn't remembered just how dramatic Sophie could be. She placed a hand on his arm. ''Come to me tonight,'' she said.

''But Sophie, I no longer love you,'' he said lightly, wondering if he was being completely truthful. ''If your passion is fueled by my love, the night might be a great disapointment to you.''

''Now you're being cruel,'' she said, sipping her champagne. She lowered her eyelids. Gustav thought he saw a glimmer of a tear in her dark lashes.

''Oh, Sophie,'' he said gently, ''why are we quarreling? Can't we be friends?''

''No,'' she said, her eyes flashing now. ''We can only be lovers. I'll wait for you at the Palace Hotel.'' She swept away in a crush of silk.

Gustav, rather overwhelmed by the evening's developments, took a deep sip of champagne. He was not going to the Palace Hotel tonight, although he was certainly tempted by Sophie's beauty. Perhaps if he sent flowers or something. He took another deep sip. Thank God, he thought, he wasn't a student anymore. It occurred to him that Sophie was perhaps a little mad.

''We need to talk for a moment,'' said Sophie to her host. ''Is there some quiet place?''

Kessler led her to a door obscured by potted palms. Inside was a small sitting room.

"Mrs. Cavendish is going to be a problem, I fear. I want her out of the way," said Sophie.

"Out of the way?" Kessler pulled at his collar and looked rather ill. "Temporarily?"

"No, permanently.

"I can see you're not up to the task," she continued after a moment. "Get me another interview with these Hindoos. I'll tell them what's needed."

"But Fraulein," said Herr Kessler, "abducting Miss Arbor, temporarily, that is one thing, but Mrs. Cavendish, an innocent party . . ."

"Need I remind you, Herr Kessler, that we are at war? Many, many German soldiers will die if we fail. Their blood will be on our hands. We are embarked on work that will keep America out of the war and afford us a swift victory. What are one or two lives in such a situation? You must take a larger view of things. Besides, Mrs. Cavendish told me she intends to pursue the mystery of her abduction."

"But Frauelin Von Gluck . . ." Kessler put a shaking hand to his forehead.

"May I remind you," said Sophie, "that it is because of your bungling that Mrs. Cavendish became involved in the first place?"

He sighed. "I will leave it all to you," he said.

"I'm afraid everything has been left to me," she said. And to herself, she thought, *There will be practically no time for Gustav. It's foolish of me to want him. But I do. Especially that he now thinks he doesn't want me.*

When they went into supper, Gustav found that he was to be seated next to his hostess. He found this rather odd, although as a baron he outranked the others in the room, but surely such feudal distinctions wouldn't be made here. After all, he was an employee of her husband. At the other end of the table, Kessler looked rather strained talking to Sophie. What a change from the leer he'd had in the office when he came back from his meeting with her. Perhaps it was Frau Kessler's presence. Still, it hadn't escaped Gustav's notice that Sophie and Kessler had arranged for a tête-à-tête in a small room behind the potted palms. What on earth could have been the purpose of that?

Mrs. Kessler told him how pleased she was to be able to speak German. "Yet Fraulein Von Gluck was speaking to Mrs. Cavendish just now, and I distinctly heard her say you were a Czech and not an Austrian."

"Bohemia is Austria," said Gustav with a smile. "We are all part of the great Hapsburg empire."

"Yes. Still, it is curious I did not know this before." Frau Kessler helped herself to a large quantity of lobster from a plate held by an immaculate butler.

"Perhaps it is because I think of myself as an Austrian," said Gustav.

"It is a great weakness of the Hapsburg empire," said Frau Kessler, "that there are so many Slavs and Magyars in it."

"Yes, it is a weakness, to be sure," said Gustav warily. *And a weakness that gives me hope for my own people,* he added mentally. "I'm glad you didn't include Bohemia as a liability."

"You Bohemians have a great deal of German blood," she said.

"My grandfather was a Viennese," said Gustav. "And of course, among the better classes the spread of German culture has been quite thorough."

"Well, thank heaven for that," said Frau Kessler. But she seemed to be eyeing him suspiciously. Damn Sophie. She had already told them he was a Czech. Would she tell them, too, how he had ranted against the Hapsburgs? If he had known then that he could best serve his cause in a secret way he never would have carried on as he had in his youth. But perhaps he would have told Sophie in any case. It had been hard to keep a secret from her. He had wanted her to know all about him, every thought, every emotion. And what had he learned about her in return? Probably very little. It had been the selfishness of youth, he reflected sadly, that had allowed him to mistake his own pouring out of his soul for a mutual intimacy.

"Of course," said Mrs. Kessler now, "it is, I am sorry

to say, rather typical of Mrs. Cavendish to ask a lot of personal questions about one's guests.''

"Well, she has a job to do," said Gustav. "Just as I do. I must confess, since I have joined the ranks of those who toil I have developed a more relaxed point of view about things. America, too, has changed me."

"Indeed?" Mrs. Kessler did not approve. Conversation with his hostess was uphill work. Gustav sighed. "Although, I do find the idea of a lady reporting on the doings of society rather a curious phenomenon."

"She is divorced, you know," said Mrs. Kessler with satisfaction.

"Yes, I know. But I am sure, Madame, that the lady was blameless. Otherwise I know I should never find her at *your* table."

There. That should shut her up, he thought.

Apparently he was wrong. "Sometimes, Herr Baron, there are circumstances that cause one to bend one's rules. My husband felt it advisable to include her tonight."

"Perhaps," said Gustav, rather surprised at this information, "it furthers the cause of German culture to have such an event in the newspapers."

"Of course," she replied. "Although naturally my husband would not want any cheap publicity."

"Naturally not," agreed Gustav. Really the woman was impossible. How could anyone who wanted to be called a lady criticize her own guests! And Kessler himself was nothing but a social climber. Although perhaps he was a spy as well.

# CHAPTER
# 9

T HEY were well into the second course when Gustav made his decision. He would have to go to Sophie. He would ask her not to tell his employer about his nationalist views. The line he would take was that Herr Kessler was a very patriotic German, caught up in a strong feeling because of the war and so forth, and he would never understand Gustav's youthful excesses. And if the price he had to pay for Sophie's silence was making love to her once more, so be it. Actually the idea rather excited him, but it repelled him, too. He forced his ambivalence to the back of his mind. This was all for the cause. Hadn't women spies done the same sort of thing? Of course, they had been called whores for it, too.

Sophie had never had a moment's doubt, apparently, that he would come to her. She was so bold as to tell the Kesslers that her old friend Baron Wechsler would escort her back to her hotel, Frau Kessler's brows shot up at this, and that meddlesome Maude Teasdale Cavendish, naturally, seemed interested as well. Would it appear in her newspaper? Gustav took his opera hat and his white silk scarf from the butler, said stiff and proper good-byes, and handed Sophie into a waiting taxicab.

They had barely pulled out into the street when Sophie

embraced him, crushing her body against his, enveloping him in her musky scent and kissing his mouth with the fierceness he had once thought was love. He had forgotten how physically exciting she could be. He wrapped his arms around her tightly and pulled her even closer.

"I thought the evening would never end," she said. "I wanted to be alone with you."

"Be quiet," he said. "Let's not talk anymore. We can talk later." And he kissed her with an urgency that matched hers.

They remained silent in the hotel lobby, in the elevator, and in her suite. She dismissed her maid—it was a different one, but she scurried from the room with as much alacrity and as little surprise as her predecessor used to ten years before—and then she began to unfasten the studs of his shirt while he undid the buttons down the back of her dress. She undressed him very expertly and quickly, flinging his clothes on the floor. When she stood in her corset and stockings and shoes, she began to pull the pins out of her hair and shake it down over her shoulders. Gustav stopped for a moment to admire her, but she pulled at the ribbons on her corset, kicked off her shoes, whispered, "Schnell, schnell" and rubbed her hands all over his naked body.

He carried her to the bed, just as he used to do ten years ago, and finished undressing her there, all except for one stocking, forgotten in the urgency of the moment.

They made love with the kind of desperation Gustav remembered from his youth, never stopping for anything teasing or languorous, slamming together, their bodies glowing with sweat, Sophie's face beneath him framed by the tumble of loose hair around her face, with the wide-open look of passion.

Afterward, as Gustav lay next to her, he felt a desire for separateness, for space between them, yet she was nuzzling next to him. He realized that though he had been terribly excited, he now felt strangely empty.

He closed his eyes for a moment and then remembered why he was here.

'Sophie," he murmured, "it's been such a long time."

"Yes," she said dreamily, "I'm glad I found you again."

"I'm a different person now," he began. How was he going to get around to the subject?

"Not so different," she said sleepily.

"Well, for one thing, I'm not interested in Bohemian nationalism anymore." He tried to make a self-deprecating little laugh.

"Oh, Gustav, you're not going to talk politics again, are you?" she said, not without some semblance of affection. "Then I'll know you never changed."

"Well, I wish you'd forget all about that part of my past," he said, stroking her hair and examining her face, her eyes closed, her mouth relaxed. "I wouldn't want it known around. It's all rather embarrassing, really, one's youthful excesses."

"What are you talking about?" she said, her voice husky.

"Well, I know it's rather silly, but my employer wouldn't like to hear about it. He's a very patriotic old fellow, and of course the war has brought it out even more. He'd hate to think I wasn't a loyal Austrian."

Sophie's eyes flew open. "Your employer? Who are you talking about, Gustav?"

"Why, Herr Kessler, of course. I thought you knew. I am an accountant at his shipping firm."

Now she sat up in bed, wide awake, clutching the sheets over her chest in a protective way. "What? You work for Herr Kessler?"

"Why, yes. Is that so startling?" He propped himself up on his elbows. Her reaction astonished him. Why should she care about Kessler's boring shipping firm? Unless, of course, she knew it was more than that. He remembered her tête-à-tête with Kessler in the room behind the potted palms.

She scrutinized him carefully. "Just what are you doing working for Kessler? Aren't you supposed to be a hop farmer?"

"I *am* a hop farmer," he said indignantly. "But as I

told you, I need capital. I've taken the work just for a short while to get a little money ahead. I have to have kilns so I can make my own pilsner. You don't know what it's like selling perfect hops to fools who brew inferior beer."

"A rather peculiar story," she said, narrowing her eyes. "Surely you could raise the money—from your family, if from no one else."

"I don't want to get it from my family," said Gustav. "It's clear you don't understand this country at all."

"And that old fool Kessler," she said. "He took you on, no doubt, because of your title. He's a very *burgerlich* little man. A terrible snob."

"That may well be," said Gustav. "But I'm a good accountant. Really, Sophie, I can't see why any of this should disturb you so."

Sophie fell back against the sheet, her body rigid. "Oh, damn," she said.

"I don't understand." He kissed her forehead. "What is the matter?"

"I just don't like the idea of your working for Herr Kessler," she said. "It's very . . . awkward."

"Awkward? Why?"

"Because. I have some business with him. His German Culture Club and so on. I wish you weren't working for him. That's all."

She turned to him. "Say you'll leave his firm."

"Of course not. If you're afraid he and I will talk about you, well, I should think you'd know me well enough to know that I would never do that sort of thing."

"I just don't like the situation."

"What's the matter?" laughed Gustav. "Is he your lover too?"

"No, of course not. What a thing to say." Sophie looked properly insulted.

"Well, this work you're doing with him. The spread of German culture, or whatever it is . . . goodness, Sophie, you come to San Francisco so seldom, what difference could this make?" He raised his eyebrows and tried to look shocked. "You aren't some sort of *spy* are you?" He laughed, and as he did he realized that laughing when you don't really feel like laughing is the most difficult kind of lying there is.

"Listen," said Sophie very softly. "I don't want you to ask any questions. I'm warning you. Right now, Kessler Shipping is the wrong place for you to be. I'm asking you, telling you as an old friend, leave that job now."

Sophie was evidently aware of the true nature of Kessler Shipping. Gustav himself hadn't known for certain that the firm was more than it appeared to be. He only knew that Mr. Voska suspected Franz Kessler. Now he had confirmation.

He wondered if Sophie knew that he knew. He hadn't a great deal of confidence in his acting ability. And he had a great deal of confidence in hers. She had moved him to tears on stage. And off, too.

"Don't be ridiculous, Sophie," he said evenly. "I'm not going to give up that job. It's pleasant work. Mr. Kessler makes very few demands on me. The pay is excellent. I'm quite happy there."

"I can't quite believe that," she said. "Baron Gustav Wechsler, a clerk."

"Just say you won't tell him about my student days, Sophie."

"It could be dangerous for you to stay there," she said, narrowing her eyes.

"Is that a threat?" He had decided. He couldn't trust her not to tell Kessler. She seemed mixed up in whatever Kessler was up to.

Sophie knew that Gustav was anything but a loyal subject of the Austrian Empire. And Sophie knew that Gustav was in a position to uncover any untoward activities at the shipping firm.

He cursed himself for not having made greater inroads in his mission at the office. The missing ledger—the one that was always punctiliously referred to in the company's books but that Herr Kessler had always told Gustav he need not bother with. He should have found it by now and read it. He had been waiting to be taken into Kessler's confidence. Those were his orders. And although Gustav had managed to make an anti-English remark now and then, or to comment on the war news in a way that made his Central Powers sympathies clear, he hadn't wanted to push. Now it could be that he was about to be exposed. He had better act at once.

He tossed back the bedclothes and surveyed the room, looking for his clothes.

"But where are you going?" Sophie's usually lovely, melodious voice was raised an octave, actually sounding shrill. Gustav took it as a sign that the situation was out of her control.

"I have to leave, darling. You don't know how these American hotels operate. Did you know they have detectives simply to spy on the guests and see that nothing irregular happens in the rooms?"

"Oh, Gustav, you're being ridiculous."

"It's true. It's a very strange country, Sophie."

He wandered into the other room of the suite and began to dress. Sophie, wrapped in the bedspread of gold and white satin, followed him. "You look like Aida," he said. She was lovely. Her skin was so creamy.

She put a hand to her abundant dark hair and pushed it away from her face. "Don't go," she said. "I need you to stay here with me. It's been such a long time, Gustav."

He turned away from her as he pushed the studs into his shirt front. If he looked at her any longer he might well stay. "It hasn't been so long," he joked. "Just about half an hour, I'd say."

"You're so cruel, Gustav," she answered. "You know what I mean. It's been so many years. And I've missed you so."

"Sophie," he said. He didn't know what else to say. He repeated her name and kissed her and then, with a great effort of will, he pulled himself from her arms.

Gustav shut the door behind him and went quickly down the deep-carpeted hall.

After he had left, Sophie rushed to a white French

telephone on a marble table. "Hello, operator. Yes, I know it's late. Please give me this number immediately. This is Miss Von Gluck. I must speak to Herr Kessler. Ring as long as you have to, it's urgent."

By the time Gustav's elevator reached the lobby, the call had come through. As he passed the desk, he saw the night operator, a tired-looking young man with an earpiece, hunched in front of a switchboard, and heard him say into his device: "Miss Von Gluck, I have Mr. Kessler on the line."

Smiling, Gustav left the lobby. He'd have to act very quickly.

Gustav had taken several precautions against such a contingency. Early on in his employment he had managed to borrow the key to the office for just a moment and make a wax impression of it. He now had a duplicate key in his card case. He had also watched Herr Kessler carefully. He had never managed to learn the combination to the office safe, a sturdy green model behind Kessler's desk, but he had noticed that when Miss Lipton, the secretary, had once been asked to fetch something from the safe, she'd consulted a little card in her own desk drawer.

The missing ledger, the ledger that Gustav constantly came across in his own accounts—"Refer to Ledger D"—was probably in that safe.

Gustav decided it would be fastest to walk down Market Street to the office. It was close to the hotel. He went at a good pace, but not too quickly. Even at this late hour there were people on the streets—San Francisco was a lively town—and he didn't want to attract attention. He reached the building in about ten minutes.

While he had the key to the suite of offices on the sixth floor, he had no key to the main door of the building. As this was always open during the day, and he hadn't realized he would be attempting to penetrate the building at night, he hadn't provided for this first lock. His original plan had been to go back to the office just a short while after office hours one evening and conduct a search then. The building's caretaker was around until ten, he had learned, supervising the cleaning women.

He took out his gold pocket watch. It was four o'clock in the morning. The place would be deserted. He went up to the door, looked around, and tried the handle. It was locked. Through the glass he could see that it was a stout lock. He thought for a moment about simply breaking the glass. There was no one on the street just now. He might be able to make it. He had to get into the building soon, because Sophie had warned Kessler, who might just come down to see that Gustav hadn't tampered with anything. After all, Sophie could tell Kessler that Gustav was suspicious. He had come right out and asked her if she was a spy, and if by implication, if Kessler was one, too.

He was about to look around for some object with which to break the glass, when a party of men in evening dress came by, accompanied by some overrouged women in cheap, shiny evening clothes. They were laughing loudly and sounded drunk. He stepped back into the shadows of the alley along the side of the building while they passed. The front was no good. He could be spotted.

He looked up at the sixth-floor windows. Gilt lettering on the panes said "Kessler Shipping Company." In the alley he pried loose a piece of brick paving. It seemed to take forever. Then he tackled the metal fire escape that went up the side of the building, climbing to meet it on a pile of old wooden crates, then pulling himself up on a projecting bit of ornamentation, and finally swinging over the metal railing onto the bottom step.

As he climbed, he'd be hidden from view along the bottom floors by the alley and the building opposite. But once he was past the fifth floor, he'd be above the roofline of the opposite building. And, while his dark evening clothes would blend in with the dark brick, the side of the building above the fifth floor was painted with a garish advertisement. It showed a smiling Cuban senorita tossing her head back and holding a smoking cigar. His black figure against the bright colors would be startling. He'd have to act quickly.

It was filthy work, the metal was sooty, and it was difficult shifting the paving brick around to accommodate his climb, but he managed, nervous only when he climbed across the broad breast of the Cuban cigar girl. He knew how conspicuous he was now. Soon he was staring into a huge red mouth full of white teeth. The advertising worked its way around a small row of windows at the side of the composition, and one of these was his goal.

He wrapped his hand in his handkerchief, turned his face away, and clinging with one hand to the railing of the fire escape, leaned as far back as he could so as to give the brick a good chance. He felt as if he were christening a ship. He threw as hard as he could—and was rewarded with the sound of breaking glass.

Then, reaching in with his wrapped hand, he undid the latch and pushed the window sash. He was inside in a few seconds, walking over crunching glass. A quick glance out the window told him he hadn't been seen. He smiled, realizing he hadn't needed the key to the office after all.

Quickly he went to Miss Lipton's desk, rummaged through it, and found the little card he'd seen her consult. Thank God Kessler was such a methodical Teutonic type. If, as Gustav had been told, Kessler was using his firm to further the ends of the German Empire, whatever business he was up to must be in those secret ledgers.

The safe was balky, but Gustav, with mounting tension, tried various ways of twirling the numbers. Finally he realized that he must pass zero between each number for the combination to work.

The safe swung open.

There were several bundles of ledgers, cloth-covered blue books reinforced with leather corners and spines. He flipped through them all. Some seemed simply to be records of previous years. Ledger D, however, had figures and notes for this year, 1916. Also in the safe was a shoebox containing hundreds of dollars in cash. If he had to escape, as it appeared he must now that he'd broken into the place, he'd need cash. Besides, this was undoubtedly used to bribe and pay off agents. Gustav would rather use it on his side. If Kessler complained, Gustav would simply turn him in as a spy. In a brief movement of exhilaration, Gustav decided this work wasn't all bad. He was beginning to enjoy it. He took another moment to investigate Ledger D. It wasn't apparently clear what financial information it contained. It seemed to be a record of shipments. He knew he should leave, but he was terribly curious.

The items shipped were an odd assortment. Besides simply a ledger of financial records, there was minute lettering indicating the nature and destination of shipments. The recipient was always the Aztec Mining Company in Aztec, Arizona. The items included metal mine supports, great quantities of canvas "for tents," said the notation, and large quantities of explosives and chemicals.

He tried to stop himself from reading the ledger. He had to leave. But what on earth was the Aztec Mining Company, and why were the records so secret?

He put the ledger on the desk and decided whether or not to take the money. If he were caught it would make him look like a common thief. When he'd taken this assignment he hadn't been told to do anything more than find out what Kessler was up to. Now he was burgling a safe. But he hadn't counted on Sophie being involved. He stuffed packets of bills in his pockets. Beneath the cash, at the bottom of the cardboard box, lay a long black revolver. He picked it up and examined the chambers. Empty.

# CHAPTER
# 10

T HERE was a rattling at the door and Gustav heard the sound of a key in the lock. Still holding the revolver, he stepped into a closet in Kessler's office. A moment later he heard Kessler's familiar heavy tread in the outer room and then the door to the room where Gustav was hiding creaking open.

Gustav held his breath. There seemed to be someone else in the room. His suspicion was confirmed when he heard Kessler say in German, "I think you're overwrought. I can't imagine that Baron Wechsler is a spy. I suppose you'll want to kill him just like poor Miss Cavendish. Really, this is becoming ridiculous."

Then, apparently, Herr Kessler saw the shambles in his office, the safe door yawning open, the broken glass, the brick where it had fallen.

"My God," said Kessler. "The money is gone—and the ledger."

No one replied. But Gustav felt sure he could smell that musky perfume. Perhaps it was just in his clothes and therefore more noticeable in the small closet.

No, because now he heard her voice. "Where does that door lead to?" she said.

"That's a closet. Why, that ledger has the whole story in it. This is terrible." Kessler's voice shook.

A second later Gustav was staring into Sophie's face. She had opened the door and was standing before him. She wore a long, black cloak with a hood, and she was holding a small ladies' gun pointed at his heart. Her beautiful face was a cold mask of rage. Now, with a gun pointed at him, he could admire her beauty. There might even be, he thought for a second, something exciting about the situation.

"You wouldn't, Sophie," he said with a smile.

She didn't smile back. "Wouldn't I?"

Very slowly, watching her eyes follow his movement, he brought his revolver up to the level of her chest. He heard a slight intake of breath, but she remained immobile.

"But that's my gun," said Kessler. Gustav kept his eyes on Sophie.

"That's right. And it's a much more powerful weapon than that delicate little thing of Sophie's."

"But," sputtered Kessler, "it's not loaded. My gun is not loaded."

"Well, Sophie," said Gustav, feeling sweat breaking out on his forehead and a cold fist in his stomach, "are you going to take Herr Kessler's word for it?"

"See," said Kessler, in an agitated voice, "the shells are all here." He was apparently rummaging through the safe.

"He's lying," said Gustav. He allowed his eyes to flicker for just a second over Sophie's shoulder. Kessler was holding out a box of brass shells in a cardboard box. "He doesn't like this business at all, Sophie. He's nervous. He wants it all to be over."

Sophie turned slightly to see Kessler, and in that second Gustav grabbed her wrist, turning the gun downward. She was amazingly strong. It took all his effort to bend her hand backwards. He was using his left hand and tried to keep the revolver steady with his right. Her gun went off with a loud crack for such a small weapon. He felt a searing pain in his thigh.

But there was still enough strength in his hand to hold

her wrist fast. With his right hand still wrapped around the revolver, he clipped Sophie on the side of her head. He watched in horror at the arc the black gun made, saw her face startled, surprised, slightly angry as it contorted in pain. He managed to get her gun from her.

"Help me, you fool," said Sophie as she staggered back.

Kessler stood terrified, open-mouthed, but a second later he began to lumber forward.

Gustav felt his wounded leg begin to collapse under him. He tried to straighten himself. He also tried to project himself out of the closet. He didn't want to be cornered like that. He fell against Sophie, his left hand still securely holding her gun. He held his arm out rigidly as he saw her hands clawing up the length of his arm trying to get the weapon. Summoning all his will, he pushed her aside, and she fell to the floor in a heap of crumpled black material.

Kessler was on him now, his chubby hands going for Sophie's gun. Gustav staggered back and tried to balance himself well enough to point the gun at Kessler. But the other man, despite his girth, was fast. Breathing heavily in Gustav's face, he wrapped his plump pink hands around Gustav's arms.

Sophie was up again, dazed. She came toward the two men as they struggled, Gustav mentally sending all his strength to his left hand as Kessler began to try to peel his fingers away from Sophie's weapon.

She was coming at them, and Gustav knew he must act. He reached into Kessler's face. His whole hand covered the cherubic features, and Gustav watched his own fingers push into the flesh, searching for the eyes, scrunching and distorting the face. The man looked as though he were made of clay. Gustav heard a horrible grunt and felt Kessler's warm breath on his palm.

Sophie was on top of them now, biting Gustav's hand. He remembered from their lovemaking what sharp teeth she had. Her canines were pointed and she bit deep into his flesh. With a little cry of pain he dropped the gun. Sophie fell to the floor to catch it, but Gustav managed to kick it across the room. He pushed Kessler down, and the man landed with a thud. Then Gustav went after Sophie on all fours. She was bent under a chair, reaching, when he seized her by the waist and pulled her away. Then, pulling himself back, he gave her a strong punch to the jaw. She screamed and fell back. Her eyes rolled in her head and she collapsed like a doll.

Kessler was up now, his face crimson with rage. Gustav scrambled back out of the office into the reception area, Kessler in pursuit. Leaning against Miss Lipton's desk, he kicked. Kessler had short arms and Gustav had long legs. The maneuver allowed just enough time for Kessler to jump back and for Gustav to seize Miss Lipton's large black typewriter. When Kessler came towards him again, he shoved the typewriter with all his strength into Kessler's stomach, knocking the breath right out of him. Kessler collapsed to the floor and Gustav stood over him a second, holding the typewriter aloft. From the weight of the thing, Gustav was certain he could kill the man if he threw it on his head.

Kessler must have felt the same way, for he began to whimper. Gustav felt he had a mental edge now, and he threw the machine down hard, not on Kessler's skull but on his bended knee. Kessler screamed and Gustav slapped him across the face, then hit him hard on the jaw. The blow was so hard that Kessler's nose began to bleed.

He scrambled over Kessler's limp form. The man was breathing hard and weeping a little. Gustav gave him a kick for good measure, and Kessler cringed in a way that let Gustav know he wouldn't have any more trouble from him.

Back in the inner office, Sophie was dragging herself, half-delirious, it seemed, across the floor towards the gun. The tips of her fingers had touched it when Gustav brought his shoe down on her hand. He realized he was using the leg that had been shot, and the pain, forgotten in the heat of battle, seared through him. His face contorted, but he managed to scoop up the gun, seize the ledger and plunge back onto the fire escape.

He plunged a little too eagerly, thrusting his body against the metal railing of the landing and falling forward. His eyes, wide open, saw the pavement below and, with a start, he jerked himself back. Then he began his descent. His leg, which had managed to behave itself during his struggle, seemed to have turned to India rubber. He favored it, and worked his way down the ladder almost hopping.

The ledger still clutched to his chest, he went down as the ladder automatically glided to the ground, but he fell off the last step and lay for a moment on his side, staring up at the cigar girl on the sign. He would have to summon enough strength to escape.

Why hadn't he had the sense at least to cut the telephone wires and give himself a chance to get away? He knew that if the police were called he'd be in trouble. Of course, there was always the possibility that Kessler didn't want too much attention paid to his business.

He stood, found that the leg worked after a fashion, and that although there was a hole in the fabric of his trousers and a circle of blood around the opening, the wound didn't seem to be bleeding.

He limped out of the alley, still clutching the ledger, his pockets bulging with bills. All in all, he was a pretty sorry sight, he imagined, what with his ripped trousers, bleeding leg, smudgy filthy face and hands. As he went out into Market Street, still unsure about his destination, he saw the same loud, drunken party of men and women that had come by as he was planning to enter the building. They were approaching in the opposite direction this time. He also heard the sound of a police siren and saw a Black Maria coming down the street. He fell in with the men and women, putting his arm around a red-haired woman, who smelled of gin.

The men in evening dress greeted him as if he were an old friend. "Hello, stranger," one of them said to Gustav. "We're looking for a taxi. Been looking for a taxi for hours. Isn't that right, girls? We've been up and down this street."

One of them yawned. "That's right. And I'm *so* sleepy."

"Come on," said Gustav. "We'll go up to the Saint Francis Hotel. We'll get someone there to get a taxi for us."

The group, strangely liquid in their movements, were easily persuaded to follow Gustav. He turned them all around, only to see the police car pull up to the front of Kessler's office building. The police rushed inside. By the time Gustav had eased his companions off Market and up towards Post Street, he saw the policemen coming back out of the building with Kessler and Sophie behind them. He took the opera hat off the head of one of his new friends (he'd left his hat in Sophie's suite, he realized), and put it on his own. From this distance he felt sure he was safe.

When he and his charges, who had now begun to sing sad songs, reached the Saint Francis, one of the party looked up in astonishment and declared, "Why, this is my hotel. Let's all go to my room for a nightcap."

As they went up the marble steps, one of the men turned to Gustav and said thickly, "Who are you, anyway?" Gustav just shrugged. He'd been planning to go with them, maybe get a bath and a shave and lay low for a while, but he decided not to chance it. Besides, he had better get to Mrs. Cavendish as soon as possible.

Despite the events of the dawn, he couldn't forget what he had overheard from Kessler's office closet. For some reason, Mrs. Cavendish's life was in danger from these people. It could only have something to do with her abduction and escape. He had to warn her. At the same time, perhaps he could be safe there for a while. And then he remembered George, the little brother who'd acted so suspicious of him, the one who had a mania about German spies.

Gustav took out his watch. It was five o'clock. There was a little traffic on the streets, now, as the city began to wake. Gustav walked across Union Square, wondering what to do next. Then he heard the clopping of hooves and the rattle of bottles. He fished in his pockets for the money he'd taken from Kessler's safe and came up with a twenty. Wearily, he handed it to the young man on the milk wagon. "You mind taking a passenger to Russian Hill?"

Gustav sat on the back of the wagon, the bouncing and the rattling of the bottles lulling him with its rhythm to a sleepy stupor. It seemed as if he had left that party at Kessler's house with Sophie weeks ago. It had been an eventful evening. And to think, when Mr. Voska had recruited him, the old man had put a fatherly hand on Gustav's knee and said: "Now remember, Baron, whatever you may have read in novels, I assure you the work is tedious. You won't end up sleeping with beautiful spies or grappling with villains." He and Gustav had both laughed.

There was no need to tell this milkman exactly where he was going. If there were questions later it would be dangerous.

"Let me off here, will you?" he said when they reached a street that he thought was near. The wound in his leg began to hurt more, and he realized that fear and the need to escape had masked physical pain for the last hour or so. Now his whole leg ached and throbbed. He limped along a street, cursed when he saw he'd made a mistake and that he meant to be several more blocks up the hill, and forced himself further along through sheer will.

When he finally came to Maude Cavendish's house, he saw a curious flick of net curtain at the opposite house. An inquisitive neighbor. He realized how horrible he looked, and that inquiries might be made, so he passed the neat little gate and went around the block to a small alley. Here was an ivy-colored brick wall. Groaning at the prospect of more climbing, Gustav pulled himself up the ivy, over the top of the wall, and fell into some shrubbery below. The ground was cold and thick with dew. Gustav found the damp refreshing. He closed his eyes for a moment. Around him in the garden he heard the birds singing, and he was dimly aware that the sun was about to rise. There was a pinkish cast to the sky. He closed his eyes for a moment and tried to gather his strength. Instead, he slipped into unconsciousness.

* * *

A train whistle screamed across the desert. Louise Arbor woke. She looked around, startled, and tried to sit up. The big, motherly-looking nurse came to her side.

"I've been kidnapped. Taken by two little dark men," said Louise, running a hand through her disheveled hair. "My God, help me."

"I know, dear," said the nurse matter-of-factly. Exactly the delusion the doctor had told her about. "I'll help you sleep." She took the needle she'd prepared, squirted the air out of the top and plunged it into Louise's arm. No use taking chances. The nurse knew how powerful the truly mad could be. She seemed like such a pretty girl. And from a good family, she'd been told. Such a shame.

# CHAPTER
# 11

GEORGE set out for school a little late. It was all right, he reasoned. He would run down the last three blocks or so and make up for lost time. His books, fastened together with a leather strap, hung over his shoulder. He hung the strap for a moment on the gate while he redid the buckles on his knickerbockers and reset his cloth cap at a jauntier angle.

When he looked up, he saw his neighbor across the street, Mrs. Sullivan, standing on the porch waving a dustmop in the air. She looked for any excuse to keep a watch on the neighborhood, even risking being seen shaking her own mop out of the front door. Next thing, she'd be hanging out the wash in the front yard. Maude said Mrs. Sullivan just didn't know any better and carried on as if their neighborhood was some kind of tenement.

"Boy!" she called out. "Come here, boy." George sighed, went over to Mrs. Sullivan's side of the street, and removed his cap. "Ma'am?"

"There's a pretty desperate character on the loose around here, you know," she said. "I saw him this morning when I was getting Mr. Sullivan's breakfast." Mrs. Sullivan never missed an opportunity to tell people how much manual labor she did. Maude said it was the worst kind of snobbery to gloat about drudgery. Mrs. Sullivan could afford good help, but all she had was a woman to do the heavy cleaning and the laundry twice a week. "He looked a desperate character, I'm telling you. All messed up and dirty and kind of staggering like he'd been in a fight or was drunk or something. And he was all dressed up in evening clothes. Maybe he was a waiter. I just thought I'd better tell you, boy, your sister being all alone in the world and all, and probably wanting to know if there's desperate characters lurking about. It's my belief he staggered into that alley behind your house."

"I'll investigate, Mrs. Sullivan," said George gravely. He went around to the brick wall behind the house. At the base was a litter of shiny, dark green ivy leaves. George knelt and examined them. "Fresh," he murmured to himself, feeling like Baden-Powell. His eyes climbed the wall and he noticed several broken branches. George smiled broadly. Mrs. Sullivan was right. Some desperate character had staggered into this alley and had climbed over the wall into their garden, leaving clues behind. George briefly considered going around and back through the house to investigate, but he decided against it. Mrs. Sullivan would want an explanation; Maude, whom he had left drinking coffee in the dining room, would want an explanation; Clara, doing the breakfast dishes, would want one, too. And while he was doing all this explaining, his quarry might escape. If he was still in the garden.

George began to climb the ivy. At the top of the wall, arms outstretched for balance, he walked a few feet to the branches of a plum tree, and then climbed down the gnarled old branches to the ground.

Stretched out, apparently asleep in the wet grass, looking as disheveled as Mrs. Sullivan had indicated but with a strangely peaceful expression on his scarred face, lay Baron Wechsler. In his hand was a flat blue book with red leather trim.

Maude pulled on her gloves on the walk just before she let herself out the gate, chiding herself for doing so. A lady never put on her gloves outside. But ladies weren't always rushing. She wanted to get her story to the *Globe* as early as possible.

At the gate she saw George's school books hanging by the leather strap he used to keep them together. She sighed. George was getting so absentminded lately. She guessed it was his age. And his preoccupation with unwholesome topics like German spies and Hindoo bandits.

She looked at the books for a moment and wondered if she should take them by his school. It would make her late, of course. No, better to let George realize his mistake and come back. Maybe he'd be less careless in the future.

She stepped out onto the sidewalk, trying to ignore that horrible Mrs. Sullivan. She was standing there with a mop in her hand. Really, anyone might take her for a maid. Mrs. Sullivan's problem, thought Maude, was that her husband had made a lot of money too quickly and his poor wife hadn't been able to adjust to her new social position. Mrs. Sullivan seemed to want to tell her something, but Maude smiled, said "Good morning," and kept walking. She was too busy for any neighborhood gossip on the front stoop. Really, Mrs. Sullivan was intolerable.

Maude's story was a fairly general account of the Kesslers' reception for Madame Von Gluck, with a lengthy description of the diva's gown, a reference to her previous acquaintanceship with the baron, and a long aside about Baron Gustav Wechsler himself, "a new face on the social scene, bringing San Francisco a much more solid and quiet example of European aristocracy than some of the Italian and French noblemen who've added their own amusing style to this city's social life. Teutonic down to his clicking heels, Baron Wechsler's handsome features bear a dueling scar according to the old German custom."

In the article Maude had spoken flatteringly of that horrible old Mrs. Kessler because, after all, Mrs. Kessler had invited her, and while Mrs. Kessler was far from the inner circle, every hostess should be encouraged to include the *Globe*'s society reporter and deserved a little reward when she did. "Mrs. Franz Kessler, with her husband a leading cultural light of our city, expressed her delight in San Francisco's ability to attract such world-famous artists as Madame Von Gluck.'' The ''Madame'' was simply a courtesy title given to artists, for as far as Maude knew, the singer was an unmarried woman, and while Mrs. Kessler hadn't spoken to Maude at all, just given her a fishy smile when she arrived, Maude thought that's the sort of thing Frau Kessler might have said. Maude had also written nice things about the lobster.

Maude wanted this piece delivered early because she wanted to get loose from Clarence P. Fogerty. He'd been everywhere she looked the last few days—even at a lecture at the Women's Century Club—hanging around outside. Every once in a while he'd come up to Maude and say something about wanting to follow up on her story. Maude had tried to shake him by walking past several of Fogerty's old drinking haunts, but he hadn't snapped at the bait. It made it impossible for Maude to pursue the story on her own.

But today she'd break loose. She'd turn in her copy at nine and leave the *Globe* before Fogerty arrived. He usually expected her at eleven. Then she was going to track down Louise Arbor. For ever since the night she and George had called Dr. Arbor, no one had heard or seen Louise. And Dr. Arbor himself wouldn't come to the telephone, either. Today, without telling a soul, and without Fogerty in tow to horn in and steal her story, Maude would take the train to Palo Alto and find out exactly what had happened to Louise. It was most uncharacteristic of Miss Arbor not to have attended her own cousin's ball—which was what had happened. Maude had heard she'd simply sent a note around with a servant, saying she was ill. It was all very mysterious, and perhaps a link with Maude's own abduction. Louise could be hiding, or she could even be kidnapped!

Maude caught the cable car down to Market Street and took a moment on the car to straighten her hat, first unpinning it from her abundant hair. It was a lovely hat, Alice blue with a tall crown and brim and decorated with soft, gray feathers. Really, she thought, pushing in the pearl-tipped pin again, I am really becoming lax—pulling my gloves on on the street, fixing my hat on the cable car.

When she reached Market Street she decided to walk the several blocks to the *Globe* offices. Normally arriving at work later, she had no idea how crowded the street could be at this hour. It was quite a crush, and it seemed she was jostled several times. Finally, while she was waiting to cross the street, she felt more than a jostle. She felt a very firm push. With a shout, she felt herself hurtle forward. Her chest and face were scraping the pavement and she'd hurt her head. She partly raised herself, pushing up on the palms of her hands, and, still on the ground, realized she was on the streetcar tracks. A trolley was coming towards her—she heard it before she got the impression of a blur of silver wheels—and then she felt strong arms around her shoulders and ankles as she was pulled off the tracks. She hid her face as the car raced by a few inches from her head. When she looked up after it had gone by, all she could see was a mangled Alice-blue felt hat, the feathers bent, their tips lifting slightly in the breeze.

She looked around at her rescuers, a handful of men, who were now pulling her up to her feet. Dazed, she thanked them. Someone handed her the remains of her hat. Shaking, she went back to the sidewalk.

A little old woman with ludicrously dyed red hair, in a dark dress with a shawl wrapped tightly around her and missing front teeth helped her brush off her skirt. Maude had been wearing a blue skirt with a matching jacket decorated with frogs in darker blue silk. The trim was all scratched and torn. Maude put a hand to her bare head and tried to push some wisps of hair back into shape.

"I saw the fellow what pushed you," said the woman in a gravelly voice. "A little Mex all dressed up in a frock coat."

"A Mexican?" said Maude, startled, looking at the old woman and then up and down the street. "Are you sure? Could he have been a Hindoo?"

"I guess. Brown skin, black hair. A little fellow."

\* \* \*

George was delighted. It was almost an answer to a prayer. A Central Powers spy, passed out in his own back garden. And clutching a mysterious book, too. Perhaps it was all in code. George bent down and tried to remove the book gently from beneath Baron Wechsler's folded arms.

Suddenly the baron's gray eyes flew open. He looked sharply at George while he continued to lie there, holding on hard to his book. It seemed as if he were unsure as to where he was. Then realization seemed to come to his face, and the intense gray eyes softened.

"Young Cavendish," he said.

"Teasdale," said George. People were always making this mistake. "My sister's name is Cavendish, because she married."

"That's right," said Wechsler, closing his eyes momentarily before he propped himself up. "Give me a hand, will you, George, I've had a rough night."

George automatically bent to help him, even though he was suspicious. "What are you doing here?" he demanded. He seized the baron under his arms and began to pull. Gustav let out a yelp of pain.

"What's the matter with you?" said George. And then he saw the wounded leg. "My goodness, you're really hurt."

"Shot," said Gustav. "I think the ball is still in there."

"Golly," said George with enthusiasm. And then he said, "We'd better get you a doctor."

"It may not be safe," said Gustav.

"What kind of trouble are you in?" said George. "Who shot you?"

"I need to talk to your sister," said Gustav.

"Maude? What for? She's gone anyway, probably."

"Well then, get me inside the house," said Gustav. "I can't spend the rest of the day lying out here in the damp." He sounded irritable. "I'll have to wait for her."

"Okay, okay," said George.

Carefully he helped Gustav to his feet.

"Damn," said the baron. "It didn't hurt so much last

night.'' He half hopped towards the house. ''Who's in there?'' he asked.

''Clara. The housekeeper.''

''Any other servants?''

''No.''

''I don't feel like explaining to anyone right now,'' said Gustav. ''But I thought you might understand.''

''Me?'' George was astounded.

''Your sister says you're interested in German spies.''

They had reached the kitchen door, now.

''You mean you're going to tell me all?'' George could only imagine that this German spy had had a fit of remorse. And George was going to be the first to hear about it. Any thoughts of school that might have lingered at the back of George's mind were now completely abandoned.

''Listen,'' said George in a whisper, ''I'll see if I can get you past Clara.'' He peeked in the window. Clara was mopping the kitchen floor and singing.

''I've got it,'' said George. ''We'll go in the coal cellar.''

''The coal cellar?'' Gustav looked exhausted at the thought. But George was leading him around to the side of the house. ''Now wait here,'' the boy instructed.

George went around to the front door. He was surprised to see Clara coming out with a shopping basket on her arm.

''And what are you doing here?'' she demanded.

''I forgot my books,'' said George haughtily. ''And while I'm here I'll just pop inside for my homework. I left that in my room.'' He took his books from where they had been hanging from the gate.

Clara frowned and closed the gate behind her. ''I'll have to mention this to Mrs. Cavendish,'' she said. ''Can't have any hooky-playing going on. And mind, George, the kitchen floor is wet, if you're planning on eating anything.''

''Oh, really, Clara,'' said George, exasperated. He let himself in with his latchkey and looked out the window as Clara set off down the street. She was probably just picking up a few things at Schulz's grocery. He might not have much time. He went to the kitchen door, went around to the coal cellar door and brought Gustav back through the kitchen.

"I know a little bit about first aid from my scouting," said George. "But you should see a real doctor," he added reluctantly.

"No," said Gustav. "There would be inquiries. I can't have that right now."

George decided that the baron must be a spy. He'd better make him comfortable, get what he could out of him, remorse or whatever, and then send for the authorities. He'd have to make sure that the baron couldn't escape. In the man's obviously weakened condition, it shouldn't be too hard.

"I'll take you upstairs," said George.

"All right. Can't say as I like the thought of stairs, though." George felt the baron's weight heavily on his shoulder. It seemed that the man was getting heavier and heavier.

"Okay," said George. "We'll try the dumbwaiter."

Somehow he managed to get Gustav into the dumbwaiter. He seemed to crumple into a little ball inside the big, square wooden box. George pulled on the ropes and heard the creaking, squeaky sound of the box going up to the next floor. He kept it going one more floor—it was hard work—until the dumbwaiter was at the very top of the house in the attic.

Then George ran up two flights of back stairs and, panting, opened the dumbwaiter doors. The baron practically tumbled out. He looked pale.

George helped him over to one of the old servants' rooms, unoccupied since Maude's divorce, when everyone but Clara had to go. There was a narrow bed in there and a sink. The baron fell onto the bed with what looked like great relief.

"Now listen, George," he said, "and listen well. I know something about spies. And I know they intend to harm your sister. I came to warn her."

"Why would anyone want to harm my sister?" said George.

"I don't know. But she must be warned. Perhaps she should leave San Francisco. These are very dangerous people."

George looked down at the circle of blood. "Did they shoot you? The German spies?"

Gustav lay back on his pillow, eyes closed. "Yes."

"Why did you come here?" said George.

"Because before I was shot I overheard them say something about harming your sister."

"And because you needed a place to hide," said George. It suddenly occurred to George that if a German spy wanted to penetrate their home to harm Maude, and if the baron was a German spy, they had already penetrated the house and George had helped. He looked suspiciously at the wound. What if it was a fake?

"I must see to that," he said.

"Never mind that now," said Gustav, but George ignored him and left the attic room. Before he did, he took the precaution of removing the key from the door and locking the room from the outside.

Inside the small room, Gustav looked up at the coved ceilings, the faded wallpaper, the varnished wooden door, the sink on its spindly metal legs. The boy had locked the door. Either he was taking precautions so as not to give Gustav away to the servant, or he was suspicious of Gustav. Either way it proved that the boy was cautious. That was probably a good sign.

He had hoped Mrs. Cavendish would be home. Of course, he had forgotten that the woman had a job. Presumably she was out gadding about finding things for her wretched newspaper. Perhaps he had better simply leave a warning with the boy and try to escape. This couldn't be the safest place for him right now if Sophie had plans to kill Mrs. Cavendish. The boy's question was a good one. Why? Why would agents of Imperial Germany want to kill an American society reporter? Something to do with her abduction, no doubt. It was probably worth his while to try and solve that mystery. But his first order of business was to get in touch with Mr. Voska. Whatever happened to him now, he had to tell Mr. Voska about Sophie. And about Kessler. The ledger had to get to Mr. Voska, too, somehow, if Gustav couldn't make out its significance himself. It was a lot to do. And difficult while he was limping around with a bullet in his leg.

He smiled a little at the thought of that bullet. There was no doubt in his mind that Sophie might have pulled that trigger when her gun was pointed at his chest. And could he have shot her? He didn't know. He'd known his gun was empty, so it had been easy to point it at her. All in all, a curious episode. One he could never have imagined the night he heard her sing for the first time and went backstage to meet her.

He heard a click at the door and the boy came back inside. He was carrying a basin filled with a roll of gauze, some scissors, tweezers, and a small, dark brown bottle. There was also a decanter of whiskey.

Maude went into the *Globe* offices and directly through the rows of desks to Mr. McLaren's office, holding the remnants of her hat.

"Well, look what the cat dragged in," he said, chewing vigorously on his cigar. "You're a mess, Cavendish. And your hat needs blocking."

"My hat is ruined," said Maude. "It fell under a moving streetcar." She had decided not to tell anyone about her misadventure. Why help Fogerty follow up on the story of her abduction? She'd wait until she had more—and she just might have more after a visit to Palo Alto if Louise Arbor was gone and she could prove it. She'd hold the whole story hostage—refusing to give it to the *Globe* unless she got a byline.

Maude debated a moment before deciding that she couldn't go to Palo Alto without a hat. It would be too conspicuous and she would feel ill at ease. She couldn't wear the remains of her Alice-blue hat, either. She'd have to go back home. As she went out into the street, a little shudder went through her. There was a difference between being pushed under the wheels of a streetcar and being held captive. Whatever these people had wanted with her before—and she was willing to guess they had really wanted Louise Arbor—they wanted something different now. Now they wanted her dead.

Gustav looked suspiciously at the basin George carried. "I'll have a go at that wound, if you'd like," said George. "Or I'll call a doctor. But Clara's going to be home any minute and I can't guarantee she won't call the police."

"No police," said Gustav. "It would only complicate things."

"All right." George came toward the bed. He cut away the fabric of Gustav's trousers. It was a real wound, all right. If he'd tried to get into the house through a ruse, this was more than he would have needed.

"Here." He handed Gustav the decanter. Gustav took a big slug. Then George filled the basin with water and washed the wound. "This part will sting," he announced, applying antiseptic. Gustav grimaced and drew his breath in quickly.

George examined the wound. "I can see the bullet. I sterilized the tweezers with some of the antiseptic." Then, while Gustav looked away towards the wall, George probed into the wound. It was rather like taking out a very large splinter, George told himself. It was hard to get a grip on the shiny metal surface with the tweezers, but finally George plunged the tweezers deep into the wound so as to push the bullet out from behind. Gustav's whole body became rigid, but he didn't cry out.

A second later, George was rewarded with the sight of the bullet popping out of the bloody flesh. It fell on the bare wood floor with a metallic ping.

George picked it up. "Here's a souvenir for you," he said. Gustav turned his face from the wall. He looked extraordinarily pale, but he managed a weak smile. Then he took another deep swig of the whiskey.

George cleaned he wound some more and then placed

folded gauze on top of it and tied the gauze in place with a strip of cloth.

"You should rest now," said George.

Gustav clutched his arm. "No. There's work to be done. I want you to help me."

"How do I know you're not a German spy?" said George.

"Listen," said Gustav. "I'm a Czech. I'm Austrian by nationality, but I'm a Czech. I want the Hapsburgs out of my country. I'm working against them in this war to make my country's independence a possibility."

George was silent. He wasn't sure he believed him.

"The Germans are planning something," Gustav continued.

"What?"

"I don't know. But part of the answer is in this book. I want you to help me get a message to my superiors. They must know about this."

"Wouldn't I be violating American neutrality if I helped you?" asked George solemnly.

"No, you would be preventing a violation of American neutrality laws," said Gustav. "For heaven's sake, don't argue with me now. These are the people who want to harm your sister."

"I suppose I should tell the authorities," said George.

"If you do that, they might send me out of the country," said Gustav. "And they might get around to investigating my charges eventually. But meanwhile, great harm could be done. And to your sister, too."

"You're right," said George. "I should handle this myself." He still had some doubts about the baron's story, but he decided to go along as much as possible until he learned more.

"Good fellow. Now listen. First of all, can you get to my apartment and secure a book there? It's just a novel, but it's the basis of the code I use to communicate with my superiors."

"Who are your superiors, exactly?" said George. "The English?"

Gustav shook his head. He spoke with great effort now. George realized he had been weakened. "No. Patriots. People like me, who hate what the Central Powers stand for—militarism, Prussian love of war and conquest."

"And when you have the code book you'll send a message to these people?"

"That's right."

"Let's have a look at that notebook. Is it a code, too?"

"I don't know. Please don't ask me so many questions. You might be in danger if you know too much."

"Let me have a look at that," George insisted. He took the book from the bed. "You can't expect me to get involved if I don't know what I'm involved in." He flipped open the book. "It looks like bookkeeping. Some kind of accounts book." George knew Gustav was too weak to stop him.

"That's what it appears to be."

"Golly," said George. "The Aztec Mining Company. I bet that's where the Schulz boy is. He sent his folks a postcard from Aztec, Arizona. I thought it was some kind of cooked-up story, because I know he wanted to serve the Fatherland and go off to war. Instead, they said he was a miner in Aztec, Arizona. And you're saying this is some sort of a German plot? Golly!"

"What?" Gustav got George to repeat his story.

"Listen," he said urgently, "don't spend any more time talking. Go to my apartment"—he gave the address on Pacific—"and pick up the red book on the bedstead."

George tiptoed downstairs and through the pantry. He could hear Clara bustling around in the kitchen. He managed to get past her and into the back parlor, where he let himself out the French windows into the garden.

A moment later he'd scrambled over the wall, had brushed off his clothes, and was walking down Russian Hill whistling, one arm swinging free, the other hand in his pocket wrapped around Baron Wechsler's latchkey.

About twenty minutes later George reached the flat, the second story of a modern white building with red tile roof and bits of Moorish architecture around the doors and windows. He opened the door with the latchkey, deciding to tell anyone who questioned him that he was the baron's office boy come to fetch some papers. No one saw him, however.

George looked around the silent flat with interest. So this is how spies lived. It was sparsely furnished, with a look of impermanence about it. The furniture was simple, dark-stained, and without much character, and there was a flowery carpet on the floor. The place was neat and tidy but strangely impersonal. There was a kitchen, a dining room, a living room, and a bedroom.

Next to the bed, where he had been told it would be, George found the book. It was a perfectly ordinary-looking book—a rather worn copy of *Girl of the Limberlost* by Gene Stratton Porter. George tucked it under his arm and prepared to leave, but a sound at the door made him freeze in his tracks. There was a metallic, scrabbly noise, as if the lock were being picked. George looked around him for another exit; there was none.

# CHAPTER
# 12

GEORGE heard the low voices muttering outside the door. He stepped back into the bedroom. It was dimly lit and hung with some heavy damask curtains. He stood for a moment behind them. This would never work. He was sure his feet stuck out from beneath the damask. He was about to decide on the closet when he heard a splintery kind of sound, and the door opening. He stayed where he was. Two people were walking through the flat. They walked through the rooms but spent just a second in the bedroom, while George held his breath.

There seemed to be two people—a man and a woman—and they were speaking German. George caught his breath. Up until now, he hadn't been sure he was really dealing with German spies. Now he felt sure it must be true. He couldn't see anything from behind his curtain, but he could tell from the voices that they were in the small kitchen. They seemed to be arguing about something, although quietly, as if they were afraid they might be overheard. George took this moment to leap across the room from under the curtain and into the closet. Of course, if these people were searching the flat they would find him there. He pressed his ear to the wall of the closet. He seemed to be hearing cupboards opening and closing. George put his eye to the keyhole in the closet. He smiled. He couldn't see anything. There must be a key. Slowly, he opened the closet door, reached around and seized the key from the lock. Inside, in the dark closet lit only by the light of a rather dirty little closet window, he turned the key slowly in the lock. There. That would buy him a little time, in any case. He began to investigate the little closet window. It was awfully small, but then, so was George.

He heard them moving about the living room now. There was the sound of furniture scraping. He wondered if they were looking for anything in particular. Perhaps the ledger that Baron Wechsler still had with him. Or perhaps the code book.

George stood on top of a laundry hamper, the wicker creaking beneath his weight, and examined the closet window. It had a simple brass latch and a little arm that held it open at right angles to the building. He leaned out. It was pretty far down to the ground and a brick-paved courtyard below, with tubs of flowers sitting around. But on the first floor and to one side was a balcony, and around the windows just below him were the ends of some heavy wooden beams, projecting from the stucco surface. George didn't know how these new-fangled Moorish buildings were constructed. He hoped that those little wooden projections really were part of sturdy beams and not some sham decoration.

He took the copy of *Girl of the Limberlost* and unbuckled his knickerbockers, placing the book inside the voluminous tweed leg, rebuckling it securely. This whole procedure made him tumble off the wicker hamper, and he landed with a muffled thump on some shirts. The baron had been negligent about sending out his laundry. It had overflowed from the hamper onto the closet floor.

The scraping of furniture in the other room ceased, and he heard footsteps coming into the bedroom. He bent down and peered through the keyhole. He saw a pair of men's trousers and the bottom half of a rather stout man. And he saw the swirling skirts of a lady. Above his head, he heard the doorknob rattle. A second later he saw her stoop down and was looking into her face. She was a beautiful lady, dark and proud-looking. George stood transfixed for half a second before he could see no more, realizing that the lady's brown eye had blocked the light from the keyhole. With a start, he drew back, but not before catching a whiff of a lovely, musky perfume. He had been just inches away from her, with that door between. George found the idea of this rather exciting. It was almost with reluctance that he replaced the key in the lock so she couldn't see him, pulled himself up on the wicker hamper and through the window. He hung facing the building for a moment and felt with his toe—hardly daring to look down—for the bit of beam. It wasn't as big as he thought. There was just room for one foot, but his other foot found a place for itself on another bit of wood. With his hands he clung to the window ledge above him. Slowly, his fingernails digging into the rough plaster, his body pressed as close to the surface of the building as possible, he bent his knees and lowered himself down onto the beams. He seized them in his hands and lowered himself still further, hanging from the wooden projections. There was a drop, now, of just another foot or so to the balcony railing. He let go, bounced onto the wrought iron, and fell awkwardly onto the balcony. Now there was just one more story to go to get to the ground.

An old lady came to the window and stared out onto the balcony. George didn't wait another second. He catapulted himself off the balcony and fell into a huge old laurel bush just a little below. The branches snapped beneath him and poked him, and he scraped himself on one of the thicker branches, but thrashing around in the shiny green leaves until he was free took just another second. He looked back up at the closet window. The dark woman was looking down at him. He waved his cap and then took off running.

Maude came home cross and annoyed. She decided as soon as she put on a new hat that she'd take a taxi to the Southern Pacific depot and go down to Palo Alto. But when she arrived home, Clara asked to speak to her about George.

"Oh, what has he done now?" said Maude nervously. She hoped he hadn't done anything to offend Clara.

"Well, ma'am, I just thought you should know that when I was going out to do my morning marketing, he was still hanging around the house. I hope he's not playing hooky."

"Oh. Well, I'll talk to him about it," said Maude, trying to sound casual.

"He said he was just coming back for his homework."

"That could be," said Maude. "I saw he left his books at the front gate this morning."

Then Clara noticed Maude's disheveled appearance.

"Why, Mrs. Cavendish—your jacket is torn. And what happened to your hat?" cried Clara in alarm, examining the crumpled felt and feathers in Maude's hand.

"A streetcar. Isn't it awful?" She held it up. "I fell and the hat rolled under a streetcar."

"Well, the feathers are ruined, but maybe I can steam out that dent in the crown," said Clara thoughtfully. "I'll put on the kettle."

"Oh, do you think you can? It would be easy to have it trimmed again." This was the first cheerful news Maude had heard all day.

"Just be glad," said Clara dryly, "that your head wasn't in it when this happened." She turned to go, and suddenly Maude found herself shaking and dizzy.

She had been putting the thought to the back of her mind—perhaps it had been the shock of the push onto the pavement—but someone had tried to kill her today. Nervously she checked to make sure the front door was secured, then she wandered into the study and found the French doors unlocked. Anyone could just come in here and . . .

Morbid thoughts went through her mind. She turned away from the doors and put her hand on her forehead. What would George do if something happened to her? She was all he had left. She stood there for a moment, trying to compose herself. And then she heard a barely perceptible rattling at the French doors. Horrified, she turned and saw a shadowy form through the heavy lace curtains and saw the shiny brass knob move slowly.

Maude started to scream, but all she could come up with was a hoarse gasp.

A second later she heard George's voice. "Maude? Is that you? Are you all right? Let me in!"

She went to the French doors and opened them. "George Teasdale! Why aren't you in school? What have you been up to? You look all raggedy and disheveled. And you scared me half to death."

"What have *you* been up to, Maude? There's a scrape on your face and all that stuff on your dress is hanging off." He pointed to the navy frogs.

"I almost got run over by a streetcar."

"Oh. I was locked in a closet and I had to escape by climbing down the sheer side of a building."

"George!" Maude looked shocked. "What *is* going on?"

"Well, I guess I'd better tell you."

"I guess you'd better."

The telephone rang.

"Maude," said George, "you're in terrible danger. From German spies."

She sighed.

"Oh, George, you've already told me your theories."

"This isn't a theory. Maude, someone came to warn you. Someone in a position to know. He told me. You're in grave danger."

"Who?"

"Baron Wechsler."

"What?"

Clara came to the door of the room. "Telephone for you, Mrs. Cavendish." She glared at George. "Why aren't you at school? I see your sister caught you."

Maude went into the hall and stood on tiptoe, her face turned up to the speaking tube. She put the receiver on her ear. "Yes?"

"Cavendish, this is McLaren at the *Globe*. Just read your copy and I see you've got a blurb on that Baron Wechsler character."

"That's right."

"Well, he's page one now, Cavendish. Seems he broke into his employer's safe last night and embezzled funds. We're doing a big spread on him on page one—gentleman cracksman—that kind of angle. I'm sending a reporter up to interview you about the fellow. Give us the ladies' point of view. Expand a little on what you said in your society story. And, of course, we'll fix that piece of yours up a little so we emphasize him more. 'Had I but known, as I spoke to the quiet, well-mannered gentleman, that he was not precisely what he appeared to be'—that sort of thing."

"Seeing as how I'm acquainted with the baron personally," said Maude icily, "why not let me handle the whole story?"

"Come on, Cavendish, now's not the time to carry on about that. I've already assigned the story. Now I trust you'll cooperate with Fogerty when he comes around to get your story."

"Fogerty!" hissed Maude. But Mr. McLaren had already hung up the phone.

She turned to face George, who had followed her out into the hall. "George! The police are looking for Baron Wechsler. He robbed his employer last night. And you say he spoke to you today? George, this could be a terrific story. This could change everything for me at the *Globe*. Where is he? Tell me where he is!" She took her brother by the shoulders. She looked a little wild. Her hair was still partly unpinned, her color was high, her eyes shone glassily.

George looked at her thoughtfully for a moment. He'd seldom seen his sister so excited. "I don't know where he is now," said George.

# CHAPTER
# 13

IT had been absurdly easy so far. All Tommy had to do was follow the railroad tracks. And in desert country like this it was a piece of cake. He shouldn't have any trouble.

He was, he figured, about an hour out of Yuma, when a terrific wind came up. He felt it push under the wings and his craft lifted up like a glider, as if it had no power of its own. Tommy knew better than to fight nature at a time like this. He took the machine up—to be more precise, he allowed it to rise. A second later, however, the aeroplane was surrounded by a cloud of dust. Tommy was flying blind. He pulled up on the throttle and shot high above the cloud. When he looked down he saw the cloud, but the ground was obscured. There was a fine layer of gritty dust inside the cockpit now. He cursed himself for not having avoided trouble sooner. The railroad tracks were some-where below, but where he wasn't precisely sure.

He reached into a leather satchel at his side. Under a few sandwiches wrapped in brown paper and tied with a string by Cousin Will this morning was a small compass. It was hard to read, with the plane vibrating as it did, but he could make out that he was flying in an easterly direc-tion. He hadn't thought he'd need the compass at all. It was a straight shot along the railroad tracks, and even if there were clouds—a rare thing in this country—he'd simply fly beneath them. He stayed above the dust clouds, hoping for a break soon so he could get lower and follow the railroad once more. Until then, he'd make what progress he could. He didn't want to overfly Tucson, but if he did, he'd have plenty of gas. One of the selling points of the plane was its range—made possible by a capacious tank. There was even a gauge, rigged up by Cousin Will, to let you know how much you had.

About twenty minutes later, he thought he was looking at the floor of the desert once more—and that he was out of the storm. It was hard to say, though. Dust was all the same color, whether it was still or flying around. He took the plane lower until he could be quite sure. Yes, he was out of the storm now, but there wasn't a sign anywhere of the railroad tracks. He didn't know how he could have got off course so quickly. Unless the wind had blown him farther than he'd thought. He checked the compass again. He seemed to be heading east southeast. He corrected his course and took a more directly eastern route.

If Cousin Will were here he would be saying, "I told you so." He was always going on about the fact that aviation would someday require more complex means of navigation than following markings along the ground. What he thought was more logical than following a road or a railroad track or a telegraph line, Tommy couldn't imagine.

For now, though, Tommy was optimistic enough. Tucson was east of Yuma, but it was south, too. If he'd been blown south as he thought he had been, he still had a pretty good chance of heading directly for Tucson. Taking care to fly the plane as level as possible, he read the gauge. He had lots of gas.

About twenty minutes later, Tommy had a little knot of fear in his stomach. He was lost, there was no doubt about it. The first sign of human habitation he saw, he'd take her down and find out where in hell he was. He felt like a drink of water, but he only eyed his canteen for a second. If he had to take her down in the desert, he'd want to have as much water as he could. He'd wait.

He simply couldn't get hopelessly lost, he told himself. Even if he managed to live—and Tommy had a cheerful faith in his own ability to stay alive whatever the circumstances—he might lose his chance to sell the plane to the army. The way that telegram was worded, Tommy had an idea other builders were flying their machines to El Paso, too. And if the army was as eager as they said they were to get their men into the air above the Mexicans, there was a good chance they'd buy the first machine they saw.

He kept his eye out for any sign of human habitation. The land was getting more rugged. There were some big red rocks around, and flat-topped mesas. It was spectacular country. There was no doubt about it. And no doubt no one—ever—had seen so much of it so fast, the way Tommy was seeing it now, unreeling below him in vivid colors, vast and wide open under a vivid blue sky. It was funny, even off course and worried, Tommy could still appreciate the freedom and the power he had flying over this impenetrable desert. Despite himself, Tommy swooped down and executed a few barrel rolls. There was no one to see them besides jackrabbits, lizards, and coyotes, but those barrel rolls cheered Tommy up right away.

And they must have been good luck, he thought a few minutes later, because below him there was a sign of life. What was going on on top of a mesa in the desert he had no idea, but directly below was what looked like a strip of concrete, or at least macadamized road. And there were some outbuildings scattered around—one of them looked like a barracks. As he came down he saw groups of men standing in clusters and pointing at him. This was the usual reception an aviator got. No doubt they'd all be thrilled to see a real aeroplane. Tommy smiled. It was swell, knowing that wherever he landed he was welcome—a hero, even.

The wheels were a scant few feet above what he took to be a road. It was long enough to be a runway, not much longer, when he realized with amazement that he was landing on a flat tar-paper roof. This building was huge. He couldn't imagine what it was doing here. And there was another in front of him, just like it. He taxied the length of the roof, vaguely aware of shouting men beneath him, wondering if he'd be able to stop in time, before he reached the edge. He was glad Cousin Will had been so thorough. The plane had brakes. He seldom used them— he'd never flown any other plane with brakes, and he was used to planning his landings without needing them, but now he used them, pushing his foot down on the pedal until it reached the floor. He felt the machine straining against them, but the brakes really held well—as well as they had when they'd tested them.

The plane shuddered to a stop. Wiping the sweat from his forehead, Tommy climbed out of the plane. The wheels were just short of the edge of this huge building. It was bigger than a football field. He was dimly aware of his boots sticking to the hot tar-paper roof.

He stood there, covered with a fine layer of grit from the storm, sweat pouring down his face from the heat, his satchel over his shoulder, his canteen in the other hand. He took a long pull. The water was lukewarm but it tasted terrific.

He looked down at the men on the ground below, waved, and gave the devil-may-care grin with which he always ended his exhibitions. But slowly the grin faded from his face. The men didn't look happy to see him at all. Finally, one of them gestured to the side of the building. "There's a ladder," he shouted. "Come on down."

"As soon as I tie her down," Tommy made quick but thorough work of that job. As he climbed down the ladder built onto the side of this building, the metal hot on his hands, he toyed for a moment with the idea of getting back on the roof, back into his plane and back into the air. There'd been a dirt road that led from this area—little more than a track, really, but he could have followed it to some other settlement or other.

There was something definitely strange about his reception. Tommy had dropped out of the sky in a dozen fields, and aside from a few farmers who'd complained about crop damage, everyone was always thrilled to see him. These men weren't. Why not?

At the bottom of the ladder, one man, standing a few feet in front of the others, was waiting. He looked like a Mexican, or at least part Mexican. He was dark, with black wavy hair and a large moustache. He had a broad nose and olive skin. He wore cowboy clothes—a loose cotton shirt and denim pants.

Tommy jumped to the ground. Two puffs of dust appeared where his laced boots hit. He smiled at the Mexican. The Mexican didn't smile back. Tommy noticed he wore a sidearm—a Colt revolver in a tooled-leather holster.

The Mexican saw him looking at the weapon. "Dangerous country around here," he said. His accent confirmed that Spanish was indeed his native language. "Plenty of snakes."

"Listen," said Tommy, "I'm on my way to Tucson and I'm lost. Can you fellows tell me where I am?"

His question was ignored. "Who are you?"

"Tommy Cutter. From San Diego." He put out a hand. The other man took it and shook hands, but he didn't offer his own name.

"And now you have the advantage of me," said Tommy, annoyed.

The other man shrugged. "It's not important. What is important, Mr. Cutter, is that you won't be permitted to go to Tucson or anywhere else. You'll have to stay with us for a while."

"What?" Tommy took a step toward the other man, but backed off when he saw the Mexican's hand go to his gun, where it rested lightly.

"Say," said Tommy, running a hand through his hair, "am I in Mexico? I don't know what's going on, but I have some business to conduct in Tucson."

"We think our business is more important than yours." The man was looking up at the plane, now.

Tommy surveyed the other men who stood around them. He thought that if he were in Mexico he might be with a band of Villistas. With Black Jack Pershing's troops mass-ing at the border, it was conceivable these men thought he was some kind of spy. He thought with chagrin of the telegram in his pocket from the U.S. Army at El Paso. It could prove he was on legitimate business, but he didn't think Villistas would approve of him helping the U.S. Army to raid Mexico by plane, either.

But most of the men didn't look Mexican. Even the man he was talking to had blue eyes. Tommy couldn't figure it out.

"Please come with me," the blue-eyed Mexican said. "We'll talk later, Mr. Cutter."

Tommy gave his ship a last, longing look. "What about my plane?" he said.

"It will be safe," was the reply.

"Listen, I want to get out of here. I don't want any trouble. I don't know who you fellows are or what you're up to, and I don't want to know." He held his hands up, palms showing, in a gesture of conciliation. "I just want to go about my business."

The blue-eyed Mexican took out his revolver. "Shut up, Mr. Cutter," he said. "And come with me. Keep your hands where I can see them."

The code Gustav used was simple. Depending on the date, a page of *Girl of the Limberlost* served as a code book. The first twenty-six letters that appeared on a certain page were the alphabet of the day. A separate number code indicated the date. And, because vowels were used so often, the last line of the page provided the letters that were used alternately as vowels according to a predetermined pattern. When sent as a telegram, the whole thing looked like an ordinary commercial code.

Gustav was composing a telegram for Mr. Voska now, explaining that his identity was now known to the Germans, and that something was afoot in Aztec, Arizona, where Gustav said he would now proceed. Also, he warned Mr. Voska about Sophie. Gustav knew that the network was very complete. All over America, waiters, ladies' maids, consular clerks—patriotic Czechs, Poles, Hungarians,

South Slavs, Slovenes—all peoples under the yoke of the dual monarchy, were laboring to help the Allied cause. Sophie would never again work unobserved.

George stood next to him, watching him as he laboriously formed the message, stopping now and then to take a bite of food from the plate George had provided. It was an odd collection—milk, some cold salad, applesauce, a sausage, some oranges, a heel of bread, and a few licorice whips.

George looked down at the completed message. "What does it mean?" he said, running his hands through his red hair.

"I'm warning my people about that woman. The one you saw at my flat. Sophie."

"Oh. Her," said George dreamily.

Gustav looked at him sharply. "She's a very bad woman," he said.

"And beautiful," said George.

"Yes, and beautiful." Gustav sighed. "All right, the message is ready. I'd like you to wire it to this address. Now I'm asking you to memorize it." He gave him the address of the Pneumograph Electric Sign Company in New York. That was the cover Mr. Voska used. "And wait for a reply."

George repeated it a few times.

"Now," said Gustav, shifting his weight on the narrow bed, "I'm going to finish eating this and then I'll sleep. But first, you must tell me, have you seen your sister? Have you warned her?"

George dashed his glasses up and bit his lip. "No. That is, I *tried* to warn her. But I didn't tell her you were here. You see, people are looking for you. They say you robbed your boss's safe."

He told Gustav about his conversation with Maude, ending with: "And I was afraid to tell her because I have the feeling that right now she'd do anything for a swell scoop. Even turn you in. She doesn't understand about these German spies like we do."

"Hmm." Gustav looked thoughtful. "That makes it

very awkward. If people are looking for me, how can I travel?"

"You can't travel until your leg is mended a bit more," said George. "I'll hide you here, then we can go together to Aztec. You'll need someone to help you. Besides, the police won't be looking for a man with a boy. And there's your accent. If I buy the tickets, no one will know about your accent."

"It's not that strong, is it?" said Gustav, annoyed.

"It's noticeable. And then there's your scar."

Gustav touched the white line with the tips of his fingers. "Yes, there's always that," he said.

"Well, I've got a swell idea," said George. "I've got this all figured out. We'll pretend you have a toothache and we'll wrap your face all up and you can kind of moan and lean on me—that way no one'll notice the limp, and I'll do all the talking for you."

Gustav frowned. "It sounds terrible. But I can't think of anything better right now. Let's see what Mr. Voska says first. I have an idea he won't want me to go to Aztec. But I want to go anyway. For one thing, I'm being sought here. For another, I blame myself for not acting sooner. I blundered badly when I was discovered by Sophie and Franz Kessler. If I can find out what the Germans are up to in Arizona, I'll feel vindicated." And besides, he thought to himself, there was Sophie. He wasn't going to let Sophie put him out of the game.

"Well, getting back to your sister," said Gustav now, "let's not forget her safety."

"But a reporter from the *Globe* is coming up to the house any minute to get a story about you from her. I didn't want her to spill the beans to the *Globe*."

"What on earth are they interviewing her for about me?"

George shrugged. "You were in her column. She wrote about you at some party. All about your heel-clicking and your scar and all that. I guess you're pretty colorful."

"This damned scar," said Gustav impatiently.

"Anyway," continued George, helping himself to an

untouched licorice whip from Gustav's plate, "she's waiting for this fellow from the *Globe* now. Then she told me she's going out. She think's I'm at school. I went out and then came back over the wall to bring you the book."

"Well, send that telegram, will you, George. And come back with the answer. We'll tackle the problem of your sister later. Though I can't say I like the idea of her going out."

"She's safer out than in, I bet," said George. "After all, those spies can find out easily enough where she lives."

"That's right," said Gustav. And to himself, he thought, *all the more reason for me to clear out of here.* Maybe the boy could help him leave San Francisco.

As George was about to leave, he whispered to him, "George, I'm very grateful. You're a real brick."

George turned and smiled. "That's all right. I'm glad to help. Wish me luck getting past Maude to get to the telegraph office."

It was early afternoon by the time Maude had managed to get Fogerty out of her parlor and get herself down to the Southern Pacific station. She was lucky that a train for the Peninsula was just leaving.

On the train she thought about Baron Wechsler. He was really the last man in the world she would have imagined was a common thief. Although the line Fogerty seemed to be taking was that he was a smooth-talking embezzler, it appeared to Maude he'd simply rifled the office safe.

All Maude knew about him was that he was handsome, proud, and that he had some sort of attraction to Sophie Von Gluck, the opera singer. It hadn't taken much to intercept the look that had passed between them. And they'd hurried away from Kessler's party with a nervous urgency obviously rooted in strong passion. It was clear they could barely control themselves in public.

Maude hadn't told Fogerty that. And she hadn't told him that George had seen Baron Wechsler since the crime, either. George was behaving very peculiar lately. She'd practically shaken him, but all he'd said was that Baron Wechsler had strolled by the gate and told him to warn her. It was all very mysterious. Maude knew well enough that she was in danger. She had a mangled hat to prove it. But what did Baron Wechsler know about it? Nothing more, she imagined, than what she had told him herself at Franz Kessler's party.

It even occurred to Maude that George had imagined it all—part of his obsession with German spies. It also occurred to her that George had lied about it to draw attention from the fact that he hadn't been in school. But she rejected that. George would never lie. A serious talk with George was in order. It was so difficult. Maude was sixteen years older, but she had needed him for a friend, especially after her marriage fell apart. One of the worst things about the divorce, she felt, was that George had liked Nicky so much. In fact, she'd married Nicky partly on account of George, who, she felt, needed a father of sorts around the house. Instead, she'd made a horrible mess of everything. All of a sudden, she felt like crying, but she blinked back the tears and stared out the train window, trying to concentrate instead on the task at hand.

If Louise Arbor wasn't to be found, she planned to write about it. If McLaren wouldn't let her write a news story, she had a way around that, too. She'd write it as a society story. He'd told her he wanted more about Louise Arbor. And he barely ever read her copy. "The Affair of the Missing Debutante," was the headline she saw in her head.

She took a taxi from the station in Palo Alto. The Arbor home was an imposing residence, unlike, she was sure, most professors' homes. It was in the English style, a great stone structure with a wrought iron gate, a circular drive, and well-tended gardens. Two stone lions guarded the massive stairs that led to a pair of stout oak doors.

Maude straightened her jacket, smoothed her gloves, arranged her features into a determined, businesslike composition, and rang the bell.

After some time, a tall, very elegant Chinese butler answered the door.

"Mrs. Cavendish," said Maude airily. "To see Miss Arbor." She handed him her card.

"Miss Arbor is not at home," said the butler. "She is on holiday." He placed the card on a salver nearby.

Maude couldn't quite believe it. Where would she be going at this time of year? "Oh?" She raised an eyebrow. "How curious. Miss Arbor was expecting me."

"I'm afraid there's been some sort of mistake," said the butler. Maude thought she detected something in his smooth, impassive face. There was a flicker of some emotion about the eyes. Was it fear?

"How very, very curious," said Maude. "Well, I'll just speak to Professor Arbor, then. I imagine he's busy at the moment, but I'll wait." She stepped forward.

The butler didn't move. He really was a jewel of a butler, thought Maude with admiration. "I'm so sorry," he said, "but Dr. Arbor is not at home, either."

"How very, very curious," said Maude. "Isn't school still in session?"

"I wouldn't know, madame."

"Hmm." Maude tapped her foot impatiently. "Well, please tell me where they can be reached."

"I'm sorry, I am not at liberty to do so," said the butler.

"Not at liberty?" Maude tried to assume a severe expression. "Now see here, my man . . ."

She saw at once it was a mistake. The butler's expression, which had been a smooth mask, took on a pugnacious cast.

"I have my orders, madame," he said curtly. He began to close the door.

"Wait," said Maude. "Do you expect to hear from them? Are Louise and her father together? Where did they go? May I leave a message for them? When do you expect them?"

The butler sighed. He held up a white-gloved hand. "Perhaps I will have some word. I'll be glad to forward a message."

"Fine," said Maude. "Have you paper and something to write with?"

"Certainly." He stepped inside and let her in. It was a very conventional sort of house of its type. There was a lot of stained oak wainscotting and above it a patterned wallpaper with a vaguely Oriental look. There was a table with letters and things on it, an elephant's foot umbrella stand, and a pair of aspidistras in gleaming brass tubs.

The butler showed her into a small reception room off the hall—the sort of place where coats could be stored at a large party, or where a lady could receive one or two intimate friends rather informally. There was a chair and a small desk there, and Maude was given paper and pen.

The butler left her side while she tried to put something sensible down on paper. Finally she decided to simply write the truth, and a message that would be sure to elicit a reply.

"Dear Miss Arbor," she began. "Please communicate with me at your earliest convenience about a matter that concerns your own safety and well-being. Sincerely, Maude Teasdale Cavendish."

The butler had also provided an envelope. She put the letter inside and sealed it.

When she stepped out into the hall again she heard low voices, and she stopped for a second. There was something rather conspiratorial-sounding about the voices. The speaker was a woman, and by the look of her, the housekeeper. She was tall, with a straight back, a very respectable dark dress, and a tight bun of steel-gray hair.

Maude leaned forward, partly in shadow.

"All the notes and the equipment he asked for are packed and ready, Mr. Lee," she said. "If you give me the address I'll have Brandon drive it down to the station."

"I'll take care of that, Mrs. Cooper," said Lee.

Over his shoulder, Mrs. Cooper had caught sight of Maude. She raised her eyebrows inquiringly.

Lee evidently caught her look, for he turned in the direction of her gaze. Maude came forward and handed him the message. "Thank you so much for your trouble," she said.

Mr. Lee let her out and watched while she walked out to the taxi she had waiting. When she got inside she told the driver, "Pull outside the wall and stay there, please."

About twenty minutes later, a gray saloon car pulled out of the gates, the Arbor chauffeur at the wheel. "Follow that car," said Maude, "but inconspicuously."

The driver turned around. He was young, with a fresh, frank look about him. "What's going on here?" he asked. "There's nothing crooked about this, is there?"

Maude smiled. "No. I'm a reporter for the *Globe*. I'm just keeping track of some society folks."

"Oh." He seemed mollified. "That's all right, I guess. What's up? Some kind of scandal?"

"I'm not sure," said Maude. "It's just that the Arbors seem to have disappeared and I'm trying to find them."

"The Arbors? You don't mean Dr. Arbor? The chemist?"

"Why, yes," said Maude.

"Oh, does Dr. Arbor live back there?" The driver had pulled the taxi cautiously out, now, and was following the Arbor automobile at a respectable distance.

"That's right."

"I'm a student at Stanford," he explained. "Dr. Arbor is one of my professors. He certainly has a palatial house. Didn't know professors lived that way."

"I don't think many of them do," said Maude. "The Arbors have always been very well off."

"Well, I wouldn't be surprised if there *was* some sort of scandal brewing," said the driver. "I saw Dr. Arbor down at the S. P. depot last week. I was waiting for a fare. He didn't recognize me, but that's not unusual. Put a chauffeur's cap on anyone and they become invisible. And not too many of us are working their way through. The man looked terrible. All white and drawn. Something's bothering him, all right."

"When was this?" said Maude.

"Oh, let me see. It must have been Tuesday or Thursday. Those are the days I'm not in class. Tuesday. That's it. It was just a week ago.''

"Did he have any luggage with him?'' said Maude.

"Seemed like he was carrying something. Nothing big. Just a small carpetbag, or something along those lines,'' said the driver.

"And he was alone? There wasn't a young lady with him?''

"If you mean the fair Louise, she wasn't there. I would have noticed. The fellows have told me about Miss Arbor. She's kind of a legend in the chemistry department, I guess. A real heartbreaker, I hear.''

"So he was completely alone?''

"That's right.''

They pulled up in front of the station. "Thanks for your help,'' she said, paying the fare and giving him a generous tip.

Inside the station, she saw the Arbors' chauffeur struggling with a large wooden packing case. She moseyed around the waiting room a little until he'd managed to get the thing in the freight office line, then she stood behind him. It wasn't hard to read the address in India ink. The crate was being sent to Dr. Arbor. Care of General Delivery, Aztec, Arizona.

# CHAPTER
## 14

"**I** TOLD you," said Tommy wearily, "I came from San Diego. I'm testing a new plane. And if you let me out of here I'll shut up about what I've seen, which is practically nothing, anyway. I don't even know what kind of a game you fellows are up to out here in the desert, and I don't really care, either. I just want out of here."

He was sitting on the dirt floor leaning against the hot corrugated metal walls of the little shed where he was imprisoned. They'd fed him a meal—beans and coffee— and now the blue-eyed Mexican was asking him all kinds of questions.

Tommy tried to tell as much of the truth as he could. He left out the part about the U.S. Army, because he still had no idea with whom he was dealing. It also occurred to him he might be in Mexican territory. He didn't like the thought of that at all, although out here in the desert, cooped up in a tin shed, he supposed it didn't make too much difference where he was.

"Let's get one thing clear," said Blue Eyes. "You're not going to leave. Not for a long time. So you may as well cooperate with us and answer our questions. Things will go easier for you if you do."

"Well, I don't always do things the easy way," said Tommy. He smiled broadly.

Blue Eyes hit him hard on the side of the head. Tommy's vision blurred for a second, then he made a fist and jabbed it forcefully into the man's gut. It knocked the wind right out of him. Tommy pushed the doubled-over figure aside and headed for the door.

Outside, the light hurt his eyes. Two big men were waiting for him, one big blond kid with bandoleros draped over him, the other a wiry Mexican. Tommy pushed against them as they pushed him back into his prison.

Over the meaty shoulder of the blond kid he saw two people staring at him. There was an old woman, all dressed in black, and next to her stood a young girl, an extraordinarily pretty girl who looked very American. Her hair was a light golden brown and it curled around her face and hung down over her shoulders like a child's. She was wearing whipcord jodhpurs and tall riding boots and a white, dusty-looking blouse torn at the shoulder. She had a delicate little face with an adorable upturned nose, blue eyes, and pretty brown brows over them. Her mouth was open as she stared at him straining against the two men, as if she were about to speak. She looked agitated. The Mexican woman hustled her back to a square little adobe hut, and Tommy saw her pushing against the woman right before he fell down on the dirt floor of his prison.

The blue-eyed Mexican stood over him and gave him a nasty kick in the ribs. "Who knows you are here?" he demanded.

"No one," said Tommy. "I wish they did." He didn't want to tell them about Cousin Will. Who knew what these crazy people were up to? Why, they might even go kidnap Cousin Will in San Diego!

One thing was certain. It looked to Tommy as if they'd kidnapped that girl. She'd tried to tell him something. Whatever happened, Tommy was going to find out who she was and what she was doing here. And when he got out, which he fully intended to do, he'd think about taking her with him.

After Blue Eyes had left, telling Tommy he'd better plan to be alone for quite a while, Tommy went over it all again. He had managed to save the compass when they'd gone through his satchel. He'd been able to get it between the lining and the leather of his jacket, along with his telegram from the army. And they'd left him his canteen—even filled it up for him that morning. But that was about it. Not much luggage for a trip. Of course, all he had to do was get back to the plane. There was always that dirt road, the one he hadn't bothered to follow when he'd sighted this bizarre encampment. It had to lead to civilization—although Tommy vowed to be a little more cautious before he landed anywhere uninvited again.

The girl just complicated matters. He sighed. In a way, he wished he hadn't seen her, because he thought he could make the dash to the plane alone—but doing it with the girl would be a lot tougher. And he wondered how he'd get her up that ladder. All of this was based, of course, on the assumption that she wanted to leave. He couldn't help but believe that. But then, he thought, running a hand over his jaw, he was a pretty disreputable sight just now, unshaven, dirty. She might not want to be rescued by him. Well, he'd decide tonight. He had the beginnings of a plan already.

They'd left his dirty dishes behind. He examined them all. An earthenware bowl with a rather sharp lip was the best tool of the lot. He began digging in the dirt floor by the back wall, trying to ignore the pain of his aching bruise. He reasoned that they hadn't expected him and so they didn't have a very secure place to put him. And, he supposed, they thought it didn't matter if he escaped from this shed because they were surrounded by desert. But if his machine were still in good shape—and he suppressed the horrifying thought that it might have been interfered with in some way—then he could fly right out of trouble.

He thought if he worked all night he could get a space big enough to crawl out. Of course, there was probably a guard posted outside. He wasn't sure. But if they caught him, he'd at least have been out for a look around. That would be something, at least. The ground was hard, but it was, after all, just dirt. There was no reason he couldn't get through it.

He had been left alone for some time, now. Presumably they were softening him up by denying him meals and company. That was fine with Tommy. But he kept an ear out for any sound.

By evening he could put a whole hand out under the metal wall. He decided it was time to arrange things so that if he were discovered he'd still have a chance. Until he'd put his hand outside the shed, he hadn't really believed his plan would work. Now he cared about making sure it would.

He scattered the earth he'd dug up around the floor, tramping down firmly on it, but silently. Now his bootprints were everywhere, as if he'd been pacing. The dirt looked too loose and fresh. He patted it down with his hand and tried to smooth it as best he could. He took off his jacket and arranged it over the hole. It looked as if it had been flung there in exasperation. He thought it would pass muster; he'd be ready in a second if he heard anyone at the door. He knew his guards were still there in front. He'd heard one of them cough just a few moments ago. But there didn't seem to be anyone at the rear of the shed where he was digging. Every once in a while he'd arrange the dirt around on the floor, just in case he was disturbed.

A few hours later he heard a light snoring from the front of the shed. He smiled. By placing his head sideways on the ground near his excavations, he could see outside. It was dark, and in the desert sky he could see brilliant stars. If he was lucky and the moon was full, he'd have enough light to fly by. But maybe he'd better wait until dawn. He'd decide when he got to the plane. He resumed his digging, less conscious, now, of the noise he was making—a dry, scratchy sound as the earthenware scraped along the impacted dirt, breaking off in shards that fell apart into dust—then pushing the dust out of the hole with the bowl.

When Maude had arrived home after her trip to the Arbors', she went to the kitchen where Clara was preparing dinner. "Mmm, pot roast," she said, going over to the stove and lifting the lid.

Clara looked over Maude's shoulder into the large cast-iron pot. "Yes, I got a good buy on a nice one," she said. Then her expression changed.

"Why, that little dickens! George must have sneaked in here while I was setting the table. There's a whole great big slice cut off there, and half the carrots are gone, too. That boy's eating more and more all the time." She turned to Maude. "I just can't plan anything if he's coming in here picking at food all the time. Why, this morning half a loaf of bread disappeared."

She twisted her apron in her hands nervously, and then looked Maude straight in the eye. "*And* that's not all. The Scotch whiskey in that decanter in the study—it's down a good couple of inches since yesterday."

"Oh!" Maude put one gloved hand to her cheek. "Goodness. I'll speak to George right away. Where is he?"

"He's been upstairs most of the day since he came home from school. *If* he did go to school." Clara turned away and clattered noisily with some dishes. Maude took this as her cue to leave.

"Blast," she said to herself as she peeled off her gloves and flung them on the hall table. "Ouch!" she had removed her hat hastily, forgetting to unpin it. George was a truant, a dipsomaniac, and who knew what else. And on top of that, he was getting Clara upset. Maude simply couldn't affort to let Clara get upset.

"George!" she hollered from the stairs, climbing up with a weary tread, her hat in her hand, its veiling trailing on the carpet. "George, I need to talk to you." In the upstairs hall she saw George coming out of the door that led to the attic steps. Curious.

"What are you doing?" she said.

"Nothing," said George blandly.

"Come to the parlor, will you, dear. Clara is out of sorts. She's worried about you, and so am I."

"Well, I've been worried about you," said George. "You're in real danger, Maude. It's a fact."

"Yes, I know. You heard about that from Baron Wechsler. I want to talk to you about that, too."

George looked squirmy and uncomfortable.

"Come on," said Maude wearily. "Let's talk."

They sat in the parlor and Maude began. "Why weren't you in school?"

"Urgent business," said George. "More important than school."

Maude sighed. "German spies?"

He nodded. "That's right."

"What exactly were you doing?"

"Talking to Baron Wechsler."

Maude leaned forward. "George, why on earth did he come here?"

"I told you. To warn us. The Germans are after you."

"But why?"

"Don't know," George shrugged.

"And what does Baron Wechsler know about it?" said Maude.

"Plenty," said George cryptically. "But I'm not at liberty to reveal all I know."

"Oh, for God's sake, George," said Maude, exasperated. She rose and went over to the sideboard. She picked up a crystal decanter. "And Clara says you've been drinking! Maybe that explains your delusions."

"No I haven't," said George. "I borrowed some of that, but just for medicinal purposes."

Maude opened one of the doors in the walnut sideboard and took out a squarish glass. She poured herself a generous shot of whiskey. "Listen," she said after she'd taken a sip, closing her eyes for a second, "I need to know about Baron Wechsler. George, he's a common criminal. And I want a story for the *Globe*. You must tell me all about it." She sat down again.

"Not until I tell you about the need for a free Czechoslovakia," said George solemnly. "That's the key to it all. Have you ever heard of a man named Jan Masaryk? Or have you read a book called *Bohemia Under Hapsburg Misrule* by Thomas Capek? I'm going to get it from the library. Baron Wechsler's been explaining these things to me."

Maude leaned forward. "You know where he is?"

"I can't tell you unless you promise not to turn him in," said George.

"Of course I can't promise that," she said, taking another sip of Scotch and falling back against the sofa cushions. "He's a criminal. And I'd be one if I didn't turn him in. And besides, it would be a terrific story for the *Globe*."

"Maude, if you just promise not to tell, I'll tell you what I've learned."

"George," said Maude, "I'm shocked. We could be arrested for knowing where he is and not telling. George, I swear, if you don't start being more forthright with me, I'll, I'll—why, I'll arrange to have you sent to a cold, drafty boarding school in New England."

"We can't afford it," said George.

Maude put her face in her hands and began to cry. "George," she said between muffled sobs, "I'm not old enough to be your mother. It's difficult for me. I can't tell you how to behave the way a mother or a father would. But I'm doing my best to see that you grow up to be square. And now you're playing truant, drinking whiskey, aiding a criminal. You're not telling me what's going on. It's all too much."

"Buck up, old girl," said George, coming over and patting her hand. "You're being pretty stubborn yourself. All you need to do is help me out. And promise not to tell about Baron Wechsler. Who, by the way," he added parenthetically, "is not a criminal but a Czech patriot and a guarantor of American neutrality. If you help out, Maude, you'll have a story for your paper that'll make Mr. McLaren sit up and take notice, I'll tell you. Yes sir, it'll be a real corker."

"Oh, George," said Maude, still crying, "the best story in the world will be worthless to me if I've raised you all wrong."

The doorbell rang. "Oh, who can that be?" said Maude impatiently, drying her tears hastily with a cambric handkerchief she kept in her sleeve. "Get rid of them, will you?"

"Be careful, Maude. It might be the Hindoos again."
George leaped from the parlor into the front hall, colliding
with Clara, who had gone to answer the door.

Clara opened the door. Nicky Cavendish stood there
with a large bunch of roses.

"Hi, Nicky," said George. "Come on in. You can help
me cheer up Maude. She thinks she raised me all wrong."

"Just wondering how she was doing, sport," said Nicky.
"Haven't heard a word from her since her ordeal and all."
He flung the roses in Clara's general direction. "Put 'em
in a vase, will you, then bring 'em into the parlor and set
'em down. Maude loves roses."

"Why don't you stay for dinner, Nicky," said George
enthusiastically. "It's pot roast." He led his former brother-
in-law into the parlor. "Look who's here, Maude. He's
brought you some swell flowers."

"Oh *really*, George," said Maude, "I told you to get
rid of whoever it was."

"Such manners," said Nicky. "Is this the example you
set for George?" He wandered over to the sideboard and
examined the almost empty whisky decanter. "Maude!
Have you been drinking?"

"Not nearly enough," said Maude icily.

"I know it's all an act," said Nicky. "You're really
crazy about me, aren't you, kiddo?"

"Nicky, must I remind you that we are no longer
married?"

"Of course we are. I don't believe in this divorce
business. We took a solemn vow. It's very serious, a vow
like that."

"Yes, and I wish you'd taken it a little more seriously
when we were married," said Maude.

"Not in front of the kid," said Nicky with a wink.
"Say, if we ring for Clara, will she bring us some more
whiskey?" He pulled at the bell.

Maude ignored him. "George, how could you?" she
said. "You know how I feel about Nicky clomping around
here like he owns the place."

"I know," said George. "But Nicky's kind of a burly

fellow. I thought we might need some extra help in case those Hindoos come back.''

Clara came into the room, looking disapproving as she always did when Nicky Cavendish came around.

"Is there any more whiskey?" said Nicky, holding up the decanter.

Clara ignored him. She liked to make it clear to him that he was no longer the master of the house. "You rang, ma'am?" she said to Maude.

"Is there more whiskey?" said Maude in a small voice. Clara had already been out of sorts about George. Now Nicky was muddying the waters. It was all too awful.

"I'll see," she said coldly, giving George a fishy stare.

"And Mr. Cavendish will be staying to dinner," said George airily.

"I see," said Clara, twisting her face into an expression of even more intense disapproval.

"I may be staying the night," said Nicky with a wolfish smile. "Mrs. Cavendish's worried about these Hindoos, or so she claims."

"Oh, shut up!" said Maude. "Mr. Cavendish will not be staying the night," she said firmly to Clara.

"All right. I'll see if I can stretch dinner with some more potatoes," said Clara. "There's not much pot roast left." She gave George another look. "But I guess George won't be so hungry, seeing as how he's already eaten and all."

"I'm starved," said George.

When Clara had left the room, Maude sank into the sofa and buried her face in her hands once again. "You're both horrible," she said. "And if I lose Clara it will be your fault, both of you."

"Give her some more whiskey when Clara brings it," said George. "It seems to do her good."

# CHAPTER
## 15

Later, while preparing for bed, Maude reflected on her own weakness. Nicky had come into her house and taken charge once again. He and George had convinced her that Nicky should stay the night.

Clara hadn't approved, but Maude had very calmly informed her that Mr. Cavendish would be staying in the guest room and that it should be prepared. "Mr. Cavendish will need hot water for shaving tomorrow morning, but he won't be staying to breakfast."

George seemed especially jumpy, and Maude thought that perhaps he felt unable to protect her from German spies or Hindoos. Maybe if Nicky were here, he would feel less pressure. He was only a boy and needed his rest. Poor George. He seemed to think he should be taking better care of her. It was really the other way around. She should be taking better care of him.

She put on her white, lace-trimmed nightdress, tied the blue satin ribbons, and sat before the mirror at her dresser. She brushed her hair rather fiercely. Perhaps she had also allowed Nicky to stay because she too was jumpy. She did feel safer with a man in the house. She shuddered at the memory of that crushed hat.

Well, no matter how frightened she was, she wasn't

going to stop. She summoned up the thought of the odious Clarence P. Fogerty and told herself that she was going to get herself a terrific story.

There was a light tap at the door. With an exasperated sigh, she put down the heavy, silver-backed hairbrush. She knew that tap. She leaned against the door and said in a loud whisper, "Who is it?"

"It's your husband, of course," said Nicky in normal conversational tones.

She opened the door a crack. The last thing she wanted was for Clara to become aware of any nocturnal prowling. "Go away," she said.

"I thought maybe you'd like me to brush out your hair," said Nicky matter-of-factly. He was wearing one of his old dressing gowns. Nicky had left behind a lot of clothes.

"Don't be ridiculous," said Maude. "I'm very tired. I've had a very difficult day. You shouldn't be in this house, let alone at my bedroom door."

"Don't be silly," said Nicky. "Oh, I see you have a new nightdress. Very pretty."

Maude closed the door firmly, just as Nicky was about to insert his foot in front of it, and turned the key in the lock. "Don't wake up George or Clara on your way back to the guest room," she hissed through the door.

"This coyness doesn't fool me a bit," said Nicky from without, but she ignored him and flung herself into bed, pulling the covers over her head. "Damn him," she thought. "He knows I still want him. But I despise him at the same time."

Presently she heard his slippered feet sauntering back down the hall, and later, quite a bit later, she fell into a restless sleep.

Directly overhead, Gustav was sleeping. He'd spent a tense evening, listening for sounds from the household, watching the door to the tiny room, exhausted, his wound throbbing. He was unable to sleep. Finally he'd resorted to reading the copy of *Girl of the Limberlost*, the book he used to encode messages. It seemed to be about a school-girl who collected moths in a swamp. Finally, he slept.

Now he was dreaming, a wild, disturbing dream about Sophie Von Gluck. They were in bed, that ridiculous bed carved like a swan, and their limbs were entwined as they thrashed about. As often happened in his dreams, his face bore no scar. Sophie was biting him with those sharp little teeth. Suddenly she had a knife. In the dream he froze, was unable to move as he stared up in terror. Sophie hovered above him, carving a scar along the side of his face, smiling at him with pleasure as she drew the point of the knife cleanly and deeply from below his eye, over his cheekbone to the corner of his mouth.

He cried out and flung himself away. He woke up cursing, having fallen onto the floor next to the narrow bed.

Below him, Maude's eyes flew open. She had heard what sounded like a moan, and then a definite clunk. It came from overhead, from the unused servant's floor. She rose, threw a shawl over her nightdress, then stopped. She should fetch Nicky. That was why he was here, wasn't it? To protect them. But then she realized she couldn't fetch Nicky. He would think it was just a ruse to get into his guest room. She'd never get rid of him after they'd investigated the sound, which was probably a creaky window banging open. There'd be a scene. George would wake up, and so would Clara, who would probably give notice.

She took a candle in a brass holder from the mantel, lit it, and crept out into the hall.

Gustav was sure he'd made enough noise to wake the house. He struggled to his feet, trying not to put any weight on the bad leg, and made his way to the wall behind the door. He waited there for what seemed like forever. When it opened slowly he had only a brief glimpse of a flickering candle, the swirl of a white nightdress, and a cloud of reddish brown hair before he seized Maude and clapped a firm hand over her mouth. He felt her straining in his arms and struggling for breath with which to scream. Fearing her nightdress would catch fire, he blew out the candle. The room was now illuminated by a bluish moonlight from the small window.

"I'll let you go if you promise not to scream," he whispered. She writhed some more, but he held her firmly until she finally stood perfectly still. He stared into her eyes, wide with fear above his hand, until he saw the fear replaced by acquiescence. Still, he removed his hand gingerly, keeping it just a fraction away from her face.

"You," she said, apparently angry, but thankfully keeping her voice barely above a whisper. "What are you doing here? Let go of me at once!"

"I know it seems bizarre," he said, "but I came to warn you."

She pulled away from him and surveyed his form. "In Nicky's pajamas?"

He shrugged. "George provided them."

"George!"

"Without your brother I fear I—"

"You're a wanted man," she exclaimed. "You stole from Mr. Kessler. Then you penetrate my house, help yourself to my husband's pajamas—"

"Your former husband, surely."

"—and involve George."

"George saved me," said Gustav. "I'm very grateful."

"Saved you from the law! You must leave this house at once." She pushed her hair away from her face in a vehement gesture. "George mustn't be involved." She glanced around the room, looking at some dirty dishes. "He's been feeding you. Oh, it's awful. Why on earth did you come here?"

"If you'll be quiet and listen, I'll tell you," said Gustav heatedly. "I came to warn you. There are German plotters in this city, unscrupulous people who mean to kill you."

"German plotters? This sounds like something George would cook up. Let's face it, Baron, you're just a thief who took advantage of a vulnerable, imaginative boy and a helpless woman. . . ." She paused, remembering that push onto the trolley tracks. "I'm not entirely helpless," she said. "And Nicky's here."

"Your rather unorthodox domestic arrangements are of no interest to me," he snapped. He seized her by the shoulders. "Believe me, there is a plan to kill you. Because of Louise Arbor. Because you're a newspaperwoman. Because you plan to investigate the circumstances of your abduction.

"Having told you this," he said releasing her, "I feel I've done my duty. But I think it would be very foolish of you to turn me over to the police until you hear what I have to say. It could be dangerous to you and to your brother."

Bemused, Maude sat on the bed, a hundred questions racing through her mind. She had better listen to Baron Wechsler. "There's no need to tell you more than you need to know," he began. "It could be dangerous."

"You tell me everything, or I turn you in," she said flatly.

"So you can write it all up in your wretched paper?"

"Of course. This could be a wonderful story. They only let me cover those silly parties, you know."

His eyes clouded with anger, he came to her side, seized her once more by the shoulders, and shook her. "This is more important than your stupid newspaper, and whether you have to go to parties you don't like," he said. "Young men, some of them not much older than your brother, are bleeding and dying all over Europe, rotting in trenches, choking on poisonous gases. Women are being raped and children are being murdered. Proud peoples are enslaved."

"Let go of me," she said sharply.

He flung her backward onto the bed, and rose, walking away from her, momentarily unaware of his pain. "And America sits complacent, ignorant of what is going on within her own borders." He turned to her, his voice full of feeling, and said, "I should have a gun in my hand now. I should be fighting a square and honest fight. Instead, I'm hiding in an attic, talking to a silly woman who won't even listen when I tell her she's in danger."

"How dare you speak to me like that," she said, rising and coming to his side. "I could have you arrested any moment now." She didn't want him to know she had been moved by his passionate speech. The man who stood before her was nothing like the cold aristocrat she had met at Mrs. Lacoste's party.

"You've put us in a dreadful position," said Maude.

"I realize that, and I imagine it's impossible for you to see that in the grander scheme of things, it matters very little. In fact, it matters very little whether any of us live or die. But women aren't usually called upon to die in war, so I thought it only decent of me to warn you. Sophie Von Gluck is planning to assassinate you."

Maude put her hand to her forehead. "All right. Calm yourself. Tell me everything."

Gustav spoke in measured tones. He told her about Kessler and Sophie, he told her about the ledger and about the postcard at Schulz's grocery store. He told her about Indian revolutionaries in an alliance with the German powers to violate American neutrality. He told her that he must investigate what was happening in Aztec, Arizona.

"Aztec! But that's where Professor Arbor went."

"What?" He got her to tell him about her adventure in Palo Alto. "I wonder what they're up to," he murmured.

"But you haven't told me everything," she said. "You haven't told me who you are and why you, an Austrian, are apparently a traitor to your country. If you're some kind of a spy, who are you working for? How do I know you aren't a *German* spy?"

"I can't tell you that," he said. "You will simply have to believe me."

"And why should I?"

"Look," he said impatiently, "don't bother about any of this. Just let me rest here for a while, and then I'll leave. If you want to take your chances with Sophie Von Gluck, that's up to you."

"Sophie Von Gluck! How do you know that Sophie Von Gluck wants to kill me?"

"I heard her tell Kessler that you were to be killed."

Tired and in pain he fell to the bed and cursed softly in Czech.

"You're hurt," said Maude, rushing to his side. "Let me see that."

"Sophie shot me," he said wearily, lying down on the bed. "Your brother dug out the bullet."

"What!"

"It hurt like hell, but he did it."

"And you're telling the truth; you aren't German or Austrian either," she said, pushing up the fabric of the pajama leg and peering at George's bandage.

"Leave it alone," he said. "The boy did a good job." He looked at her from beneath lowered lids, lying flat on his back, his arm over his forehead. "How do you know I'm not German or Austrian?"

"Because you swore just now. And it wasn't in German."

Gustav managed a half smile. "There are four things one does in one's first language," he said. "Count, pray, swear, and make love."

"This is a very dangerous business. You'll have to go. I'm sorry, but I can't have you in the house." She pulled her shawl around her. "I can't have George involved in this."

Wincing with pain he managed to sit up. "You have to keep me here for a day or so until I can walk better. You have to help me prepare to go to Aztec, Arizona. You have to get rid of that husband of yours and the housekeeper. And you can't write a word about this until I say you can. I'm too tired to argue with you any more."

"How can I trust you? You've already told me you don't care about your own life. Why should you care about mine?"

"You're an absolutely impossible woman," he said. "Now listen to me." He seized her again. "If you don't do as I say, there will be a scandal. George will be involved. You will be involved. Everyone will know that you entertain your former husband here, on the most intimate terms, with the boy in the house. Of course it won't matter much, because Sophie Von Gluck will kill you.

Your brother will be all alone in the world.'' His face was close to hers and he spoke in a menacing whisper.

''You're blackmailing me into helping you,'' she said. ''It's despicable.''

''Yes, I am thoroughly rotten, but there's nothing you can do about it.'' And then, to his own surprise and hers, he twisted her hair in his hands, bent her head back, and kissed her passionately. She didn't resist, she even fell against him for a moment, and they felt the warmth of each other's bodies through their nightclothes. Then she pulled herself away. ''And I suppose that's supposed to persuade me, too,'' she said bitterly.

''Be quiet,'' he said. ''I hear something. Someone's coming up the stairs.'' He stared at her, alarmed. ''Your husband woke and found you weren't by his side.''

''He was in the guest room,'' she said. ''It's all over between us.''

He didn't seem interested in any explanations. ''Be quiet,'' he ordered.

From outside they heard Nicky's voice. ''Maude? Are you up here?''

He watched her face in the moonlight, anxious to see whether she would betray him. She waited a moment before answering. ''It's all right, Nicky. I just came up here to close a window. Now go back to your room.''

Gustav smiled. She had lied for him.

''I'll help you,'' she whispered to Gustav. ''But I'm coming to Aztec with you. I want my story.''

''Maude, where are you?'' called Nicky playfully.

''Go away,'' she said firmly.

''Oh, if you insist.'' He sounded tired and annoyed. They heard his footsteps recede down the stair. Gustav took her hand, kissed it very correctly, led her to the door, and shut it behind her.

# CHAPTER
# 16

THE next morning, Sophie presented herself at Madame Cecile's shop in Maiden Lane.

Madame Cecile was a plain little woman with a pointed nose and wispy, pale hair. She had an obsequious manner and a bent, fluid way of moving.

"I've been recommended to you by one of your clients," she began. "A Mrs. Cavendish."

The woman looked immediately wary.

"Of course," began Sophie, "I've since heard you sold her a model you sold to another lady." Sophie raised her eyebrows in query.

"A terrible mistake, something that will never happen again," said Madame Cecile. They spoke French, Madame Cecile with a strong Belgian accent.

"How could such a thing happen?"

"Well, the other lady saw the model. And she insisted." Madame Cecile looked as if she might burst into tears. "I meant to tell Mrs. Cavendish that the model didn't suit her. But I . . ." The woman wrung her hands.

"Never mind. It is unfortunate. But you are a good dressmaker, and I wonder if you could show me some of that stuff in the window. The apricot-colored silk. If you were to make me a tea gown of that, could it be trimmed with some stuff of the same shade but more intense in color?''

''Oh, but that is the wrong shade for Madame.'' The dressmaker took on a more authoritative tone. ''Here, let me fetch Madame something similar but more appropriate for her exotic coloring.''

She scurried into the back room, and when the curtain separating the front fell back into place, Sophie leaned over the counter and plucked several address labels from the desk. She also took note of the roll of wrapping paper that hung on a bar there. She stuffed the labels into her bag as Madame Cecile returned, struggling with a bolt of persimmon-colored taffeta.

''*Non*,'' said Sophie. ''That's not what I had in mind at all. And you're right. That apricot silk won't do, either.'' She nodded curtly. ''Thank you for your trouble.'' She turned on her heel and left Madame Cecile rather nonplussed, shifting from the weight of the persimmon taffeta in her frail arms.

Tommy didn't let himself hope there was enough room to squeeze through. He made himself scoop out a few more bowls of dirt. He'd abandoned tamping it down long ago. He didn't expect to be disturbed now—and besides, he was too excited about his escape.

Finally, he flung the bowl aside and pushed his head under the wall. The metal dug into his neck, but he twisted around sideways until he had his head completely free. Now if he could just get his shoulders through, he figured he'd be just about free. His face was smashed against the ground outside, rubbing in the gritty earth. He turned it sideways to get a breath.

The fresh air out here smelled good, and he didn't see a soul around. There were some buildings with lit windows, and he heard men's voices from within them, but the whole encampment seemed buttoned down for the night. He turned his whole body around, trying to get his shoulders through. He chided himself for not having dug more, but he simply hadn't had the patience. He'd get through even if it meant pushing the earth up like a mole. With a great effort he churned sideways back and forth, making the opening bigger, clawing at the dirt with his fingers. Finally he was free. The whole procedure reminded him of seeing animals give birth. He lay for a moment, exhausted, alongside the shed where he'd been imprisoned. If anyone should come by, he thought, he'd be practically invisible, covered from head to toe as he was with fine reddish dust.

Gingerly, on all fours, Tommy crept around the side of the shed. In front of it sat the big blond kid he'd seen earlier. He was fast asleep, his large head hanging limply forward.

There was a space of about ten yards to the adobe hut where he thought the girl was being kept. For a moment he tried to tell himself that trying to take her out too wasn't worth the risk. He thought of Cousin Will, of all the work they'd put into that plane, of the army contract that might be waiting for them at El Paso.

"Aw, hell," he muttered to himself. He brushed some of the dirt from his eyebrows and wiped his mouth with the back of his hand. Then, like a little kid nervous about crossing the street, he looked both ways and made a dash for it.

He practically collided with the adobe hut. He crept low again and worked his way around the structure. There was a tiny window up high. He pulled himself up by the ledge. There was no window there, just a wooden shutter, but he could see between the slats. The girl lay on her back on a narrow bed. She had her hands tied in front of her and her eyes were wide open. She looked terrified.

Next to her, on an uncomfortable wooden chair, sat the old lady he'd seen before. She wore a prim black dress—a typical Mexican matron—and had her dark hair in a madonna-like arrangement, parted in the middle and looped low over each ear. She was hemming some white garment—it looked like a man's shirt. On a table next to the work basket lay a long black revolver.

Tommy wondered whether the old lady knew how to

use it. The history of Mexico being what it was, he reckoned she just might have had some battle experience. Still, she was a small woman, and old. If he was fast enough . . . There wasn't really time to do much else.

The roofline was only a foot or so above the little window. He reached for the roof, got a good handhold, and hung there by his hands for a second. Then he brought up his legs and pushed them through the wooden louvers. A second later he was on the floor of the room, crouched so as to make himself a little less of a target. He flew at the table just as the woman was reaching for the gun. He didn't want her to scream for help.

With his left hand he pushed the table over, sending the gun out of her reach. With his right fist he gave the woman a powerful sock to the jaw. He didn't hold back, giving the old girl everything he had. He was surprised with himself. Tommy had never hit a woman before. He found it alarmingly easy. He reached over and tucked the revolver in his belt.

The girl on the bed didn't scream. She lay there, still quiet, still terrified, watching him with big blue eyes, her pale wrists twisting back and forth.

"It's okay," he said. "I'm an American. I'm going to get you out of here." She began to sob a little. "But I won't take you if you aren't absolutely quiet," he told her, scowling. "You saw what I did to that old party, didn't you?"

The girl nodded and stopped sniffling. He undid her ropes. He was shocked at how raw and red the marks beneath them were.

"We're going to get out of here in my plane."

"Plane?"

Until she'd said that he hadn't been sure she understood him.

"Follow me," he said.

"Where's your plane?" she asked, swinging her legs out of the bed.

"Down on top of those huge buildings. About a hundred yards or so. We'll just hope and pray no one will spot us."

"Won't work," she said decisively. She had a well-bred little voice that irritated him. He began to regret having decided to rescue her.

"Well, we'll have to try it," he said. "There's a ladder up the side of the buildings. We're going to climb to the top and get in my plane and fly away."

"If you do that we'll both get killed," she said.

"Do you want to be saved or not?" he said, exasperated.

"Not if it'll kill me," she said rather heatedly. "Listen, they've let me out for walks with the old lady. I know where they keep the cars. Model T's they use to get from one end of this place to another. It'll give us a head start."

"The plane'll give us a better head start. Now, are you coming or not?"

"But those big buildings are guarded day and night. Lots of men with guns."

"Well, let's not stand around here arguing, let's get out of here and take a look," he said.

"How do I know you aren't as bad as they are?" she said. "Or worse?"

"How could I be any worse, anyway?"

She gestured toward the Mexican lady, sprawled rather grotesquely on the floor. "They at least gave me a chaperone. They haven't . . . harmed me in any way."

"Oh, for God's sake," said Tommy. "Are you coming or not?"

"I'm coming," she said. He took her hand and led her out the door. It opened with a simple latch. They swung the door open and poked their heads out.

"The cars are parked around at the back, by the fence," she said, pointing.

"We've got to try for the plane."

"Suit yourself." She shrugged. "I'll take a chance with those cars."

"Don't be crazy," he said. "Stick with me."

He took her hand and yanked her toward him. They went behind a series of buildings, moving from shadow to shadow, until they reached the huge, looming building where Tommy's plane was tied down. He saw its silhouette against the night sky. "Thank God," he said. "She's safe—my plane." Then, crouched behind a stack of barrels, he observed the general layout. The girl had been right. The area was heavily guarded, no matter how lax these people had been with him and with the girl.

"There's got to be a way," he said.

"There is. The cars," she whispered, huddled against him. "I've thought about this carefully. I've been here for days now."

"Who are these people?" he asked her.

"I wish I knew. I can't imagine. They must be lunatics."

"And what do they want with that building? It's the biggest thing I've ever seen. Why, it must be as big as the Coliseum."

"At least," she replied. "I've seen the Coliseum. But they haven't let me get near this. All I've seen is barracks and barbed wire."

"These fellows have my plane," said Tommy, agitated.

Men, dwarfed by the colossal structure, stood around it in military fashion, rifles on their shoulders. Behind them was the steel ladder Tommy was sorry he'd ever climbed down. Frustrated, he pounded his fist into his palm. "We've got to get up that ladder." He fingered the revolver in his belt.

Her eyes followed the gesture. "It's suicide," she said. "Those men have rifles. And there are plenty of them."

"Maybe if we create a diversion," he said.

"Let's just sneak over to those cars," said the girl impatiently.

"If we push these barrels over or something."

"No. I can think of something better, I'm sure of it."

"Oh, shut up," said Tommy. "I'm going to push these barrels over, then we're going to run like hell to the ladder after they come over to investigate. And we'll shoot our way up the ladder." He paused. "You can go first."

"What good will that do if you get shot?" she whispered contemptuously. "I can't fly a plane."

Tommy got the impression this girl was used to getting what she wanted. A spoiled brat. Just what he needed now.

"A minute ago," he said, "you were all tied up and starting to bawl. Now you're being obstinate. This is the thanks I get for saving you."

"You haven't saved anybody yet," she retorted.

"I'm pushing these barrels over on the count of three," he said. "Then we run like hell to the ladder." He took out the revolver, broke it open, and noted with satisfaction that all the chambers were loaded.

"You know how to shoot that thing?" she asked.

"I hit a few tin cans off a few fence posts in my time," he said. "I'm counting now. One. Two."

"Fool," she said.

"Three." He gave the barrels a huge shove. They were stacked two or three high. Some sort of liquid came out of some of them.

They started to run, still under cover of the rolling barrels. Ahead of them, a soldier gazed surprised at the spectacle of barrels rolling towards him. He was joined a second later by another sentry, who'd been stationed a little farther away. The second man stared, too, and threw down a cigarette, not bothering to stamp it out. Slowly, the liquid made its way towards the smoldering cigarette.

Tommy and the girl were about to be exposed now, and headed for the ladder. Tommy held his revolver in his sweaty hand, sure he'd have to use it. But before he had a chance, the blast came, and a huge sheet of flame leapt into the air. He threw the girl clear, slamming her against a building. They were only a few feet from the bottom of the ladder. From everywhere men came to the fire. There was a great deal of jostling. The man with the cigarette was rolling on the ground, his clothes leaping with flames. They heard him scream.

"Don't look," shouted Tommy. "Climb up." He gave her a push and she started up the ladder.

On the roof was the outline of a man. He wasn't looking down at the base of the ladder. His eyes were drawn to the fire below.

"Now shall I tell you where the cars are?" said the girl. Tommy raised his gun, squinted and took a bead at the figure. A moment later he was joined by another man with a rifle.

"You can't kill them both," she hissed, and she pushed him onto the ground. "Come on." She took his hand and ran. She was fleet of foot. She led him away from the fire, away from the huge building, to a small yard where four Model T's sat in a neat row.

"We'll take one and disable the rest," she said. "I hope this is all of them."

"How do we even know there's a road?"

"How do you think I got here?" she said.

"Okay, okay. I'll shoot out the tires."

"No." She thrust her small hand to his. "Too noisy. And we might need the bullets."

A second later she was on her back underneath one of the cars. Deftly, her fingers found the radiator drain and she undid the valve. Water gushed out onto the ground just after she rolled clear. By the time she'd completed the operation on two more cars, Tommy had the hang of it and had disabled the last car.

"Just for the hell of it," he said, "let's take these valves with us." He scrambled over the ground picking them up. "I guess everyone's at the fire. We're in luck."

"Good idea." She grinned. "Okay, are you ready? I'll start it if you crank."

"As ready as I'll ever be." He cranked up one of the vehicles and rushed back to the driver's seat. He looked at the dashboard and touched the wheel, his grimy features in a startled expression. "Oh my God," he said. "I don't know how to drive a car."

"But I do," she said. "Get in. I'd rather drive, anyway."

He brushed his hair back from his forehead. "How do you know how to do all this?" he said, scrambling around to the passenger side.

"My chauffeurs taught me lots about automobiles," she said. "Ready?" She put the car in gear and put her foot down hard on the accelerator.

They careened around through the compound. The girl seemed to know exactly where she was going. All around them, men were running towards the flames. Nobody tried to stop them.

Soon they had left the main area and were making their way down a dirt road.

"I don't know what we'll do at the gate," she said. "They made a great deal of fuss when they brought me in. Stopped the car. Searched it."

"They seem more interested in keeping folks out than keeping them in," said Tommy. "Maybe if we just act like we're one of them."

"Maybe," said the girl dubiously, working the gears expertly. With one hand she twisted her abundant hair behind her and tucked it into her collar. "Maybe they won't notice I'm a girl if I tuck my hair in." Tommy thought this unlikely, although they were both so grimy they might not be spotted immediately as escaping prisoners. He cocked the revolver.

"Hey, watch it," he said. "Forget about the hairdressing and keep this thing on the road."

"Not much of a road," she said. "Full of ruts."

"I guess they bring a lot of things in," said Tommy. "What is going on up here, anyway?"

"I haven't the faintest idea," she answered.

"And who are you?"

"Louise Arbor."

"Louise," he said. It was a pretty name, he thought.

"You may call me Miss Arbor."

They approached what looked like a military guardhouse next to a wide, barbed wire fence.

"All right, let's just slow down and kind of wave and see if they care. Then I'll jump out and try to open that fence," said Tommy.

"I don't think we'll have time. I think we can go right through, but I'd hate to damage the radiator." She screeched to a stop and turned the car around so that its back was to the fence. "There should be a reverse gear pedal around here somewhere," she said. "One of Daddy's lab assistants had one of these and he let me drive it. I think I can remember."

"You *think* you can remember?" Tommy's voice rose. Up at the guardhouse, about twenty-five yards away, a man had come outside, looking startled at the maneuvers being executed by the Model T. He had a rifle in one hand, but he didn't look as if he'd thought about using it yet.

"All right," said Louise, "brace yourself." She put her foot on the accelerator, and twisting behind her to navigate, she barreled the car backwards toward the gate.

The man at the gatehouse leveled his rifle and Tommy aimed, closed his eyes, and squeezed the trigger of the revolver. A second later his fire was returned. "Get down," he shouted to Louise, "but keep your eye on the road."

"How can I do that? Shoot him, for heaven's sake. Shoot him."

Tommy squeezed off another round as the car crashed through the barricade. A piece of wire had caught itself on the door handle. "Keep shooting," said Louise as she leaned out the car and wrenched the door handle free. She cut herself badly in the process, but she kept at it until the car was loose, then she took off in reverse down the gently sloping road until she was out of sight of the sentry.

"I think I winged him," said Tommy doubtfully.

"If you'd open your eyes when you shoot you'd have a better chance," she said. "I'm going to get us turned around." She put the car back into a forward gear and made a wide U, bouncing in some ruts as she did so, and narrowly avoiding a ditch. Then, with a little whoop of victory, she took the car down the road at a good clip.

# CHAPTER
# 17

**B**ACK on top of the mesa, the fire had been put out by men with buckets and a small fire pump. The blue-eyed Mexican, Carlos Gottlieb, wiped his brow and put his hat back on. He sat in his own Model T, one of a small fleet used to drive throughout the vast area.

His body sagged with relief and exhaustion, but he was interrupted by an aide. "Someone's just driven through the south gate," the man shouted. "The guard has been wounded."

"What? Let's get after them. Take the cars. Get me a group of men who can drive and some who can shoot and meet me by the cars."

He took his own car to the adobe hut where Louise Arbor had been kept prisoner, and burst inside. There he saw the fallen figure of the woman in the black dress. "Mama," he cried, kneeling at her side. She was barely conscious. She looked up at him groggily. "A man came and took her," she explained. "Through the window. He has the gun."

Gottlieb set her on the bed. "I'll be back, Mama," he said. "I must stop them."

He leaped back into his vehicle and met a group of men

who were piling into the Model T's. "Come on" he said. And led a speeding caravan towards the gate.

They drove past the guard, who lay there with a bleeding arm, crashing through the remains of the gate.

Gottlieb was in the lead car. He'd barely cleared the gate when he turned and saw that the car behind was in difficulty. Steam was pouring out of the radiator and the driver was gunning the car, producing a lot of coughing, clicking sounds. It was completely stalled.

Behind him, the other cars were similarly engulfed by steam. Gottlieb's car, though, still ran. He assumed the others had been tampered with, but his own Model T had been parked next to the lab for the last hour or so.

Cursing in Spanish and then in German, he kept on down the road. It must have been that aviator. Perhaps he'd been sent to free the girl.

Well, as long as Dr. Arbor didn't hear about it it didn't matter. He just had to make sure she didn't get to civilization and sound the alarm. Fortunately, she'd taken the road from the south gate—the road that led into Mexico.

As Carlos Gottlieb cleared the gate and sped off down the road after them, Tommy and Louise were coming to the bottom of the mesa. She turned to him. "Did Daddy send you?" she said.

"Who? No one sent me. I landed, planning to ask for directions. I'm trying to fly to El Paso."

"I was hoping Daddy had sent you," she said quietly.

"Look, we'll talk later. For now, let's put a few miles between them and us."

"Daddy probably hasn't noticed I'm gone yet," she said bitterly. "He's probably still out in his lab muttering into his test tubes."

"I wonder where this road leads?" said Tommy. "I saw a road from the air, but I don't think this is it."

"Well, until there's a fork in the road we won't have to worry," said Louise. "All we can do is keep going."

"What's a road doing out here, anyway?" said Tommy. "I'd give a lot to know what those fellows up on that mesa are up to. And they have my plane!"

"The road doesn't seem to be going anywhere," said Louise. Ahead of her were two tall, sandstone rocks, as tall as buildings. Between the two of them, where the road should be, was a mass of dried tumbleweed. It looked almost as if it had been wedged between the rocks on purpose.

"I'll get out and clear that away," said Tommy.

"Hurry," she said. She turned and looked behind her as he heaved the dry, crackling foliage aside.

Behind her she saw Carlos Gottlieb's Model T. "Oh, no," she shouted. "Someone's coming."

He looked up the road. "I thought we put those cars out of commission."

"One of them must have been somewhere else. Give me the gun."

"It's on the seat, next to you." Tommy raced back toward the car. "But let me handle this."

Louise seized the gun. "Let me try," she said. She kneeled in the seat and pointed the gun at the approaching car. "I'll aim for the car," she said breathlessly. "It's a bigger target."

She fired. The bullet found its mark, penetrating the Model T's radiator. Hot water began to shoot out, but the car wasn't disabled yet. It kept coming. She fired once more, lower, and hit one of the tires. Because of the speed of the car, the tire was soon reduced to flapping, torn, dusty rubber.

Gottlieb lost control of the car. It went off the narrow road and bounced off a sharp rock. It came to a stop, steaming, smoking, and sitting crookedly in the sand.

Gottlieb staggered out of the car just as Louise started hers up again and smashed through the remaining tumbleweed.

"Now what?" she said, panting.

"Keep going," said Tommy.

"All right, but there's not much more road."

"We'll find something. But we've got to keep going."

Behind them they heard Gottlieb tearing away at the remaining tumbleweed.

"Pretty persistent fellow," said Tommy. "Where's that gun?"

"Be careful," she said. "We've only got two bullets left."

"Where is the damn gun?" demanded Tommy.

"It's in here somewhere. Maybe you're sitting on it."

He found the revolver at his feet and crouched in the seat facing the rear. "Keep going," he said. "Just keep going."

"Where?" she said. "The road ended."

He turned to look. They were about forty yards from the sagebrush, now, and they were facing a railroad track.

"Hooray!" said Tommy. "A train line."

"Well, that's just fine," she said. "If there's a train coming, that will get us out of here."

"Eventually there'll be one," he said. "That must be why they have a road out to here. They've been off-loading supplies."

"They didn't off-load me here," said Louise. "I came into a regular train station."

"Well, let's just follow the tracks for a while. That fellow can't keep up with us on foot. And if we follow a rail line we won't get lost out in the desert. Someone will find us sooner or later."

"All right. But I can't guarantee how much more punishment this automobile can take."

"Don't drive on the tracks, just keep alongside."

She prepared to turn when a bullet flew over their heads.

"Oh, hell," said Tommy. "There he is. My God, it's old Blue Eyes himself." He returned the fire, and the Mexican leaped back into the sagebrush.

"I know who you mean," said Louise, shuddering. She took off along the rail line.

After about half an hour of tense silence, Tommy turned to her. "I reckon it'll take him about forty-five minutes to get back up the hill. Maybe more. And then he'll get some more men and come back. Maybe on horses."

"Well," she said, "we'll just have to keep going until the gas runs out."

"How much is there?" He looked at the instruments. "I don't see a gas gauge."

"There isn't one," she said.

"We never finished our introductions," said Tommy. "Tommy Cutter."

"Oh."

"You can call me Tommy," he said. "Most people do."

"All right," she said, frowning in concentration at the wheel. The country was rough, hard-packed sand, though it made an adequate roadbed. She had to swerve a few times to avoid rocks and an occasional saguaro cactus.

"I guess you're pretty lucky I was around to rescue you," he said, stretching out and feeling a little more relaxed for the first time in hours.

"I guess *you* were pretty lucky *I* was around to rescue *you*," she said.

"Well, that's pretty nervy. I planned to just fly away, but I decided to take you with me. You aren't the least bit grateful."

"You wouldn't have made it, though, would you?" she said sweetly. "You can't drive a car. And you didn't know where the cars were, even. *You* wanted to climb up on the roof. You would have been killed."

"I might only have been wounded." He frowned. "And I would have been able to get out alive. *With* the plane."

"What's so important about the plane?" said Louise. "You can get another one. When we're safe, I'll ask Daddy to buy you one."

"You can't just go to a store and buy a plane," he shouted. "My cousin and I built that one. It took years to perfect the design. And we were going to sell it. I'm supposed to be in El Paso now, selling it to the army."

"Well, if you were going to sell it anyway . . ."

"Just shut up," said Tommy. "You don't seem to understand."

"Well, there's no need to be rude," she said primly. "Really, Mr. Cutter."

The car gave an ominous sputter.

"What's that?" he said.

"Sounds like we're running out of gasoline," she said. They kept on listening to the demoralizing sound of the engine gasping for fuel, until it came to a dead stop.

"Well," said Tommy, trying to sound brave. "Can't expect to find a drugstore that sells fuel around here, can we?" He slumped down in the seat.

"What do we do now?" she said.

"Wait for the train," he said.

"You know," she said, "you'd think I'd be terribly blue about all of this. After all, I've been through a tremendous amount of danger. And it was horrible being taken against my will, tied up, drugged."

"Drugged?"

She nodded. "But now, now that it's over, and we escaped and shot at those men and outdrove that horrible man with blue eyes and everything, well, I feel good. I feel like it's been almost worth it."

He looked at her, incredulous. "You've been out in the sun too long without a hat," he said.

"You don't understand, because you're an aviator and you get to ride around the sky in a plane. I've led an awfully dull life."

"You're not old enough to have led much of a life at all," said Tommy. "And nothing could be dull enough to have made all this seem fun."

"I must look a fright," she said, rubbing at her face with her sleeve.

"You do look pretty horrible," he said.

She frowned at him and fussed a little with her hair. "I couldn't look worse than you do."

"I guess I look pretty bad. I had to tunnel out of that shed where they were keeping me."

"Maybe they won't let us on the train, if it comes," she said. "We look like a couple of desperados. Oh, and I haven't a cent for the fare."

"Well, maybe we'll have to travel third class," he said sarcastically. "Listen, Louise, we'll be lucky if a train comes before those men come back. Or before the vultures get us. We're out in the middle of the damned desert."

"Oh, a train will come," she said. "I'm sure it will."

"I don't know about that. I don't even know if we're in the U.S. or Mexico. If we're in Mexico, we're smack in the middle of a revolution."

"Oh, we must be in the United States. They took me off the train in a funny little place called Aztec. It said so on the station. And there was an American flag flying. I tried to get the people there to help me, but I was half drugged and groggy, and the nurse just hauled me past all the people there and said I was a 'delicate nerve case.' And then a car came to fetch us, and they gave me another injection, and I woke up later in that adobe hut with that woman who only spoke Spanish. It was a nightmare."

"But they let you out. I saw you walking around."

"That's because I forced them to. I told them I had to have a little exercise or I'd get sick and die. Then I screamed and fussed and stamped my foot until I had my way."

"I can imagine," said Tommy.

"You see," said Louise, "I gathered early on they didn't want me to die. They seemed to want me to be fit. They fed me well and fussed over me. I imagined they were going to ask Daddy for a ransom or something. But I couldn't figure out why they had to take me so far away. Where is Aztec, anyhow?"

"I think there's one in Arizona. We're too far west for Aztec, New Mexico.

"I know one thing," continued Tommy. "After I get my plane back and take care of my business at El Paso, I'm going to find out just who these people are and what they're up to. Imagine, just grabbing American citizens like that. Who the hell do they think they are?"

"Do you hear something?" said Louise. "I think I hear a sort of singing sound coming from the tracks."

Tommy went over to the rails and put his ear against them.

"There's a definite vibration," he said smiling.

Louise got out of the car and the two of them stood together looking down the track. A plume of smoke soon appeared on the horizon.

They looked at each other, overjoyed. "You see," said Louise. "I told you." Her arms flew open and she embraced him. For a moment they hugged each other and jumped up and down and laughed.

Then, self-consciously, they parted and Louise made some ineffectual passes at her hair, trying to arrange it in tidier order. "You need a shave, Mr. Cutter," she said, trying to sound light. "Your whiskers are awfully scratchy."

When the train came into view they jumped and hollered and were rewarded by its wheezing to a halt. It was a freight train with about ten box cars and armed Mexicans sitting on top. They all observed Tommy and Louise with interest.

"Better be careful," said Tommy. "I don't know if I can guarantee your safety on a train full of Mexican troops. We must be south of the border."

"Who are you?" boomed out a very American voice.

At the end of a train, in a domed private car, a smooth-faced man in a white suit and a straw hat hung out of a window. He had a tall glass with something cool and bubbly-looking in it.

"We're lost. Can you take us to safety?" said Tommy.

"This should be quite a story," said their rescuer, looking pleasantly amused. "My, you look like a couple of real ragamuffins."

"I'm sorry we have to press ourselves on you like this," said Louise, "but my companion and I are badly in need of assistance. We'd be awfully grateful for your help."

"Of course, dear lady, of course. Come right in. Join me for lunch. I'm heading north to Mexicali. Will that suit?"

"Sounds like paradise," said Tommy. He was mentally

calculating the distance from Mexicali to wherever he was. He had to come back for his plane as soon as possible.

Terence O'Houlihan was a ginger-haired man with a brogue so thick Sophie could barely understand it. She sat opposite him in a squalid little room, barely furnished with a heavy ebony crucifix on the cracked plaster wall. He leaned over the battered oak table that stood between them, pointing with delicate hands, red at the knuckles, at a slim, metal cylinder, a cigar-shaped device.

"And so," he continued, "when this chemical eats through this copper disc and into the compartment with this other chemical, the combination produces a flame as hot as the sun. It's a very effective incendiary bomb. And small. Easily concealed."

"But how can you tell when it will go off?" said Sophie, frowning in concentration.

"The thickness of the copper disc regulates that," he said precisely. "You just have to tell me when you want it to go."

"And this knob?"

"When it's broken off the device is set."

"If it were wrapped in clothing? Would that put out the fire?"

The Irishman laughed. "Not at all. We slip 'em into pockets. Hang a jacket on a nail aboard a British ship and . . ." His hands spread delicately out like two flowers. "And anyone in the way is on his knees outside the pearly gates in a few seconds flat."

Sophie rose and scraped back her chair. "Show me how the knob works."

He made a quick, twisting motion.

"Fine. I want something that will go off within ten minutes."

"Cutting it rather fine, aren't you?"

"I'll worry about that," she said. "I'm used to working with cues. My entrances and exits are timed to the measure. And I'm counting on the fact a lady will try on a pretty dress right away."

"I'll give you ten minutes, then," he said. "I make 'em. I don't set 'em."

"Mr. Kessler will take care of the final arrangements," she said, pulling on her gloves. "Someone will fetch the device in the morning."

"All right." He rose and opened the door for her.

"Long live the Kaiser," he said to her, grinning broadly.

"Up the Irish," she replied.

"You don't give a damn about the Irish," he said, still grinning. "Nobody does. But I don't care. The enemies of my enemy are my friends."

# CHAPTER
# 18

GEORGE set off for school whistling. In his pocket was a note from Maude. "Please excuse George's absence for the next week. Urgent family business requires his presence elsewhere."

As soon as he'd delivered the note, George would go down to the Southern Pacific depot and buy railroad tickets for Gustav Van Damm (they'd decided to make him a Dutchman), his wife Maude and his brother-in-law George. They'd let George make up the names, but Gustav had insisted they use their own first names so they'd be able to speak to each other naturally.

Then he'd go back to the house and they'd all take a taxi—that was the riskiest part of the business—down to the depot. The papers were still full of the missing baron.

Maude had taken the precaution of sending Clarence P. Fogerty, who seemed to be always on her track, a lurid message, purportedly from the Hindoos who'd kidnapped Maude. The message asked for a meeting in Petaluma. They figured that would keep him busy for a while.

George picked up a stick and rattled it along a metal fence, producing a nice clattery sound.

He knew Maude still didn't want him to go, and Gustav had stayed out of it, but in the end George had won. "I'll tell Nicky," he said.

175

Maude was furious, but after a while she'd calmed down and said if they were going to do something dangerous, perhaps it was best if they all did it together. Then she'd cried and said she was bringing George up all wrong. Gustav had told her George had turned out fine so far, and that made her even more angry.

George had told Gustav privately not to pay any attention to Maude, but Gustav didn't seem to hear him.

None of this bothered George unduly. The great thing was that they were off to catch German spies. George was brimming with excitement and so happy that even the fact that Maude insisted on coming failed to dampen his spirits. Maude might fuss at them, he thought.

Back at the house, Gustav was putting on a blue suit, which had been among the collection of clothing that Nicky had left behind. It fit reasonably well. Gustav was intrigued by the way Mrs. Cavendish had handed him the clothes, stroking the lapels and treating the clothing as if it were some part of her husband. It was a curious business all round. The woman seemed to hate Cavendish, but she also still seemed to feel a powerful attraction to him. Gustav had noticed that the first time he met her, at that party of Mrs. Lacoste's.

In a way, he imagined, it was rather how he felt about Sophie. He sighed and knotted his tie. Why did love have to be so painful? Though perhaps it wasn't love—it was some bitter anger laced with lust that clung on after love had gone.

He brushed himself off. He felt immeasurably better since he'd shaved and washed properly and got into clean clothes. The leg was healing nicely—the wound looked healthy and pink. The bullet, it was clear, hadn't touched the bone, just torn into the flesh and bruised the muscle.

He descended the stairs slowly. The leg hurt, and he limped slightly, but it wasn't too bad.

At the bottom of the stairs, Maude Cavendish waited for him. "You look as if you're almost healed," she said. He smiled his lopsided little smile.

"Come and have some breakfast," she said. "I'm afraid

with Clara gone you have to take what you can get around here. Neither of us is a very good cook, but I've scrambled some eggs, and there's toast and coffee.''

As they entered the dining room, he put a hand on her shoulder. ''Having any second thoughts?''

''I've decided,'' she said. She looked unhappy.

''You're worried about George, aren't you?''

''Of course I am. And at the same time I want that story. It's what I've wanted for a long time. Oh, in some ways I wish you'd never come.''

''You can't come with me unless you're sure. I can't be saddled with a whining female. Either you're in completely or you stay out.''

''I'm in,'' she said with some spirit. ''I wonder how far you'd get without me? They're looking for you everywhere. I could turn you in, just like that.''

''But you won't,'' he said confidently.

''Not if you take me with you.''

''It will be easier to leave town with you and George, there's no doubt about that.''

''And I stay with you all the way,'' said Maude. ''That's our agreement. So don't even think about giving me the slip halfway to Arizona.''

The doorbell rang.

''Step into the parlor,'' she whispered. ''I'll see who it is.''

He ducked into the dimly lit room.

A moment later she joined him, carrying a large, flat parcel wrapped in gray paper and tied with mauve ribbon. ''How peculiar. It's from Madame Cecile. Listen to this.'' She held up a note. ''Please accept this gown in apology for my unfortunate mistake of last week. I assure you, Mrs. Cavendish, this is an exclusive creation, as all my gowns for you will be in the future.''

''Isn't that the limit? The old shrew. Thinks she can buy my favor with a gift.'' She began to tug at the ribbons. ''I wonder what it's like. If it's nice, I think I'll keep it.''

Gustav looked wary for a moment.

''You know,'' said Maude, tugging hard at the knot,

"she sent a new shopgirl around with this. She should have gone around to the back. And she was wearing too much perfume."

Gustav stepped into the hall and sniffed the air. "Sophie!" he said. He went back to Maude's side, grabbed the half-opened package, flung it into the fireplace, and threw Maude down on the sofa, covering her with his body.

"What are you doing?" she demanded, squirming out from under him. She was pretty strong, he noticed, as she thrashed beneath him.

But a second later a huge roar and a flash of bright light came from the fireplace. They both sat up. The fireplace was a mass of white flame, and amber tongues of fire were licking the carpet before it. Gustav scrambled to his feet, seized a potted palm, and flung the dirt from it around the carpet. Maude got up and began to stamp at the flames.

"No!" he cried, but it was too late. Flames had touched the hem of her skirt and were threatening to engulf her completely. She screamed. He seized her, threw her down, and, beating at her with sofa cushions, managed to put out the fire. Maude sat there for a moment, her blackened skirt and petticoat arranged wildly around her legs. "My God," she said, "these people are dangerous, aren't they?"

"Yes, they are." He turned his attention back to the area around the fireplace, using the sofa cushions to beat out the remains of the fire. The conflagration in the fireplace had died down, now. There was simply a pile of cinders where the package had sat. Some furniture around the hearth was blackened, and the carpet had a huge sooty hole in it.

He turned, exhausted, to see her scrambling to her feet, arranging her ruined clothing around her. "You can change your mind about coming with me, you know."

"Not on your life," she said. "I want to find out who these people are and stop them. I take it this was the work of your friend Sophie Von Gluck?"

"I think so. She's an accomplished actress. I'm sure she was the shopgirl at the door."

"Well, all I can say is she'd better look out. She can't get away with this sort of thing. Not in this country. I'll change now and pack a few last things, and then we'll go." At the door to the room she turned and said, "I imagine that woman has been bad all her life. And nobody noticed because she was beautiful."

The train pulled away and they both sighed with relief and smiled at each other.

"Junius Witherspoon," said their new acquaintance. "From Wichita." Confronted with his rescuer, Tommy felt especially grubby. Mr. Witherspoon was immaculate. He was portly but fit-looking, with smooth skin burnt pink by the sun. His smooth-shaven jaw looked as if it had a trace of talcum on it. His face was bland and pleasant, with light brown eyes, a slightly snubbed nose, and a wide, rubbery mouth.

"Oh, we're so grateful to you, Mr. Witherspoon," said Louise. "We've had the most amazing adventures. I'm Louise Arbor."

"And I'm her brother Tommy."

Tommy was afraid Mr. Witherspoon might not want to get mixed up in anything with the blue-eyed Mexican, who might well be pursuing them. He put a hand on Louise's shoulder and said, "My sister and I were out touring and we ran out of gas."

"Your sister?" said Mr. Witherspoon. He cast an appraising eye over Louise. "Wouldn't you two like to get cleaned up a little? There's a bathroom at the end of this car. Then you can join me for lunch. I've had my breakfast."

"That would be wonderful," said Louise. She gave Tommy a severe look. He gathered she hadn't wanted him to lie. But he thought now that he had she wouldn't tell Witherspoon what they'd been up to.

"Right this way, young lady," said Mr. Witherspoon. Tommy brushed off his clothing a little and sat down on a plush-covered chair. The private car was sumptuously furnished—paneled in light wood with some sporting prints on the wall. There was a collection of furniture all in the same blue plushy stuff, and a dining table off to one end. At the other end was a green felt-covered card table.

Overhead was an electric light with a fixture of crystal, and there was a big glass dome that made the car look airy and bright in spite of the rather oppressive furnishings.

When Mr. Witherspoon returned, he offered Tommy a cigar. Tommy was more interested in breakfast than in a smoke, right now, but he accepted, partly because he imagined Mr. Witherspoon's cigars would be excellent. Mr. Witherspoon fastidiously clipped the end of his with a little gold cutter; Tommy simply bit off the end of his and accepted a light.

"Like it?" said his host, leaning back and executing a perfect smoke ring.

"Sure do," said Tommy. "But isn't this a rather dangerous part of the world to be traveling in so luxuriously?"

"Ha! Not if you have friends in high places. I'm an arms dealer, Mr. Arbor. I do business with all the factions down here in Mexico. I've got letters of passage from all of 'em. I've got letters testifying to my good character and indicating I travel under the protection of Carranza. And of Villa. And of Zapata, Madero, Huerta—all of them, past and present." His eyes practically twinkled.

"You're a braver man than I am," said Tommy. He added mentally that Mr. Witherspoon was more of an idiot, too. "Mixing in Mexican politics isn't a good idea any time. But *now* . . ." He shook his head.

"In my business, the worst times are the best times."

"Seems a shame, though, doesn't it?" said Tommy. "I've spent a fair amount of time south of the border. I grew up in San Diego. And it seems a shame. The Mexican people never had much—they work hard just to feed themselves. To see them fighting among themselves, too— well, it just seems a damn shame."

Mr. Witherspoon shrugged. "A good case could be made that I'm doing my country a service. Did you know the Germans have been down here arming all my customers to the teeth? Trying to get on the winning side of this revolution so's they can have an ally right on the U.S. border." He shook his head. "They'd like nothing better than to get these Mexicans united so they can start a border war that will tie down U.S. troops and keep us out of that war in Europe."

"Well, that war in Europe should cheer you up," said Tommy. "I imagine there's plenty to be made selling arms over there."

"Yes," said Mr. Witherspoon, either not knowing or not caring that Tommy's disapproval tinged the remark. "But the Mexicans pay in gold. And they pay more. It's a real bonanza down here right now.

"What do you do for a living?" Witherspoon gestured at Tommy with his cigar.

"I'm an aviator," he said. "My cousin and I have just developed a new aeroplane and we're planning to sell it."

"Oh, interesting. Say, I wouldn't mind getting into that field myself. I imagine the machines have some real military potential."

Tommy shrugged. "I guess so. I just like to fly them." He wasn't about to tell Mr. Witherspoon he planned to sell the thing to the army. Witherspoon would be selling planes to the Mexicans next, he imagined, so they could massacre each other even more efficiently.

At that moment, Louise came back into the room and both men looked astonished at her transformed appearance. She was still wearing her grimy riding habit, but she'd somehow managed to brush it and sponge it so it was presentable. Her face was glowing from a vigorous scrubbing, and her hair was twisted up and arranged becomingly around her face.

Tommy realized that while she'd looked like a kid before, she was actually a rather sophisticated young lady. He had a sudden urge to get himself as clean as she was. "Have you a razor I could borrow, Mr. Witherspoon?"

But Mr. Witherspoon ignored him. "Do sit down, Miss Arbor. I must say you look lovely considering all your misadventures. I know it's early, but don't you think a glass of champagne is in order? To celebrate your rescue?"

"How about a razor?" said Tommy rather gruffly.

Witherspoon touched a button in the wood paneling, and a few moments later a Mexican servant appeared. "Give this young fellow a shave, will you?" said Witherspoon.

Tommy followed the man through a door into an elegantly appointed bathroom. There was even a barber's chair. Steamy towels were applied to Tommy's face. He sat while the servant whipped up some lather in a mug.

"Aren't you a little nervous, traveling around in the middle of a revolution?" asked Tommy in his passable Spanish.

"Señor Witherspoon makes it well worth my while," said the servant, stropping the razor carefully. "And I feel safe with him. He has many friends."

When Tommy was shaved and had washed himself as well as he could, he went back into the front of the car. Louise was giggling and handing her glass to Mr. Witherspoon for a refill. Tommy frowned. There was a kittenish expression on her face that annoyed him. The wine couldn't have affected her so quickly. As soon as Louise had washed her face and dressed her hair, she'd turned into a cheap little flirt. This was hardly the tough, sarcastic girl he'd escaped with from that encampment. Maybe she was only nice to rich men who traveled around in private railway cars.

"Oh," she said, turning. "Tommy. You look so different."

Tommy had taken considerable trouble with his appearance. "So do you," he said.

"I'll just go and see about something to eat for you," said Mr. Witherspoon. "Have a glass of champagne."

When Witherspoon had left, Tommy took the bottle by the neck and splashed some into his glass. "Been having a cozy time?"

"Mr. Witherspoon is charming," said Louise. "Don't you think?"

"No, I don't."

"Well, it's awfully decent of him to save us. And why on *earth* did you say you were my brother? It's absurd."

"Seemed like a good idea. Isn't it a little early for you to be drinking, Miss Arbor? Is that what they taught you in finishing school?"

"I think considering the circumstances, the rules can be broken. Anyway," she said with a toss of her head, "people who know the rules know when to break them."

"Well, stop flirting with Witherspoon. It might give him ideas. I don't think he's a straight shooter."

"Well, the least I can do is be charming to him seeing as he's saved us and all."

Witherspoon came back into the room. "There. It's all settled. I'll have the food sent in as soon as it's prepared. But could I see you for a moment? There's something I'd like you to take a look at. Interested in horses?"

"Well, as a matter of fact I am," said Tommy.

"There's a couple of beauties I got down in Mexico I'd like you to see."

Louise gave him a little look that seemed to say, "Humor him," so Tommy shrugged and followed Witherspoon out of the car. They went through another car with a little kitchen—Tommy longed for some of the sumptuous food he saw being prepared there—and then they went through one more door, buffeting about in the wind between the cars, into a car where two magnificent horses were tethered. They looked like Arabians—one was glossy black, the other was a palomino. They were beautifully curried, with silky manes. Tommy patted their noses and felt their flanks.

Suddenly, out of the corner of his eye, he saw Mr. Witherspoon rush at him. A second later, before he had a chance to react, he felt a huge weight at the base of his skull and he fell unconscious to the straw-covered floor.

Mr. Witherspoon removed a heavy object from a silk pocket handkerchief, smiled a little, and left the car.

Back in the saloon his face took on a worried expression. "I'm awfully sorry," he said. "But your brother just got kicked by a horse. Stood right in back of the thing—damn fool thing to do, I'm sorry to say."

"What!" Louise rose, knocking over her glass. "Where is he?"

"He's being taken care of. Manuel is an excellent nurse. I think it's best to keep him quiet for a while. He'll be all right. You just stay here with me and have breakfast."

"I want to see if he's all right," said Louise.

"He told me to tell you not to bother him and to get a bite to eat. Said it's been some time since you did."

Louise sat slowly down. "Oh, but I'd rather see if he's all right," she said.

"Don't be obstinate, young lady," said Mr. Witherspoon waggishly. "Look, here's Manuel with our breakfast."

Louise's concern momentarily vanished as she saw silver covers lifted from steaming plates of scrambled eggs and bacon. There was also a basket of rolls and some magnificent fruit—grapes and peaches.

"I really should see if he's all right," said Louise faintly.

Manuel retrieved Louise's fallen glass—it hadn't broken on the soft carpeting—and said something to her in Spanish.

"What?" said Louise, still abstracted by the turn of events.

"Don't you speak Spanish? Your brother does," said Mr. Witherspoon.

"No, I don't," said Louise. Mr. Witherspoon smiled and spoke to the servant in that language. The servant looked startled, gave Louise a curious glance, and withdrew.

"I must see him," said Louise. "Please take me to him." She went to the door and rattled the handle. It was locked.

# CHAPTER
# 19

"PLEASE, Miss Arbor, won't you sit down and eat your breakfast? Let's make this a civilized trip. We'll have a good meal, some more champagne, and we'll get to know each other better."

"Really, Mr. Witherspoon," said Louise haughtily, but with the strain of fear in her voice, "I want to see my brother."

"Your brother? I don't think he's your brother, Miss Arbor—if that's your name. I could tell by the way he looked at you. You're racketing around the countryside with some young man and you're no better than you should be. Now that's the truth, isn't it?"

"What do you want with me?" said Louise, bringing a knuckle to her mouth and looking at him with horror.

"What do you think I want?" he said blandly. "Nobody rides for free on my train. I wouldn't have got what I wanted out of life if I hadn't simply taken it. Oh, don't look so horrified. I'm not interested in anything crude or violent. It will go a lot easier on you if you simply cooperate. And don't pretend you don't know what I'm talking about. Well-brought-up young girls don't end up out in the middle of the desert with scruffy young men."

He held out his hand. "Now come back to the table and

we'll resume our conversation. I want this all to develop naturally." He smiled. "You really have no choice in the matter. It's my train."

Choking back tears, she accompanied him to the table. "There," he said as they sat. "Now why don't you indulge me a little and let your hair back down. It's very lovely hair." He reached over and pulled out a hairpin.

Louise stood stark still. "What a delicious-looking brunch!"

"That's the spirit," he said, as if he were a teacher encouraging a pupil. "Just act natural. We have plenty of time. You know, my dear," he leaned over and squeezed her knee, "I think you'll find a mature man has so much more to offer than that rather disreputable young friend of yours. You'll see." His eyes shone. "Now let me put a little butter on this roll for you. And by all means, have some more champagne."

Back in the freight car with the two horses, Tommy came slowly to consciousness. His head lolled heavily on his neck. He opened his eyes cautiously. It took him a second to remember where he was. He felt the back of his head. It ached horribly. He shifted a little and felt another ache in his ribs where old Blue Eyes had kicked him. He was tired and he hurt. He struggled to his feet and then he saw he wasn't alone. Witherspoon's Mexican servant was there, holding a stout rope.

He came toward Tommy and pushed him back down. Tommy was still weak and dizzy, and before he had a chance to collect himself he was being very expeditiously bound, hand and foot.

"What are you doing?" he said in Spanish. "What the hell are you doing? What does Witherspoon want, anyhow?"

"The woman," said the servant, pulling tight on the rope.

"What! The man's insane." Tommy twisted around but the work was almost finished.

"Perhaps he is. But he always gets what he wants and

he wants your woman. You're lucky he didn't throw you off the train.''

"That woman is my sister," said Tommy. "Do you have any sisters?"

"I have five," said the servant, sitting back on his heels. A look of obvious concern crossed his features.

"And you are helping this man to dishonor my sister," said Tommy, trying to put a lot of Latin feeling into the words. Then he narrowed his eyes. "If this is allowed to happen, I will come after your sisters someday."

"You'll never find them, señor, and even if you could find them—"

"You are a disgrace," said Tommy. "And you will be cursed for this."

"Calm down," said the man. "Listen, I don't like this either." He paused. "And if the girl is your sister, well I can understand . . . I'll tell you what. I want you to hit me very hard." He was rapidly untying the ropes, now. "Very hard." He tapped his jaw. "It will go all right with me if they find me bruised and knocked out. All right?"

"All right," said Tommy, grinning and pulling the ropes off himself.

"But you still might fail. He has a gun. It's in the desk drawer."

"That's all right," said Tommy. "I've got one, too." He pulled out his revolver. "With one bullet."

"Are you going to kill him? I know you have cause, but . . ."

"No. If I was a Mexican I might," he said. And he added to himself, *if she really was my sister I might.* "Ready?" He pulled back his fist and landed a roundhouse punch. The fellow had a glass jaw. A second later he was flat on the floor.

Tommy looked over the horses. They had observed all these proceedings with a calm Tommy envied. Quickly he saddled them, realizing that they were well trained.

He looped the rope into a neat coil and hung it on his shoulder. He checked the lining of his jacket; the compass and the telegram were still there. It wasn't much, but it was a start. Tommy planned to take Louise off the train. He'd debated the wisdom of trying to take the train over, but he'd decided against it. There were all those armed men sitting on the boxcars behind him—presumably guarding a cargo of arms. Or maybe a cargo of Mr. Witherspoon's gold. And there was the fact that Witherspoon apparently had important friends in Mexico.

He went to the door of the car and out onto the small platform that connected them, then into the next car. In the kitchen, he helped himself to a roast chicken, which he stuffed in his jacket, and a bottle of wine, which went into a pocket. Then he went out of the window and clung to the side of the train. He wished he wasn't so overburdened with supplies, but he had only a short distance to go. Making sure he couldn't be observed by the men on top of the cars, he worked his way forward to Witherspoon's car. When he'd made it there, he peered into one of the windows. Louise was sipping champagne but he could tell already that she knew she was in trouble. Her eyes were as big as saucers. Witherspoon had his back to Tommy. He was leaning over Louise and kissing her hand. Tommy tapped on the window ever so slightly. She saw him and looked overjoyed. Then Witherspoon's head began to turn. Before Tommy had a chance to duck, he saw Louise take Witherspoon in her arms and kiss him. Witherspoon forgot about the window.

Tommy didn't know why he was working so hard to save this girl from a fate worse than death. She seemed pretty well able to handle herself under all the strain. Although it was clear she'd kissed the old fool to keep him from seeing him, Tommy was still shocked at the lack of maidenly reserve that would allow her to think of such a thing and to carry it out so convincingly.

At the side of the car was a small ladder to the roof. This would be the trickiest part. Still clinging to the moving train, he fastened one end of the rope to the ladder. Then he went up, with the other end of the rope in his hand.

Inside te car, Witherspoon drew back from Louise appreciatively. "Well, now, that wasn't so bad, was it? I can see you know what you're about, my dear. It was silly of you to have been so coy." He reached for her and Louise held up her butter knife.

"Oh, but you said we should finish breakfast first," she said archly. She was wondering if the butter knife could do any harm. She'd dearly love to sink it into the base of his throat above the creamy silk collar. He batted it out of her hand and pushed her down on the divan and began to pull at her blouse.

Tommy's boots crashed through the glass dome at the top of the car and he swung down on the rope, aiming himself at Witherspoon. He knocked him off the divan, and a minute later Tommy was on the floor on top of him with his hands around Witherspoon's throat.

Overhead they heard the pounding of feet, and then they saw a circle of brown faces looking down at them through the broken glass of the domed window. The faces were crisscrossed by drawn rifles with bayonets fixed.

Tommy pulled out the revolver and held it against Witherspoon's temple. He crouched next to him, holding the man around the neck. In Spanish Tommy shouted: "He'll die if you fire."

"No, no. Don't fire," said Witherspoon in a choked voice. Tommy eased up on him just a little to let him talk.

"Okay, we're going to see your horses now," said Tommy. "Louise, open that door."

"It's locked."

"Well, break the glass with something. Quickly. I don't know how attached to their boss these fellows are."

Louise picked up a huge lamp and threw it through the glass pane in the door. Then she reached through the broken glass and opened the door. "It works."

"Good. Now open doors for me. We're going through one more car and then we'll be leaving."

He gave Mr. Witherspoon's neck an extra squeeze. Witherspoon's face turned red. "Tell them," hissed Tommy into his ear, "to back off. Tell them to stay on the roofs of the freight cars."

"If you kill me, they'll kill you," said Witherspoon.

"Yes, but you'll already be dead, won't you, Witherspoon? And if I'd lived the way you seem to, I'd try to put off meeting my maker as long as possible. Now tell them. And remember, I speak Spanish."

Witherspoon choked out directions to the troops. The brown-faced men all disappeared from the window.

Louise and Tommy and Junius Witherspoon struggled down the length of the next car. Tommy pulled the emergency brake that hung there. The train came to a jarring halt.

They went on into the freight car. Here Tommy took Mr. Witherspoon by the shoulders and slammed his head hard against the wall. After the third blow, Witherspoon fell in a heap next to the unconscious Manuel.

"Hope you know how to ride a horse," he said to Louise.

"Of course," she answered. "Why do you think I'm wearing a riding habit?"

Tommy gave Louise a leg up on the palomino. "I trust these are well-behaved horses," he said. "They seem to take a certain amount of commotion in stride. Now as soon as I open this door, ride like hell."

"What about you?"

"I'll be right behind."

"All right." Louise patted her horse's head and leaned over its neck. "You'll like a nice hard ride, won't you?"

Tommy slid open the door next to the boxcar, and Louise's horse flew out, jumping into the desert and landing on the sand with a wallop. A second later, Tommy, on the black horse, was behind her.

They rode hard without looking behind them for twenty minutes. When they did look behind them, they saw the train was starting to move again in the opposite direction.

"I guess he gave up," said Tommy. "I don't think those fellows would do anything until he came around again. But they can't come after us now. We're too far away. Not unless Witherspoon wants to follow on foot."

"Oh, Tommy," said Louise breathlessly. "Thank God we got away. He was horrible. Really horrible."

"I knew he was a nasty customer right off. But you said we should be charming to him."

"Never mind what I said. I've been through enough. I don't want to hear what I said before."

"That's twice now I've saved you," said Tommy. "and my plane is still sitting up on that mesa somewhere, wondering why I'm not saving her."

"But *I'm* not saved yet," said Louise. "We're out in the middle of the desert. We might die out here."

"We might," said Tommy, "but I'm beginning to think nothing can kill us." He fished out the tiny compass from his pocket. "What do you say we just take a chance and ride straight north? I think I'd like to get back to the U.S.A."

Dr. Arbor was trembling. He stood in front of the desk in Carlos Gottlieb's little office, and the sweat poured from his brow. For a moment Gottlieb wondered if the heat and the pressure would affect Arbor the same way it had affected the late Dr. Kohler. But despite his shaky appearance, there was a firmness to the scientist's voice as he spoke.

"You've got it. You have what you want. The factory is working at full production, and my system panned out. It was just a theory, but by God it worked and you have enough gas for your needs. My work is done. Now, please, let us go."

Gottlieb averted his eyes. "You'll be able to go when we've completed the project. Day after tomorrow."

"But you haven't let me see Louise for a day. Is she all right?"

"Of course she's all right." Gottlieb had allowed Arbor to see his daughter every night. Drugged with veronal, the girl looked simply as if she were sleeping soundly.

"Well, I want to see her. I can still stop, you know. I can shut it down. I can." In spite of his brave words, Dr. Arbor's voice shook.

Gottlieb sighed. "We're so close now, doctor," he said, trying to sound slightly impatient, instead of frightened. "I thought it would be best if you stayed away from her until we launch. It would give you the extra push we need to make sure that our plans will be on schedule."

"You're insane. All of you are insane," said Dr. Arbor.

"You may think whatever you like," said Gottlieb, his smoky blue eyes glowing. "All I require from you is another five hundred tons of the stuff in time. When we have what we need, you and your daughter are free to go."

"But how can I be sure of that?" said Dr. Arbor.

"We are not barbarians. We realize you'll be reluctant to tell the world that you've been a traitor. I'm sure your silence can be assured." Gottlieb leaned forward to drive home his point. "In any case, we can find you again. And your daughter, too. You'll be safe as long as you keep quiet about your work here."

"I just want to see Louise again," said the doctor. He looked as if he were about to burst into tears. Gottlieb turned away. After all this, they'd never be able to say he, Gottlieb, was soft. He'd done more for the Fatherland than many who thought he was only half a German.

"Five hundred tons more and you will," he said, gesturing to the guards. They hustled Dr. Arbor out of the room.

Gottlieb buried his head in his hands. Three more days. Three more days and it would be over. He'd be so glad to be out of this godforsaken place. He'd force them to take him to Berlin. He and Mama in a cozy little apartment there. A nice quiet job in the foreign ministry. It was all he asked for the hell he'd been through.

Wearily he began to code a telegram to be sent to the Kessler Shipping Company in San Francisco.

He hadn't been totally frank in the telegram. If it were only Herr Kessler to deal with, it would be one thing. But that woman! He didn't want to excite her. She was capable of anything. A word from her and he could be back in that miserable little Sonoran village—inherit his father's old job of consul—trapped forever.

Instead, he had written glowingly of the fine work Dr. Arbor had done. It was amazing. They were still on schedule. It was as if Dr. Kohler had never died on him like that. God. Kohler. All the work he'd done with the man, keeping him alive, keeping him sane. And then the fool had wandered off in a fever. Considering all that, it was amazing what had been accomplished here. He thought the Iron Cross, plus a post in the foreign ministry would hardly be enough. Maybe an ambassadorship to a Spanish-speaking country. Mama would like that better than Berlin.

The final line of the telegram was optimistic. "Operation will take place as scheduled." Very German, he thought. Nothing flamboyantly Latin, nothing self-congratulatory. Because whatever had happened to Louise Arbor and the strange American who had descended on them out of the sky, the operation would take place as scheduled. Dr. Arbor would get that five hundred tons out of the factory on time. Carlos knew he would.

# CHAPTER
# 20

"**I** THINK I'll step down to the dining car and have another sherbet," George said. "I'm feeling kind of peckish. Got any more of that German money, Gustav?"

Gustav peeled off a few bills. George grinned and set off, hands in his pockets, whistling.

"George," said Maude mechanically, "don't put your hands in your pockets like that. And don't whistle."

"Golly, Maude. Stop picking on me," said George cheerfully. He left the compartment. And Maude turned to Gustav, exasperated. "Will he ever act like a gentleman?" she asked.

"George is a remarkable young man," said Gustav.

"He is, isn't he?" said Maude thoughtfully. "I've done my best. I feel as if I have only a little while more to shape him and then it'll be too late."

Gustav laughed. "I think it's too late already. George is already shaped."

She smiled. "Ten years ago I was nineteen. And George was four. I practically carried him across town. After the fire. We got ourselves a ride on a garbage cart away from Russian Hill, through all the smoke, all the way up Geary to Golden Gate Park. And while they fought the fire, we lived in a tent and stood in line for our meals. And I cried and tried to tell him about Mama and Papa, and about the town burning. You know there were some people who thought the whole world was ending? And George was only four years old and he said, 'Mama and Papa are in heaven and they'll build all the houses back up again.' And I thought he was just a baby and didn't know any better, but later I realized George was absolutely right.''

Maude had begun to cry. She fished in her sleeve for her handkerchief. ''Oh, my,'' she said. ''I'm sorry. I must be all red and blotchy.''

Gustav leaned over and took the handkerchief from her and wiped her tears. ''You and George may be called upon to be brave once more,'' he said. ''You'll be able to do it.''

''I hear the conductor,'' said Maude after a moment. ''Better put that toothache bandage back on.''


The horses were tethered to a large cactus. Tommy and Louise lay on the ground. The remains of their picnic—the chicken bones and the empty wine bottle—lay nearby. They were side by side, on their backs, staring up at the starry desert sky.

''Now over there,'' said Tommy, ''is Orion. See? Those three stars are his belt.''

''I'm scared,'' said Louise.

''Me, too,'' said Tommy. He put his arm around her. ''And it's going to be cold tonight. But in the morning it will seem all right again.''

''But it might not,'' said Louise. ''We might die. Really.''

''We might. But we probably won't.''

''How do you know?''

''Because I just know. Ever since I crashed. Did I ever tell you I crashed once? And I rolled out of the crate just before she burst into flames. And ever since then I knew, I just knew, I'd die an old man with lots of grandchildren sobbing around my bed.''

''Your arm is around me,'' said Louise.

''Want me to move it? I thought you'd be cold.''

''I'm out here all alone in the desert with a strange man. Anything could happen.''

Tommy yawned. "But it won't. I'm not exactly a Junius Witherspoon. And I'm pretty tired besides. And scared, too." His nonchalance was a little studied.

"But it could happen," said Louise. She lay rigid beside him.

He rolled over and propped himself up with one elbow. "Here. Take my revolver. There's one bullet left, remember? You're safe."

"You idiot," said Louise. "Listen. I'm nineteen years old. And I might die out here in the desert. No one will ever know what happened to me. And," she said in a whisper, "I will have died never knowing the experience of physical love." She turned her face away from him.

Tommy sat up, startled. Then his face relaxed into a smile. "I guess I better keep that gun myself," he said slowly. "Just one bullet stands between me and dishonor."

She turned to face him again, her eyes wide with anger. "Oh, you're perfectly horrible," she said. "How could you say such a thing? Of all the men to die with, I end up with you."

He took her by the shoulders and kissed her rather roughly. Then, his lips hovering just above hers, he said huskily, "Louise, you're just a kid and you're scared and you don't know what you're talking about."

"I'm not just a kid," she said breathlessly, touching his cheek with the tips of her fingers.

"And besides, we're not going to die out here. I'm not going to let you die. You got that?"

Trembling and silent, she nodded slowly. He stood and drew her up with him. "We're going to get back on those horses," he said, "and keep going north. I was wrong to want to stop." He picked her up and carried her over to the palomino. He helped her up onto the horse and patted its nose. " 'Course, if we're still wandering out here tomorrow night, well then maybe you got yourself a deal." He winked and she glared at him. "You're awful," she said.

George leading the way, Gustav and Maude walked

from the quiet little station at Aztec, Arizona, up the main street of the town. It was hot and dusty and dry.

"Hardly looks like a hotbed of German spies, does it?" said Maude, beginning to wonder if she hadn't come on a fool's errand. There was one unpaved street—and a cluster of buildings with dirty and broken windowpanes. "Why, it's practically a ghost town," she said. Gustav helped her step up onto a wooden sidewalk. A red dog was napping in the middle of the road.

"Up here," George called back to them. "There's a hotel."

The three of them pushed through the swinging doors out of the sun into the dark interior of the Aztec Hotel. There was a rather elaborately carved bar along one side of the room, and a sea of tables on the polished wood floor, but the place was pretty well deserted. There was one table of men playing cards, and a bartender polishing glasses and watching the travelers' arrival with interest.

"Golly," said George. "It looks like something from a Bronco Billy movie." He set his suitcase down heavily. The card players turned to look at them.

"What can I do for you folks?" asked the man polishing glasses. He had leathery skin, a bald head with just a fringe of grizzled hair on it, and flat, narrow, yellowish eyes.

"We'd like rooms," said Gustav.

Silently the man fished around under the bar. "I got a book here somewhere," he said. Finally, he produced an old leather-bound book. "You got a pen?" he asked.

Gustav signed the book, "Mr. and Mrs. G. S. Van Damm and George Smith."

"We'll want two rooms, please," he said, while Maude averted her eyes, embarrassed. She hadn't really thought about sleeping arrangements. They hadn't much of a plan at all, she realized. They'd tried so hard to get to Aztec that they hadn't given too much thought as to how to proceed once they arrived.

The man seemed to be looking for keys, now. "That'll be three dollars as a deposit," he said. Gustav gave him the money. "Now, the rooms might be a little stuffy. But we'll air 'em out for you and they'll be okay by tonight. Haven't been used much." He slapped two keys on the bar.

"So I see." Gustav was examining the register. "You haven't had any guests for some time."

"This is practically a dead town. Ever since the mine closed down five years ago. Kind of makes me wonder what you folks are doing here." He gazed at them frankly.

"Oh." Maude smiled and put her arm around George. "My poor little brother suffers so from asthma. We were told the desert air would be just the thing for him."

George gave a wan smile and wheezed.

"Strange," said Gustav, screwing the cap back on his fountain pen. "I thought the mines had been reopened. The Aztec Mining Company is around here somewhere, isn't it?"

Suddenly the man's eyes grew wary and he slammed the book shut. "You in the mining business?"

"No, no, just all kinds of business. It seems I heard something of the Aztec Mining Company."

Behind them they heard the scraping of a chair on the wooden floor. A short man with a spiky brown beard was coming over to them. He wore a blue checked shirt and red suspenders and faded Levi pants.

"He asking about the mine?" the newcomer asked the man behind the bar.

"That's right."

"Sheriff'll be mighty interested to hear that."

"The sheriff?" Maude was surprised.

"That's right. He's always on the lookout for nosy parkers coming and asking about the mine."

"Why?" demanded Maude.

"He doesn't want to see any trouble. No union men coming in here, causing trouble, and nobody coming in trying to learn what's going on there. Just a word to the wise." He winked.

"Gee, that's too bad," said George. "I was hoping we could go on a tour of the mines. Might be kind of interesting."

Maude glared at him. George never knew when to shut up.

"You in or out?" came a query from the card table.

"I'm in, I'm in." The short man with the brown beard clomped back to the corner. One of the card players had his back to the bar, the other, who seemed to be watching Maude, Gustav, and George intently, was a tall Indian with black hair to his shoulders, parted in the middle and tied around his forehead with a bandanna. Without taking his dark, unshaking eyes off them, he flung a card down on the table.

"Say, is there anyplace in this town we could get a good lunch?" said George now. "I'm famished."

"Desert air seems to be doing the boy a world of good," said the man with yellow eyes. "He's already got his appetite back. I can fix you up with lunch. Take a seat."

"Thank you," said Gustav.

"And if you still want the rooms, I'll take your bags up now," he said.

"There's just one little problem," said Gustav, holding up his hand. "I seem to have used up all my small bills. Can you exchange a hundred dollar bill?"

The man with yellow eyes, bending over the suitcases, paused and looked up. "We'll work something out," he said.

"See," said the short, bearded card player, laughing in a strange, snuffly way. "Whoever said the mine don't bring money to town? Why, this gentleman's plenty interested in the mine and he's got hundred dollar bills to throw around."

"You talk too much, Charlie," said the Indian. "Play cards and shut up."

"What are you trying to do?" said Maude in a whisper as they sat down. "Get us killed? I have a feeling they've got a few desperados in this town willing to do just about anything for a hundred dollar bill."

"Just trying to save some time," said Gustav. "From what I can see, the mine hasn't brought much prosperity to this hole. I can't think the people here feel much loyalty to the place.''

"Apparently the sheriff does," said George.

"Probably graft and corruption behind that," said Maude. Gustav hushed them all up as the man came back with a coffee pot. "I'll get you started with coffee now," he said. "Don't pay attention to Charlie." He poured syrupy looking coffee into three heavy, white china cups. "He makes a big fuss about everything. It comes of this being such a quiet place and all. Nothing much happens here."

From outside the swinging doors they heard the pounding of horses' hooves.

Outside, Tommy and Louise were barrelling down Main Street on Mr. Witherspoon's horses. The sleeping red dog woke from his slumber and ran arthritically out of the way.

Louise's head was back, she was laughing and saying, "We did it. We did it. We're all right." Tommy, grinning at her side, said, "I promised you I'd save you, stupid."

They reined in their horses outside the Aztec Hotel. "There's got to be a telephone here," said Louise. "I'll call Daddy long distance right away and tell him I'm safe. And then we can have a bath and something really scrumptious to eat."

Tommy eyed the unpainted facade dubiously. "We'll see," he said. "It's not exactly the Ritz."

They dismounted and looped the reins over the old hitching post that stood there.

"Oh, Tommy, I don't care. It looks like the Ritz to me."

She was just about to push through the swinging slatted doors when Tommy reached out for her. "Wait a minute," he said. "Have you got any money?" They stood facing each other at the threshold.

"Of course not," she said. "Have you?"

He shook his head. Louise shrugged. "Daddy will wire us some. Until then, we'll just have them keep everything on account." She tilted her head to one side and smiled up at him.

"Your face is dirty," said Tommy. "You think they'll give you credit with a dirty face like that?"

"Don't be silly, of course they will," she said. "You just watch. We'll manage somehow. Don't worry."

They started inside once again and Louise touched him on the arm. Her merry little face looked very serious all of a sudden.

"Tommy, what I said last night in the desert. I'm so embarrassed. You must think I'm the worst kind of little fool."

"Louise . . ."

She held up her fingers and touched his mouth lightly. "I just want to say how grateful I am to you. I really must have sounded idiotic."

If anyone was idiotic, I was, said Tommy to himself. To Louise he said, "We'll forget all about it."

Louise's eyes blazed with anger. "You *will*? Well, I may be dirty and untidy, but in San Francisco there are plenty of men who wouldn't forget it for a second."

"Louise, you're pretty, all right, but you're a lot of trouble," said Tommy, his voice rising too. "Now just shut up, okay?" He took her in his arms and kissed her long and hard.

Inside the saloon bar of the Aztec Hotel, Maude, Gustav, George, the yellow-eyed hotel owner and the three card players watched the swinging doors. Beneath them they saw two pairs of boots, the tall riding boots on tiptoe, very close to each other. Above the doors they saw the tops of two dusty heads in an embrace.

The doors swung open, and Louise and Tommy were framed in the doorway, lit by the harsh sunlight from outside.

"My God," said Maude standing up at the table. "It's Louise Arbor."

"Mrs. Cavendish," cried Louise in a strangled little voice. "I suppose you've heard everything I've said and it'll all end up in your horrible newspaper. Oh, this is terrible."

# CHAPTER
# 21

$S$OPHIE Von Gluck wore a burnt-orange gabardine traveling suit. Her matching hat was trimmed with soft, brown doves. She leaned out of the window of her train, blowing kisses to her admiring public. There was a good crowd there—mostly young men. Sophie was en route to New Orleans, and the train had already begun to emit regular, heavy puffs of smoke; the wheels began to turn and the car jerked. Her hand went to her hat, and she held on to it charmingly while waving with her other hand, gloved in light brown glacé kid.

Just as the whistle blew, Franz Kessler ran to the side of the train and thrust a bouquet of yellow roses through the window at her. Sophie smiled prettily and took them. "Read the note," said Franz Kessler, running alongside the train. "There's a message from Aztec."

Sophie sat down heavily, flung the roses at her maid, and opened the envelope that had been fastened to the bouquet. A slow smile passed over her features. Gottlieb seemed to have pulled it off. And, if the train wasn't delayed, she'd be able to be there at the final moment. She pressed the message to her breast and cast her eyes upward in a rather operatic gesture of joy.

Of course, she thought, after the moment of ecstasy had

passed, there was still plenty of unfinished business to attend to. The scientist and the girl had served their purpose. They would have to be disposed of. And then there was Maude Teasdale Cavendish. There was no evidence that the bomb had done its work. She was altogether too lucky, that Maude Cavendish. And finally, there was Gustav. Sophie wanted to settle that score herself. But whatever had happened to him, he'd never succeed in stopping the plan now. Within days, all the revolutionary factions in Mexico would be united against their neighbor to the north, and the United States would be hopelessly embroiled in a war on her own border. There was plenty of time for the Cavendish woman and for Gustav after that.

Sophie watched her maid leave with the roses. She leaned back on the seat and smiled a contented smile. In a few days, the course of history would have been changed. And Sophie would be singing Dalilo in New Orleans. No one would know how important she had been. It was absolutely delicious.

Gustav, George, Maude, Tommy, and Louise were finishing up their lunch in the Aztec Hotel. "But it's marvelous," said Maude, leaning over the table, her eyes glistening. "I'll wire Mr. McLaren immediately." Gustav put his hand on hers. "Not so fast. Let's talk about this a little more."

"But the escape across the desert, the daring young aviator—why, it's incredible."

"I must speak to Daddy right away," said Louise. "I want him to know I'm safe."

"Louise," said Maude softly. "He isn't home. I looked for you in Palo Alto. He's gone. And your butler wouldn't tell a soul where he's been. He left on the train, very agitated. And then apparently he sent for some things from his lab. Your butler sent a crate of things here—to Aztec, Arizona."

"But that means—"

"He must be back there," said Tommy in a whisper.

"But what's Daddy got to do with all this?" said Louise.

Gustav spoke gently, with a wary eye on the door back into the kitchen, "Miss Arbor, what kind of a scientist is your father?"

"He's a chemist. He specializes in gases. But what's that got to do with it?"

Tommy glanced at Gustav and the two men seemed to telegraph some idea. "I wonder," said Tommy, "if he's up on that mesa?"

"Working for them? Helping them with whatever it is they're doing up there? It's impossible." Louise shook her head.

"Not if they had something to make him help them. Something very precious. Like you."

"Daddy? A prisoner? And I left him up there!"

"It's just an idea," said Gustav tensely. He cast a glance over to the table where the trio of card players had been. Now only the Indian sat there.

"Well, if he's there," said George, tucking heartily into his steak, "there's just one thing to do." He looked around the table and grinned. "Get him out."

"We'll have to call the authorities," said Gustav.

"Not until I get my story," said Maude.

"Not until I get my plane," said Tommy.

"Not until we get her father." George pointed at Louise with his knife.

"Don't point, George," said Maude absentmindedly. "Maybe the baron is right. Maybe we should let the authorities rescue him."

Tommy shook his head doubtfully. "That place is an armed camp. Louise's father could get caught in the crossfire."

"Well, what can we do on our own?" said Maude. "Let's be realistic. Maybe we'd better call the authorities."

"What authorities?" said George with his mouth full. "The sheriff?"

"Well, why not?" said Louise. "It's a start."

"The sheriff's a crook," said George. "On the mine payroll."

Tommy's eyes opened wide. "He is? You sure?"

Gustav nodded. "It's possible. He does look out for the mine's interests. Although, it now appears it's no mine."

"Well, what about the folks in this town?" said Tommy, looking around the empty room. "Maybe we could get a posse together or something."

"We'll have to pick our friends in this town very carefully," said Gustav.

"Oh, it's all my fault," said Louise. "I got Daddy involved in some horrible danger." She began to shudder and then to cry.

Maude rose. "I'll take Louise upstairs. She'd like a nice hot bath, wouldn't you, dear?"

"Oh, yes," said Louise gratefully.

Maude led her upstairs. Tommy watched her go with apparent reluctance. He turned back to Gustav.

"Now, let me get this straight. You think this has something to do with German spies?"

"That's right," said George. "They're up to something out there, all right."

"Gases. Huge buildings. Hmm. It's all very strange," said Gustav. To himself he thought, *and Sophie is behind all of it.*

Tommy shook his head incredulously. "It's amazing. How can they get away with something like this?"

"They can't," said George, finishing up the last crumb of his apple pie. "We're here. And we're going to stop them. I think we should somehow get a look at this place. Isn't that the first order of business?"

"I've had a look, and I'll tell you it's pretty damn grim," said Tommy. "I'd just as soon never go back there. But those sons of bitches got my plane."

"Think there's any more pie?" said George plaintively.

Gustav was pensive. "How many men do you think they have?" he asked Tommy.

George rose with his plate and moseyed toward the kitchen. He gave the tall Indian a frankly curious stare as he went by, pushing his glasses into position. The Indian's arm shot out and restrained him.

"You people want to take a look at that mine?" he said, turning his dark eyes upward.

George sat down eagerly. "What kind of Indian are you?" he said.

The Indian smiled. "Apache."

"I'm George Teasdale." He thrust out a hand. "I've never met a real Indian. I'm from California and they all died out."

"So I heard." The Indian's gaze returned to Gustav and Tommy leaning over their table in intense conversation.

"What's your name?" George put down his plate and sat down.

"Joaquin. Joaquin Cruz. I've got a longer one white people can't say."

"I *am* sort of interested in that mine," said George. "Folks around here seem kind of closed-mouth about it, I gathered."

"Why don't you introduce me to those other fellows, George? Maybe we can do some business."

Maude answered the knock at the door of the room. The Aztec Hotel proprietor, who seemed to comprise the entire staff, handed her another large kettle of water.

"Thank you," she said. "If you'll just wait and heat up one more kettleful, I'm sure that will be satisfactory."

She went into the room where Louise sat, knees to her chest in a large cast-iron bathtub, and poured the water in around her. "Watch out," she said, "it's hot."

"It's wonderful," said Louise rhapsodically.

Maude went back to the door of the room. "And we'll need plenty of towels." The man with yellow eyes nodded, and left with the empty kettle.

Maude went back to Louise's side, crossed her arms, and leaned against a chest of drawers. Louise was working hard to get more lather from a cake of yellow kitchen soap. It was an old-fashioned room with dark oak furniture, a big brass bed and gray and white striped paper.

"You've been through a horrible ordeal," said Maude, thinking of the story that presented itself: "Debutante

Fights for Life in Savage Wilderness. Our Reporter Soothes Brave Victim of Dastardly Plot.''

"But you know," said Louise, "I was telling Tommy—Mr. Cutter, you know, who saved me—well, I saved him, too, a little—anyway, I was telling him that after the dull life I've led it was rather exciting.''

Maude revised her mental headline: "Thrill-crazed Debutante's Brush with Death—'I Love Danger.' ''

"Oh, I know it seems silly," continued Louise. "I'm worried sick about Daddy. But it has been rather thrilling, hasn't it?" She extended a pink leg from the suds and examined it thoughtfully. "I mean, everything I've done before has been so *respectable*. That is, Tommy isn't at all like the young men one meets in society, but he's so—well, rugged.''

Maude sighed, and her arms fell to her side. "You know, Miss Arbor, it's really very curious. I'm not very respectable, and I try so hard to be respectable. And you are respectable—a pretty young thing with a good family behind her—and you try so hard *not* to be respectable. I wonder what it all means?''

Joaquin Cruz was now sitting at the table with Gustav, Tommy, and George, who had forgotten about his second piece of pie.

The Indian was sketching a map with Gustav's fountain pen on a piece of paper. "It's about a day's ride away," he was saying. "Down the San Cristobal valley and then a little to the west in the Pinta Playa mountains.''

Tommy pounded his fist on the table. "A day's ride. Why, in my plane I could do it in half an hour.''

Cruz looked up from his drawing. "I've seen your plane," he said. "It's tied up on one of those buildings.''

"You've seen her?" Tommy reached out and grasped the Indian's hand. "She's all right?''

Cruz nodded.

"I want her back.''

"I can't get her back for you," said the Indian. "But I

can take you there. I can show you a place where you can see the whole area."

"And why would you do that?" said Gustav.

"For money," said the Indian simply. "You have money, don't you?"

# CHAPTER
## 22

"**T**HERE, don't I look much better?" Louise had finished dressing her hair with some of Maude's hairpins, and she wore one of Maude's dresses—a lilac-sprigged print. "You know, I feel sure we'll get Daddy out safely. Everything else has worked out. I wasn't sure it would, but Tommy said it would and he was right."

Maude tried to answer Louise's brave little smile with an optimistic one of her own. She hoped the girl was right. "Well, we'll do our best," she said. "I'm sure it will all end happily." Louise, she reflected, was used to having her own way. She probably couldn't even imagine failure or disappointment.

"This dress looks ridiculous with these boots, doesn't it?" said Louise, lifting the hem a little and looking down at her toes.

"Come on," said Maude, "let's not worry about fashion now." She had been as patient as she could, trying to be considerate of Miss Arbor after her ordeal in the desert and her uncertainty about her father, but Maude wanted to be back downstairs to talk to the men about what course of action they would pursue. "Mr. Cutter won't notice, anyway," she added a little tartly.

Back in the saloon bar, Tommy rose and went over to

Louise. Maude had been right. He didn't spend a second admiring her toilette. "We're going to clear out right away, Louise," he said. "We're going to find your dad."

"Keep quiet," said Joaquin Cruz rather severely. And then he took a long look at Louise. "That isn't the nerve case that escaped from up at the mine, is it?"

"What do you mean?" said Gustav sharply.

The Indian regarded him coolly. "Sheriff's been on the lookout for a young lady who wandered away from the compound. The story is she's the daughter of one of the mine managers. She was brought through here a while ago. Apparently the girl's a lunatic who needs to be taken back there for her own good. On some kind of a rest cure."

"I'm not a lunatic," said Louise stoutly.

"The sooner we get out of town the better," said Gustav decisively. "Mr. Cruz can take us to the mine. He knows an observation point in the hills nearby where we can take a look at the situation unseen."

"How far away is it?" said Maude.

"About a day's ride. We'll need a few supplies and some horses."

"Back into the desert?" said Louise. "I just got *out* of the desert."

"Well, if they're looking for you around here, I think you'd better stay with us," said Tommy.

Gustav said, "Mrs. Cavendish is free to stay here. It will be a rough ride, I'm afraid. The terrain is rugged."

"Stay here? Don't be absurd. Why do you think I came to Aztec? For my health?"

Gustav smiled. "Excellent," he said. "Then you'll want George along too, I imagine. Can't leave him behind to get into mischief."

"I don't care who comes along," said Joaquin Cruz. "But I think we'd better get a move on. That fellow I was playing cards with—Charlie—he's got a big mouth."

"Well, the hotel proprietor can tell people we're here just as well as that Charlie," said George.

Cruz shook his head. "Not likely. He'd like a few

guests for as long as he can get them. And besides, the sheriff's not too popular right now. Thing is, everyone expected the mine to mean lots of jobs in the area. But so far, the only one who's made any money on the deal is the sheriff. His wife's always going up to Phoenix and coming back with trunks of new clothes from Goldwater's.''

''All right,'' said Gustav, ''let's get a list of provisions drawn up. You sure you can procure these things locally?''

''As long as you can pay for them.''

''I can pay for them. And I can pay you to take us to the site.''

George had taken the fountain pen and begun to compose a list. ''Food, blankets—it gets cold in the desert, right?—canteens, field glasses, first-aid kit, horses, of course. And—shouldn't we have some kind of weapons?''

''I've got a revolver,'' said Tommy. ''Compliments of the Aztec Mining Company. But there's only one bullet left.''

''Me, too,'' said Gustav. ''A Colt .45. We should probably get ammunition.''

''You're expecting violence?'' Maude was asking Gustav.

''No. I just want us to get a look at the place. But I want to be ready, just in case. I don't want to be unprepared again.'' He touched his wounded leg.

''You know the Scout motto, don't you?'' said George.

''Never mind, George,'' said Maude, but she said it kindly.

A little over an hour later, they were on their way. They headed south, through the broad San Cristobal valley. On either side of them were mountains—the Mohawk mountains to the west, the Aguilas to the east. They rode too hard for conversation, and it was hot, dusty work.

Maude was relieved when Joaquin Cruz signaled to them to halt. But then he said, ''We're going to have to make a little change in the route. A party this size leaves a pretty good track. We'll go west, onto rockier ground, to throw them off. It'll make us harder to track. Of course, if they know where we're going—and they'll have guessed—it might not work, but I bet we can lose them in the hills. I know this country pretty well.''

"Them?'' asked Maude.

"Take a look.'' Cruz gestured to the horizon. There was the merest trace of dust hanging above the horizon against the deep blue of the sky.

"Might be that sheriff,'' said George.

Cruz led them to the foothills of the Mohawks. Their pace slackened as the animals picked their way through rockier terrain. Maude rode alongside Gustav. "How's your leg?'' she said, brushing back sweat-soaked hair from her forehead. She was tired.

"It's all right. How about you? Sorry you came?''

"Not a bit,'' she said. "I want to know what's out there.''

"Well, whatever's out there, I can tell you one thing,'' piped up George. "It's some dirty German plot. Those fellows are pretty unscrupulous. Even the ladies among 'em are unscrupulous.''

"George,'' said Maude with feeling, thinking about her brush with a fiery death, "that opera singer is no lady.''

"You think this has something to do with that war in Europe?'' said Joaquin Cruz.

"That's right,'' said George. "But they don't know Americans. We'll whip them good when we get into the war. Don't you think?''

"No concern of mine,'' said the Indian flatly. "There's a spot up ahead where we can water the horses and lie low for a while. I've got a hunch those men have picked up our trail.''

He led them up a winding rocky path that didn't look like a path at all, and to the mouth of a narrow cave in the sandstone cliffs.

"Look,'' he said, pointing to a damp patch in the stone at the entrance to the cave. "There's a spring in there. It's a big place. We can go in one by one and there's room for all of us.''

He dismounted and led his horse into the cave. The others followed suit. It was a relief to get out of the hot sun, but Maude felt a closed, eerie feeling in the darkness, barely discerning the shapes of the horses around her.

"How much longer is it?" said Tommy.

"A few more hours until we reach the base of the hill. Then we spend the night there, and at dawn we can climb up. There's a spot where you can see the whole layout," said Cruz.

"Any idea what they're doing there?" asked Gustav.

"It was a copper mine. Mine was played out. Then the new owners came. Brought in all their own men. Built a rail spur from Aztec. Said they were using a new method to get out the ore that was still in there. The process was so secret, they said, that they were afraid others would come and steal it. That's why they're always trying to keep strangers away. I got curious so I went up and took a look one day."

"And what did you see?"

"Big buildings. Plenty of men. With guns. That's all."

"And gases," said Gustav. "Curious, isn't it? All those things Kessler's ledger says they brought in—mining struts, explosives, tents—it all fits with the mine story. But what are they *really* doing?"

"Better fill your canteens now," said Joaquin Cruz. "And let's go outside and see what the sheriff's up to. Where are those field glasses?"

They trooped outside the cave, and from behind the shelter of a large rock they passed the glasses to each other in turn. After a while, Cruz allowed himself a slight smile. "Take a look," he said, passing the glasses to Gustav. "There they go. Charging through the valley with the sheriff in the lead. We'll be safe now. It's a slower way, my way, but it's a secret way."

In the Aztec Mining Company camp, Carlos Gottlieb sat at his desk and gnawed at his cuticles. Everything was going smoothly—except they hadn't found that young couple. He imagined if they were still alive they were wandering around down on the Mexican side somewhere. But everything else was going fine.

The news that Fraulein Von Gluck would arrive personally had put him extremely on edge. The woman had probably slept with every important man in Berlin if the stories were only half-true. He'd have to put on a pretty show for her if he wanted his reward to be commensurate with his efforts. He'd have to get the men into their stuffy German naval uniforms and run up the flag. That's what they'd want to hear in Berlin. It made it all so much more complicated. And he'd arrange for some kind of viewing platform for her. She'd like that. It would add a higher tone to the proceedings.

It meant pulling some more men off patrols, but now that they were so close, he could afford that. And of course, he'd need hundreds of men when the final moment came. He'd find out tonight, when they had their dry run. Thank God she wouldn't be there for that, although the crews and the engineering staff, as well as Dr. Arbor, had assured him everything would go well. He checked his watch. If all went well tonight, or to be more specific, early tomorrow morning, well then, he'd be able to rest a little easier when Fraulein Von Gluck arrived.

There was a rap at his door and a young German came in. "It's Dr. Arbor," the man said. "He wants to see his daughter again."

"Tell him no," said Gottlieb, his voice sounding shrill. "Not until after the ceremonies tomorrow."

By nightfall Maude was exhausted, but she wasn't going to complain, even though the prospect of a night sleeping on rocky ground sounded wretched after a long day on a horse. Gustav had been quiet, there was a look of intensity about him throughout their ride that had made him seem even more distant than usual. He seemed preoccupied, yet doggedly determined.

George had seemed to find the experience a delightful lark, commenting cheerfully on the scenery—which seemed to Maude the bleakest she had ever seen—acres of parched earth relieved only by grayish, scrubby bits of vegetation and odd, sculptural rock formations.

Louise Arbor, however, had aired her complaints loudly. Maude couldn't feel too sorry for her. Louise's declarations of exhaustion were delivered with an energy Maude herself could only envy.

"No sooner do I get a bath and put on a decent dress," the girl complained, "than I get back into these filthy riding clothes. It's simply awful."

"Aw, Louise, let up, will you," said Tommy Cutter. "We should have left you back there so's the sheriff could cart you off to the Arizona state mental home. Then you'd be wearing a straitjacket instead of those clothes. I've been out in the desert as long as you have, and no one gave me a bath or a pretty dress to wear or anything. I didn't even get a champagne breakfast with that charming Mr. Witherspoon."

"Who's Mr. Witherspoon?" asked Maude. There was still so much of the story she hadn't heard. She couldn't imagine how it could all be put into a coherent newspaper story. She'd have to do a whole series. And Mr. McLaren would have to put it on page one. But of course he would. This was terrific stuff. And the story wasn't even over yet. The best might be yet to come.

"All right," interrupted the Indian. It was getting so dark Maude could barely make out his face. "Here's where we sleep. We have to make camp in the dark because I want to be ready to start climbing at dawn."

"We'll build a fire right away," said George. "To keep the coyotes away, right Mr. Cruz?" He sounded thrilled about the coyotes.

"We don't need to worry about them," said the Indian. "Mostly we worry about snakes."

"We're going to sleep here?" said Louise. "You know, it's much more exciting escaping than going out on an expedition like this. I didn't notice how uncomfortable we were on the way out of that place, but the way in is simply murderous."

Joaquin Cruz held the bridles of two horses and led them away. He turned to Tommy and said, "Maybe we should have left her back in Aztec."

"Lay off, will you?" said Tommy irritably. "Louise has been through a pretty bad patch lately. And she's worried about her dad."

"Why don't you and George see about the fire," said Gustav quietly to the Indian. "George's scouting experience should come in handy."

"You were picking on me a moment ago yourself," said Louise to Tommy. Maude noticed a tense edge to her voice and wondered whether the girl's nerves were about to snap.

"That's 'cause I like you," said Tommy. "Even though you are a lot of trouble. We'd better hobble these horses for the night. Where's that rope?" He and Gustav went about this errand.

Maude went over to Louise and put an arm around her. "You'll feel better when you have a bite to eat," said Maude. "Come on, let's put something together. Although my efforts on cook's night out haven't been auspicious."

Louise gave Maude a grateful smile. "I'm afraid I *am* a lot of trouble," she said. "I'm so nervous and weary."

"I should think so," said Maude stoutly. "My goodness, you've been through a great deal."

"You seem so calm," said Louise.

"Well, I'm rather worried myself," said Maude. "I want desperately to discover what is going on at that camp, but I feel as if I shouldn't have involved my brother. He's only a boy."

George arrived with Joaquin Cruz, carrying some dry brush. "Oh, Maude, are you going on about that again? I wouldn't have missed this for the world. What's for dinner?"

Dinner, it transpired, was canned beans, some tough biscuits charred by the fire, powerful coffee boiled up in a saucepan, and oranges. They ate quickly and without much conversation.

"Isn't this terrific?" said George. "Now I guess we'd better bury the scraps so the coyotes will stay away. And then we'll get our bedrolls out and tuck in. I know some swell ghost stories to tell around the campfire."

"This isn't a Boy Scout trip," said Maude wearily.

"No, it's better," said George. "I can't wait till the fellows in my troop hear about *this*."

Maude yawned, too tired to remember to cover her mouth. "They can read about it in the *Globe*." She smiled sleepily. "*Everyone* will be reading about it in the *Globe*."

"We should get some rest," said Gustav. "Cruz says we should plan our ascent at dawn. It's safer. Besides, I don't want to wait too long. I'm anxious to get a view of the camp."

"The sooner the better," agreed Tommy. He turned to Cruz. "You think we could slip in there? Just one of us? I'd like to get my plane out—and there's a seat just behind the pilot's seat for Dr. Arbor."

The Indian frowned. "We didn't talk about a raid. I'm just taking you up there to look."

"Just a thought," said Tommy.

"We'll reconnoiter first and think later," said Gustav. "For now, let's organize some sort of watch system. I propose the men take turns. The ladies may be excused."

"Miss Arbor and I can help," said Maude. "If I'd thought I would be a liability I wouldn't have come."

"Very well. But you won't object to having a man on your watch with you?"

"If you want," said Maude, relieved she wouldn't be on watch with Louise.

"Fine," said Tommy. "Louise and I can be together and George and Cruz, and then Wechsler here and Mrs. Cavendish. How's that sound?"

Everybody agreed, and George said eagerly to the Indian, "We can talk about the Apaches. I'd like to learn some Indian lore."

George and Cruz were each armed with a revolver. The others spread out bedrolls on the flinty ground and prepared to sleep. "Now, George," admonished Maude, "don't chatter at Mr. Cruz the whole time and keep us awake."

"We'll keep our voices low," said George. "Get some sleep, Maude. You're going to have to wake up well before dawn, you know. 'Night, all."

Three hours later, George, still animated, was shaking

Louise Arbor. "Your turn," he said. "There's plenty of hot coffee. Oh, it's been terrific. We heard coyotes yowl and Joaquin said we heard a mountain lion, too. And the stars are fabulous. You've never seen anything like it. Joaquin taught me how to make arrows."

Louise's blue eyes opened wearily.

The Indian stood over Tommy and nudged him with the toe of his boot. He handed over a revolver and Gustav's pocket watch in silence.

"It's pretty cold," George was saying to Louise as she struggled to her feet. "Better take those blankets. Want me to tell you about the fire? You gotta keep feeding it, but slowly."

"We'll manage, son," said Tommy, running a hand through George's hair in a gesture that had more male camaraderie than fatherly condescension.

"I'll try," said George, "but I'm so excited."

"I know," said Tommy, smiling. "So am I. This is a hell of an adventure, isn't it?"

Tommy and Louise settled down near the fire, and Tommy tucked blankets around them. He noticed that George had handed her a revolver, too. "Well, I already saw you shoot," he said, "so I know you can handle that if you have to. Think you can stay awake?"

She nodded and regarded him from beneath languorous eyelids, managing a sleepy smile. "But I'm too sleepy to talk," she said.

"Okay. I'll talk. I'll tell you all about airplanes."

She groaned.

"All right, all right. I won't tell you about airplanes. Want some coffee?"

"No, thank you."

He poured himself some in a tin cup. "Are you cold?" He didn't wait for an answer, but put his arm around her. "This is where we were last night. Out in the desert. Looking at stars. Remember?"

"Don't remind me," she said. "I made a fool of myself."

"No, you didn't. You know, Louise, I've been thinking. San Diego isn't that far from Palo Alto. Not in a plane, it isn't. How about if I came up after all this is over and Will and I have concluded our business with the army? I *know* they'll buy the plane if I can just get it to El Paso. After all that, I could fly up and see you and take you for a ride. You'll love flying, I know it.'' He paused and sipped his coffee.

''And Louise, there's something I want to tell you. I know I've been hard on you, kid. But I really admire you. Even when you complain.''

He turned to her. ''Well, Louise, what do you think?''

She was fast asleep. Her head had fallen on his shoulder, her eyes were closed, and she was breathing a little heavily. ''Mmmm,'' she said in her sleep.

Tommy smiled, stroked her hair, and kissed the top of her head. He arranged her more comfortably on his arm. ''Good night,'' he said softly.

Louise slept through the whole watch, but when she woke Maude, she managed to convey an impression of brisk efficiency. ''I'll be grateful for some sleep, Mrs. Cavendish,'' she said.

Gustav stood up stiffly on his bad leg, and Maude saw him wince. ''Still hurting?'' she said.

''No,'' he lied. ''I was just surprised to find it wasn't working the way I'd expected. I forget about it when I'm asleep.'' He handed her a revolver. ''Can you shoot?''

She shrugged. ''No. But I just aim and pull the trigger, right?''

''That's good enough,'' he said. ''I don't think we'll need to.''

They arranged themselves under their blankets and sat a few feet apart. ''What exactly are we watching for?'' said Maude. ''Wild animals or German spies?''

''I don't know,'' said Gustav. ''It just seems wise to be vigilant.'' He turned to her. ''I'd hate to think I've involved you or your brother in anything truly dangerous.''

''Oh, honestly,'' said Maude. ''Stop apologizing. If this turns out well, I'll be a famous reporter. And George is having the time of his life. And besides, you couldn't have done it alone.''

"No, I couldn't have," he said. "George's trick with that toothache bandage was ingenious."

"He's very resourceful," said Maude. "Thank goodness he's reasonably honest, he's such a good liar."

"He overdid it a little on the train," said Gustav, smiling at the recollection. Maude watched him in profile and she realized his smile was off center because the scar pulled at one corner of his mouth. "Carrying on as if I'd die on the journey." George had insisted Gustav lean on him and moan as they boarded the train. "And telling the conductor that I was convinced only my own dentist in Phoenix could pull the tooth." He laughed. "Perhaps that fiction saved me from having a perfectly sound tooth removed by those helpful people on the train."

"Did it hurt?" said Maude.

"My tooth? Of course not."

"No, I mean—" She traced the outline of the scar on his cheek. He took her hand in his and pulled it away.

"Oh. That. No. It was a clean cut. I was lucky. Sometimes it's pretty messy." His tone had changed abruptly to a reserved chill.

"Forgive me," said Maude. "I didn't mean to—it's just that it all seems so unreal out here in the desert. I shouldn't have asked such a personal question." She looked away from him.

"But that's your job, isn't it?" he said. "Finding out about people? Well, actually, it's not that I mind your asking. Most people stare at it and think about it and don't say anything, but they notice. It's just that it was such a silly thing to do. Part of a cult of German manhood. I was desolated afterward. I thought no woman could ever love me." He laughed. "It's a memento of what a fool I was. There to remind me every time I shave." He touched his cheek.

"Well, we've all made mistakes," said Maude. "Mine was Nicky, and he's always there to remind me of what a fool *I* was." She sighed.

"I've been curious about that," said Gustav. "Don't you think you still love him?"

"Nicky?" Maude's eyebrows rose. "Why, it's not like that at all, it's—"

"Shhh!" interrupted Gustav. "Do you hear something?"

They froze, listening. There was a mechanical sort of humming, a gentle throb as if from an engine. And it came from above them.

They looked up into the starry sky. Then a huge shadow blotted out the moon. Gustav began throwing sand on the fire, his eyes still turned upwards. Above them hung a huge cigar-shaped object as big as a battleship but long and smooth and rounded.

"My God," said Maude pointing, "there's another one."

At the horizon another of the immense ships sailed slowly and steadily through the night sky. "And another," said Gustav. "Look! Three in all."

"I've seen pictures of them, but I never knew they were so huge. Why, they're monstrous," whispered Maude.

"A zeppelin factory in the desert," said Gustav. "It's unbelievable."

One of the ships was overhead, now, and in the moon-light it cast a giant shadow on them that lasted for minutes as the ship cruised by. When it had maneuvered past them and headed back over the mesa with its two companions some time later, Tommy, Louise, Joaquin, and George were awake and staring skyward, too.

# CHAPTER
# 23

O N the ground up on the mesa, Carlos Gottlieb was jubilant. The maneuvers had gone splendidly. The crew, fresh from Munich via Mexico, declared the machines excellent. The whole camp had cheered when they'd seen the monsters straining at the lines, hovering above the ground outside the enormous hangers. It was the first time the craft had been outside, the first time the men had seen the ships in their entirety. It was indeed a stirring sight. Carlos Gottlieb himself had been moved to tears.

He hadn't been prepared for the awesome size of the things, nor for their buoyancy. The three zeppelins wanted to rise up into the air, and it took the combined strength of at least a hundred men each to keep them on the ground before the launch.

He was ready now for Fraulein Von Gluck. Indeed, he was almost happy she was coming, he was so proud of his work. And the final problem, the ability of the plant to produce enough hydrogen in time, had been solved, despite the failures and the death of Dr. Kohler. Carlos Gottlieb pushed Dr. Arbor to the back of his mind, however. He knew that after the official launch tomorrow, Dr. Arbor wouldn't be needed again. And the girl was missing.

The problem of the old man and his daughter seemed

insignificant now, of course, but still Gottlieb didn't care to dwell on it. He was making plans to drape some bunting on the viewing platform. He was sure Sophie Von Gluck would be very impressed with the arrangements.

Maude actually awoke feeling refreshed, though she'd had little sleep. Dawn had drenched the rocks around them in fabulous colors. And the bleak landscape of the day before seemed to have been transformed. The sky was a softer blue, the rocks were pink and rosy, more like living things. And the air was so clear and crisp and dry that it was bracing.

They made short work of preparing the camp for their ascent. The horses were fed, watered, and tied up in the shade. All the signs of the group's overnight stay were cleared away. They garlanded themselves with a few essentials—canteens of water, a bite to eat, field glasses, and their two revolvers.

"The secret is so simple," said Joaquin. "We must pass through a narrow space between two tall rocks. Most people would never notice it. But behind this space is a way to the top. And at the top there's a place to hide and see below. You'll get a fine view."

"I'm still reeling from the view last night," said Tommy. "Of course that's what those big buildings were—hangars."

"And those metal mine supports probably form the framework of the ships," said Gustav. "And all that tent canvas was really to cover the zeppelins. It's overwhelming."

"Well, I guess we know why they needed the explosives," said George. "Aerial bombardment. They're just waiting for us to get into the war, then they'll terrorize us from the air. They're fiends."

"And Daddy's been helping them." Louise's face was ashen. "Oh, it's all my fault. If I hadn't insisted on driving everywhere alone . . ."

"We've been over all this before," said Maude. "Let's get *going*. Don't you want to take a look at this place?"

Joaquin Cruz had made it sound like a casual stroll. It was hardly that. Once they had squeezed through the space between the two tall rocks they were faced with what looked to Maude like a sheer cliff. On closer examination, however, she saw that there were enough irregularities in the rock to afford climbing places.

Cruz led the way. There actually was a way up, a narrow, rocky path between the face of the cliff and smaller rocks on the other side.

They traveled single file—George following Cruz, then Maude and Gustav, then Louise, and finally Tommy. As they made their way up, Maude resisted the temptation to look down. It was steeper now, and she was making more and more use of handholds in the rock. She wiped the sweat from her forehead and reached up above her on the side of the stone wall. George had already scrambled to a level slightly above hers.

Suddenly she saw George with a huge rock. He had it held high above his head and seemed about to crash it down on her hand. She pulled back, staggered a little, and fell onto Gustav just as the rock landed where she had been holding on.

"George!" she shouted. "What are you doing?"

"Golly, Maude," said George, "it was all coiled and about to go for your hand." George held up a long snake with a pulpy, bloody head and an impressive rattle at the end of its body.

Maude regained her composure, and through sheer effort of will forced herself to look at the repellent thing. "Thank you, George," she said. "You saved my life."

The enormity of this fact seemed lost on George. "Think I should skin it and keep the skin as a souvenir?"

"Good idea," said Gustav. "We can put it next to the bullet you dug out of my thigh."

"How much farther is it?" asked Louise with a trace of apology in her voice.

"Not much," answered Joaquin Cruz flatly.

To everybody's surprise, he was right. A little while later they were gathered at the top of the cliff, unburdening themselves of canteens and satchels. Cruz led them a little farther along and they all positioned themselves in a narrow space between rocks. "Look," said the Indian.

Five heads peered over the rock. Beneath them was the compound. From their perch they could see everything. The area below was a rough circle, fenced in with barbed wire about three quarters of the way around and walled in the rest of the way by the rock face that harbored the watchers. Two roads led from the area—one a long dusty strip that Louise and Tommy recognized as the way they'd escaped. Another, shorter and steeper, led north to a rail spur that went the length of the San Cristobal valley.

"We're right on the Mexican border," said the Indian. "One road leads south, another north."

The compound itself was a collection of small buildings dominated by the three massive hangars. Some of the buildings looked like barracks. Others were small adobe huts, and one long, low building, set apart from the others, had a smokestack on it. Small groups of men walked between the buildings.

"They changed a lot of the old mining compound," said the Indian. "Built these new buildings."

"The zeps must be in their hangars," said Tommy. "Or maybe they've taken off."

"Wouldn't we have heard them?" said Louise.

"I don't know. Not if they headed south." Tommy frowned.

"But Mexico is south," said Maude. "Why would the Germans want to head south with their zeppelins?"

"Where are those field glasses?" George handed them to Gustav. "They're doing something in front of one of those hangars. Building something."

Indeed, workmen could be seen pounding nails into a boxy structure.

"Look over there," said Maude. "On the road from the rail spur. Someone's coming."

Gustav trained his glasses on that area and followed a Model T Ford as it made slow progress up the winding road. At the gate a small party of men stood, almost as if at attention. A woman got out of the car. Gustav drew in his breath sharply.

"Give me the glasses," said George. "Is it her?"

"Is it *she*," corrected Maude. "Let me see."

She took the glasses from Gustav's hand. It was Sophie Von Gluck, all right. And Maude could tell from the posture of the man greeting her that he was fawning all over her.

"Who are you talking about?" Louise was squinting at the faraway figure in an orange traveling suit.

"That must be Sophie Von Gluck," said George enthusiastically. "The beautiful and dangerous German lady spy. Let me see. I've only seen her through a keyhole— and out of a window for a few moments. I want to have a look at her."

Maude handed the glasses over to George.

Throughout all this, Tommy had been staring at his plane, a look of longing on his face. She was tied down properly. As far as he could see, she hadn't been tampered with. If only he had wings now—if he could float right over and get behind the controls.

"I wonder who that man is," said Gustav, still watching Sophie.

Louise squinted some more. "Give me a turn with the field glasses. It might well be the blue-eyed Mexican."

"Oh," the Indian spoke now. "Señor Gottlieb. The mine manager."

George reluctantly relinquished the field glasses.

"Señor Gottlieb?" said George. "My goodness."

"They call him the *aleman*," said the Indian.

"The German," translated Tommy. "And he's got my plane. He also kicked me in the ribs when I was down." He made his hands into fists.

"But where's Daddy?" said Louise. She was scanning the compound with the glasses.

"What does your father *do* exactly? I mean, I know you said gases," began Tommy.

"Well it's clear to me now why they wanted him," she answered. "Usually I don't pay much attention to Daddy's work. But I know what he's been working on lately. He's been so preoccupied with it. He's developed a new method for more efficient production of hydrogen. That's what's in zeppelins, isn't it?"

"That's right," said Tommy. "Why don't you keep your eyes on that factory building? Maybe he'll come out." Privately, Tommy thought it likely that Dr. Arbor's usefulness had ended. He'd seen the airships on maneuvers. And what these people would do with Louise's father once they had wrung his scientific knowledge out of him, he shuddered to think.

"When we escaped, did we knock over barrels of the stuff?" said Louise.

"Not likely." Tommy was surveying the camp with his naked eye. "That was probably diesel fuel. You need those for the engines on a zep. The hydrogen keeps 'em up, the diesel keeps 'em going. Hydrogen would have made a much bigger explosion."

"Yes, I know it's very volatile. Daddy said so."

"You mean the slightest thing might set it aflame?" said George.

"Too bad we don't have one of Sophie's little incendiary bombs," said Maude.

"Wait a minute," said the Indian, "what are you folks talking about? I don't want any trouble. I just took you here for a look."

Gustav had been thinking, and appeared to come to some sort of a decision. "I want you to clear out," he said to the Indian. "Can you send a message for me in town? At the station?"

"You send any message it'll be all over town," said the Indian.

"It's in code," said Gustav. He rummaged in his satchel and came up with his dog-eared copy of *Girl of the Limberlost*. "I'm going to tell Mr. Voska what's going on here."

He tore out the flyleaf of the book and began to compose a message.

Maude watched him, and presently she said softly, "You think there's a possibility we can't get out of here, don't you?"

Gustav didn't answer. He looked up and said, "You can't wire your paper, Maude. Not unless you have a commercial code."

"It'll wait," said Maude. "I hadn't planned on any posthumous glory. My journalistic ambitions don't extend past the grave."

"Come on," said Tommy, irritated. "What's all this talk? We're sitting pretty right now. All we have to do is figure out a way to get Louise's father out of there." He paused. "And my plane. And then you can tip off whoever might be interested in this little stunt these fellows are pulling out here. The cavalry can come in and clean out these vermin."

"You think you can go in and get Daddy?" asked Louise breathlessly.

"The odds are terrible," said Gustav. "There are guards posted all around the compound."

"Not as many as there were," said Tommy. "And besides, they're getting ready for some kind of show. Look."

He pointed to the platform the carpenters were finishing up. A large, black-clad Mexican lady was draping yards of crimson fabric over the structure.

"They must be planning an ascension. For Sophie's benefit," said Gustav. "Don't you think?"

"I see him!" said Louise, still glued to the field glasses. "Look. Over there. Near that long building with the smokestack."

They saw a tall, bearded figure flanked by two young men.

"Oh," said Louise, excited, "it's Daddy. He's all right."

"We've got to get him out of there," said Tommy. "We *will* get him out of there."

# CHAPTER
## 24

SOPHIE Von Gluck was feeling the heat. She made a mental note to loosen her corset stays at the first possible moment. She was also beginning to regret her decision to send her maid on to New Orleans. She wanted someone to take care of her—to bathe her wrists in cologne and dress her in something cool. She should have realized how primitive the conditions at the camp were, but she was still annoyed at the discomfort. Sophie was in a little sitting room furnished with nothing more than a couch with a Mexican blanket stretched across it, a couple of straight chairs, and a low table.

Carlos Gottlieb sat on one of the straight chairs and next to him sat his mother, a short, stout Mexican lady in a heavy black dress. She had black, shoe-button eyes in a round, wrinkled face, and a severe coiffure. Her hair was almost completely black, with just a few strands of silver. *She has plenty of Indian blood,* thought Sophie, and some of it showed in her son's face. It was as lean as his mother's was round, but the cheekbones were high, his coppery skin smooth and beardless-looking, except for a scraggly attempt at a moustache. Only his dusky blue eyes betrayed his father's German blood.

"It will be about an hour before we are ready," said

Señor Gottlieb in his carefully accented German. "Our tests at dawn were most successful. The German crews pronounced the machines excellent—as good as anything they've flown before."

"You can be very proud of your work here," said Sophie. A servant entered, wearing the uniform of a German sailor. He left a tray with a large pitcher of lemonade and glasses on the table.

"Yes," said Gottlieb. "We are *very* proud."

Señora Gottlieb remained impassive. Sophie had already been told she spoke no German. The old lady began to pour out the glasses of lemonade.

"I will tell you frankly, Fraulein Von Gluck, it has not been easy," continued Gottlieb. "The conditions here, as you can see for yourself, are primitive. And the production problems—especially for the hydrogen gasses—were most difficult."

"That's why I sent you Dr. Arbor," said Sophie.

"Yes, and we are most grateful. It was not easy to persuade him at first—" Gottlieb left this topic hastily, and Sophie detected a moment of squeamishness.

"In any case, it has been difficult for us—for Mama and me. I'm looking forward to another assignment. I hope," he said stiffly, "that I will be permitted to serve the Fatherland in another capacity very soon."

"Oh, but you have done so much already," said Sophie. "That is, if all goes according to plan, you will have served the Fatherland well. What we want from this operation is nothing less than a formal state of war between Mexico and the United States. That should keep the Americans out of our business in Europe long enough for victory to be ours. Then, of course, we will help you here in Mexico. The injustices you have suffered over the years from your northern neighbors will be avenged with the help of a victorious Germany."

"My concern is the well-being of Germany," said Gottlieb stiffly. "I am a German citizen. My loyalties are with Germany."

"So," said Sophie, draining her glass. "When are the ceremonies to begin?"

"We shall be ready in two hours," said Gottlieb. "Until then, perhaps you'd like to rest and refresh yourself? I'm sorry we can't provide the comfort to which you are no doubt accustomed."

"I understand," said Sophie, rising. "We are at war."

"Just so, Fraulein. But I think you'll agree that military discipline has not been forgotten, even in this place. You will see that our officers will be sent off like the heroes they are, with full honors according the importance of the occasion."

"Very well," said Sophie offhandedly. Gottlieb's German was becoming more pompous all the time.

"I hope," he said eagerly, "that your report to Berlin will be a favorable one. It has been very lonely, if I might say so, working so far away, never knowing if my efforts have been appreciated."

"Many of us work without recognition, Señor Gottlieb," said Sophie stiffly. "We must find satisfaction in the knowledge of important work well done rather than in personal glory."

"I have never forgotten my duty," said Gottlieb with a slightly fawning smile.

"And by the way," said Sophie. "We must do something about Dr. Arbor and that daughter of his as soon as we are sure we don't need them anymore. Do you understand?"

"Yes, of course." Gottlieb pulled nervously at his moustache. "But there will be plenty of time. Let us concentrate on the launch, now."

"It's a loose end and it must be tied up," said Sophie.

"Let me show you to your quarters," said Gottlieb weakly. "I must excuse myself. There are still some last-minute preparations."

"I'm sure everything will be in perfect order," said Sophie.

"How are we going to do it?" said Louise. "We can't just rush in there and take him."

"Well, we know where he is, now," said Tommy. "In that funny little building over there. With two guards."

"Armed guards," said Gustav. He was propped behind the rock with the field glasses. "It won't be easy."

"You'll need a diversion," said George. "Tommy and Louise got out because of the fire. Something like that will make it easier."

"What's this?" said Gustav, still glued to the field glasses. "Something's going on down there."

They all peeked over the ridge. Several men had arrived in the open space in front of the zeppelin hangars where workmen were putting finishing touches on the bunting-draped platform. The newcomers carried large bundles wrapped in brown paper. From around the compound men began to gather there. The bundles were opened. They contained dark blue clothing.

"The men seem to be forming some sort of a line," said Maude. "But I can't see what's in those bundles."

Gustav adjusted the focus of the field glasses. "They're uniforms." He observed one man shaking out a garment and holding it up against his body to check the size. "German naval uniforms."

"Naval uniforms," said Maude. "In the desert?"

"That's who's in charge of zeppelins over there," said Tommy. "The Germany navy."

"It must be some kind of ceremonial thing," said Maude. "All put on for that horrible woman."

"This is our chance," said Gustav, turning to Tommy. "It's the perfect opportunity. As soon as a man puts on a uniform he becomes anonymous."

"What's the idea?" said Tommy.

Gustav spoke swiftly. "You and I get in there. You'll need me because I speak German and I know German military drill. We get in that line and get ourselves a couple of uniforms. Then we bluster our way in to where Dr. Arbor is kept and hustle him over to your plane."

"I've got a scheme," said George. "All that canvas that the Aztec Mining Company records say was for tents—well, it was to cover the zeppelins. And the hydrogen is inside, in bags. Now what do you want to bet they drag the zeps out for this ceremony? It's probably like christening a ship or something. And last night Joaquin showed me how to make Apache arrows. We made a couple of them." George rummaged in the leather satchel at his side. "Now, with some of what I've got in the first-aid kit—"

"George," said Maude. "Be quiet." She turned away from him. "There's something else that concerns me. Even if you get Dr. Arbor up into that plane, how can you get out? That plane only seats two."

"Can we get three in the plane?" asked Gustav.

"No," said Tommy. "It's especially constructed to take two men and a gun and that's it."

"Then I'll have to get out another way," said Gustav.

"How?" demanded Maude.

"Look," said Gustav. "I think we can lower ourselves down this cliff on a rope. Maybe I can get up the same way."

"Up takes longer than down," said Maude. "You'll be a target for too long."

"Well," said Louise, "there may be another way. Give me those field glasses."

"I'll just go in alone," said Tommy.

"You'll never make it," said Gustav. "You need me. I'll put on one of those uniforms and start shouting German orders—thank God I've brought that silly monocle—and I'll be able to get whatever I want. I understand the German mentality."

"You do look the part," agreed Maude.

"I got out of there once—I can do it again," said Louise. Everyone in the camp is lining up to get their silly uniforms.

"Look, the cars are still parked where we left them. And we still have the radiator valves. Right Tommy? But from here I can see that the whole collection is in one place. I'll go down with you and wait by the cars. Daddy and Tommy can get into the plane and Baron Wechsler can meet me there."

"I can do that myself," said Gustav.

"Can you drive an automobile?" said Louise.

"Perhaps you can tell me how," said Gustav.

"Don't be absurd," said Louise.

"I'm going with you," said Maude to Louise. "I can take one of the guns and shoot while you drive."

"It's unnecessary," said Gustav. "We don't need you."

"My story won't be any good if I tell it from up here," said Maude.

"What about me?" said George.

"You go down and meet us with the horses," said Maude. "We'll be going out that north gate. A car can't get us all the way to Aztec. It's too rough."

"I'll arrange for a diversion," said George. "If you'll just let me explain—"

Gustav interrupted him. "This is a hastily conceived plot, but we haven't much time. We must seize the opportunity. Let me look down there." He took the glasses.

"Hooray!" said Gustav. "They've got some officers' uniforms down there. Just the ticket. Let's get that rope and arrange to get down there."

"All right," said Tommy. "Is everybody clear, here? Louise and Maude, you wait with the cars. I'll fly Dr. Arbor out, then Gustav will run like hell to that car. In a uniform he just might make it out of there with a fuss. If not—well—Louise and I did it once. It can be done again."

"Let me explain," said George.

"George," said Maude, as the men uncoiled rope. "Whatever you do, don't go into that compound."

"My plan doesn't call for that at all," said George.

"Well, what is your plan?" said Maude impatiently.

"George," interrupted Gustav, "I want you to go down with the horses. We'll come and fetch you as soon as this is over."

"Will this scheme work?" said Maude to Gustav.

"It'll have to," said Tommy.

"It'll work," said George.

George, I hope you don't think I'm crazy going down

there," said Maude, "but I've just got to do it. Do you understand?"

"Yes, I do," said George.

Tommy and Gustav were attaching ropes to a mesquite tree. "Now, George, as soon as we're down there," said Gustav, "pull these ropes up and get down there. If we aren't back by nightfall, go into town and get help. Understand?"

George nodded, Maude gave him a big kiss, and Gustav tied one end of the rope around his waist. "We'll go down first," he said to Tommy. Tommy nodded and tied the other rope around himself. The two men began clambering down the rock, half hanging, rappeling themselves from the rock wall, half falling. It was a short drop, but enough to kill them without ropes. It took them several seconds to get down, but to Maude and Louise up above it seemed like forever.

When they were down, George with the field glasses, and the two women scanned the compound for any sign that the men had been spotted. "It worked," said George. "Get ready."

Maude felt absolute terror, but she didn't stop to think. Louise seemed equally unthinking. They tied the ropes around their waist with George's assistance—"Double half hitch," he murmured—and crawled down. The sensation was rather like that in an elevator, a sinking feeling in one's stomach, followed by the actual sinking of the body itself. When Maude landed, with a strain of the rope around her waist and a horrible thud, she realized for the first time what she had done. She looked back up the cliff at where George was, but she didn't see him. She might never see him again, she thought, in a moment of panic. The women untied themselves. The ropes inched their way back up the cliff, and Louise took Maude's arm. "Come on," she said. "We've got to hurry. Got the gun?"

Maude nodded. It was tucked in her belt.

"Follow me," said Louise, and she flashed a wide smile—a smile Maude had never seen on Louise's rather pouty features before.

At the top of the cliff, George had coiled the rope neatly and begun to whistle. He took his pocketknife and selected a stout, flexible piece of wood from the mesquite tree. He cut it off. Then he unlaced one of his tall boots and held up the lace, examining its length.

Tommy and Gustav ran a few yards, then slowed their pace and fell in with a group of men making their way to the central open area.

Gustav overheard men talking in German. "We've managed for years without our uniforms, now all of a sudden they want us to get into those scratchy things. What's up?"

"I heard they arrived from Berlin six months ago and they've been in storage ever since."

"Ever worn one?" said another man. "They'd kill you in this heat."

"Not me," was the reply. "I was a merchant seaman. My ship was laying over in Baltimore for repairs when the war broke out. I did my duty, signed up at the German consulate, and next thing I knew I was here. I thought I'd be sent home. Or at least get a berth on a German navy ship. This is a crazy war."

"What are they saying?" muttered Tommy.

"Never mind," said Gustav. "Just follow me."

Gustav turned to the merchant seaman who'd been stranded in Baltimore. "Quit your grumbling," he said. "Once we get you *matrosen* in uniform we'll be running a tighter ship, I can guarantee you that. It's high time we had some discipline in the ranks."

The sailor from Baltimore swallowed hard and shut up.

The line inched forward, and at the end of it chaos reigned as men threw bundles of uniforms randomly at the other men, who tried somehow to put together a uniform.

Someone shoved a sailor's kit into Gustav's hands and he flung it at Tommy. "I'm an officer," he snapped. "A captain. Where is my uniform?"

The man handing out the clothing shrugged, and Gustav

rummaged in a pile of clothing. "This is a disgrace," he said to everyone around him. "Berlin shall hear of this."

Another group of men were sorting through a collection of shoes.

"Let's skip the shoes," whispered Tommy. "It'll give us a head start."

"Right," said Gustav, fastening a row of brass buttons. "All right, you just follow me and when I bark at you, watch my hands. I'll try and get my meaning across."

Gustav set off at a brisk, military pace, his features a mask of military correctness.

Near the rock wall they had just descended, Maude and Louise scurried along swiftly, darting behind a series of buildings until they reached the small area where a row of Model T's sat. They were completely alone. Maude felt exposed and vulnerable. "Get inside one of these and lie down," hissed Louise. "I'll check and see if they've fixed the radiators."

Maude climbed into one of the machines and crouched down on the floorboards. She was relieved it was all she'd have to do for now. To distract herself from her fear, she began mentally writing about this portion of her adventure. "Your reporter, crouched inside the machine, her heart pounding hard . . ." she began.

Louise fished in her pockets for the radiator valves that Tommy had carried out of the compound. She rolled out from under the car and, still staying low to the ground, felt above her for the cap on top of the radiator. It came off as easily as a jar lid. She emptied the contents of two canteens into the opening.

"Let's give it a test," she said to Maude in a loud whisper. "I'll crank and you press on the button above you. We'll see if it starts."

Maude poked her head out from the kneehole space she was in and, biting her lower lip in concentration, followed Louise's directions. They heard a sputter from the engine.

"All right," said Louise. "It seems to work."

From her hiding place, Maude saw the car door open

and Louise joined her down on the floor. Maude couldn't help but feel that the driver's side with its pedals had to be more uncomfortable.

"Now I guess all we do is wait," she said to Louise, who was curled up next to her.

Louise sighed. "It's not so scary when you're actually doing something. Oh, Mrs. Cavendish, do you think this will work?"

"It had better," said Maude.

"If it does," said Louise, "I'll be seeing Daddy very soon. Oh, isn't it thrilling, Tommy going and getting him for me? Men are so brave."

"We're pretty damn brave ourselves," said Maude.

# CHAPTER
## 25

I<small>T</small> took Gustav and Tommy no time at all to find the little adobe hut, similar to the one that had served as Louise's prison, where Dr. Arbor was being held.

Tommy slackened his pace for an instant, but Gustav turned and barked some order at him and beckoned, and kept walking towards the two men who stood there with rifles slung on their shoulders.

Gustav spoke to them quickly in German and they managed two sloppy and bemused salutes. He said something else to them—Tommy caught a word that sounded like "ooniform"—and the two left hastily. Gustav called them back, however, and Tommy stood there trying to look as severe as Gustav while inwardly cursing his companion for prolonging their contact with the guards. Gustav gave the guards another order and the two men handed over their rifles. Gustav gestured to Tommy, who stepped forward and took them. The guards scurried off.

"What did you tell them?" hissed Tommy.

"To go get in uniform," said Gustav. "Come on, let's go."

Tommy, a rifle in each hand, kicked open the door and stepped aside so Gustav could enter. Something about the way the man carried on like some comic opera Prussian made it easy for Tommy to play his own part. And if he looked scared, well then, anyone observing them would just assume he was frightened of this overbearing officer.

Inside the adobe hut, Dr. Arbor was sitting at a small desk. His head was in his hands. He looked up, terrified, and ran his bony hands through his stiff white hair.

"Dr. Arbor," said Gustav, "we've come to take you out of here."

"I knew it," said the doctor, standing now, his eyes blazing. They were, Tommy noticed, the same electric blue of Louise's eyes. "You damned Germans have got what you wanted and now you're going to kill me. You're swine."

"Relax, Doctor," said Tommy. "We're Americans. Gus here just looks like one of them. And sounds like one of them, too."

"If this is some trick to make me go quietly . . ." began the doctor, looking suspiciously back and forth at the two men.

"Louise is safe," said Tommy, wondering if it were true. "She sent us to get you out of here."

Dr. Arbor ran out from behind the desk and grabbed Tommy by the shoulders. Tommy tossed one of the rifles to Gustav and gave the doctor a clumsy half embrace. "I helped her get out of this place a few days ago," said Tommy. "She's a remarkable girl, Dr. Arbor."

"Thank God she's safe," said the doctor. There were tears in his eyes.

"We haven't got time to talk," said Gustav tersely. He was examining his rifle, breaking it open and noting with satisfaction the loaded chamber. "We're taking you out by plane. You're going to have to climb. It'll be risky but it's our only chance."

"No, wait. I can't go now," said the doctor. "Now that I know Louise is safe I can't let it happen."

"Let what happen?" said Gustav, his attention drawn from the rifle in his hands. "What exactly is happening here?"

"Zeppelins," said Dr. Arbor wearily. "They've got . . ."

"We know," interrupted Tommy. "We saw them on maneuvers. We'll notify the authorities."

"But they're leaving any moment now."

"Where to?" said Gustav.

"To Mexico. They're attacking Mexico."

"Mexico! But they've been trying to develop an alliance with Mexico."

"That's right," said Tommy, remembering his conversation with Junius Witherspoon about German agents arming Mexicans.

"The zeppelins," said Dr. Arbor, "I've seen them. They have American markings."

"What!" said Gustav.

"They've had to tell me a lot," said the doctor. He looked pale and weak, and he braced himself on the desk. "I had to know the range of things. They had me help them produce enough hydrogen to lift the things in the air." He paused and looked helplessly at both men in turn. "They had Louise. Otherwise, I never would have—"

"We know that," said Tommy.

"They want Mexico to think it's been attacked by the United States," said Gustav in awe. "It's a fantastic plan."

"What else would unite all the warring Mexican factions?" said Tommy excitedly. "It would ensure Mexican unity and war between the U.S.—out of a European war," finished Gustav. "It could work."

"You bet it could," said Tommy. "I've spent some time down there. They're a proud people. Big fancy machines like this dropping bombs—and our record down in Latin America. Why, every Mexican above the age of eight would be fighting American soldiers. And those Mexicans can fight pretty damn hard when it's a question of honor."

"My God," said Gustav. "Aerial bombardment of innocent civilians."

"We've got to stop them," said Tommy.

"Yes," said Dr. Arbor. "And now that I know Louise is safe I have to help you do it. Those ships are set to take off any moment with a load of bombs for Mexico City, Cuernavaca, and San Miguel Allende."

"But it will take some time to reach those targets," said Gustav. "If we alerted our government . . ."

"Listen," said Tommy, putting a hand on Gustav's stiff uniform, "it mght take months for the word to get out to the hills that it wasn't really the U.S. And then they wouldn't believe it." He turned to Dr. Arbor. "I know a little bit about these birds. There's a flyer in England who took one down from his plane. It can be done."

"I've watched and listened," said Dr. Arbor. "These fools don't know I speak German. I know where they keep the guns."

"What kind of guns?" said Tommy.

"The guns they're using on the ships. Some are already on the ships, but with typical German thoroughness they have spares, although I can't think the Mexicans will be firing at these things when they fly over. They have Lewis guns. Automatic guns with a belt of cartridges that spit out bullets. They use them over in France."

Gustav smiled. "That's right. But they build them here in America. I happen to know something about them. My last assignment was to infiltrate a weapons factory and keep my eye on potential German saboteurs. I've tested enough Lewis guns to keep my ears ringing for years."

"If I fly you around those machines, you can fire at them," said Tommy to Gustav.

"That's right," said Gustav. "If we can get to the plane." They smiled at each other then, and simultaneously a flicker crossed their faces and they both looked at Dr. Arbor.

"I know what you're thinking. Forget about me. Now that I know Louise is safe I don't care. Well, that's not entirely true. I had a lot of scientific work I wanted to finish. But I've been a traitor to my own people. If I can stop what I've done I don't care."

"Louise can take him out," said Tommy.

"Louise! She's here?"

"There's a little fenced-in area with a fleet of Model T cars about a hundred yards from here, along the base of that cliff," said Tommy. "Louise is waiting there with a car."

"She shouldn't be here. What's the matter with you boys? You said she was safe. You said you got her out of here."

"We did," said Tommy. "but she wanted to come back and get you."

Gustav took Dr. Arbor by the shoulder. "We'll march you over there and hand you over. Then you can take your chances by land and we'll take ours in the air. And maybe bring down those ships."

"If you don't bring them down," said Dr. Arbor, "I'll wish I was dead."

"You might be in any case," said Tommy. "But for Louise's sake, try your best to get out of here."


Up on the mesa, George had practiced a little with his improvised weapon. It wasn't for nothing he'd earned his archery merit badge. Maude hadn't had time to sew it on his uniform yet, but he had it. And although he had only two arrows, George was confident.

He untucked his shirt and tore at the shirttails with his teeth, tearing off two long strips of cloth. He bet it would work. He put down his work for a moment and went over to the rock that shielded him from the compound. He raised the field glasses around his neck to eye level and peered through them. The women were well hidden in the car—he'd observed that a while ago. And the little adobe hut was without its two guards. He imagined that part of the plan was working too. Now he just needed one thing to happen and he'd set things off.

He whistled thoughtfully to himself as he opened the first-aid kit and selected a bottle of disinfectant. This was the only part of the plan that might not work. He was no chemist. If they hadn't all rushed off he might have got Miss Arbor to help him. She seemed to know something about it. Well, he'd see. He wrapped the fabric carefully around the shafts of the arrows and went back to take a look through the glasses.

In a sea of navy blue—for the entire camp seemed to have been put in uniform in record time—he saw a splotch of orange. It was that lady. Smiling, he observed her through the glasses. She was walking through the compound flanked on either side by the man who'd met her—the man Joaquin had identified as Gottlieb—and the old Mexican lady in black.

George adjusted the focus and looked at Sophie's beautiful face.

Carlos Gottlieb consulted a gold pocket watch and placed it fastidiously back in his pocket. Everything should go exactly on schedule.

Fraulein Von Gluck at his side fanned herself furiously with a black silk fan Mama had provided. She looked flushed with the heat, but there was more to it than that, Gottlieb decided. There was a glassy look about her eyes and a twisted, voluptuous smile on her face that gave him the impression she was terribly excited about what she was about to witness. They took a decorous pace, and he watched Fraulein Von Gluck pick her way delicately through the dust in her orange slippers.

He thought to himself that he should use this opportunity to put in another word for himself, but it seemed futile. The woman had cut him off at every turn. Perhaps after the launch. Then she would see what he had done for the German Empire. It even occurred to him that perhaps he could channel some of the excitement he saw in her face his way. After all, he was the man who had made it all possible.

He smiled and offered her his arm, and she gave it to him mechanically, without looking at his face. Then, out of the corner of his eye, he saw Dr. Arbor. He was being hustled away by a very Prussian-looking officer. The man even had a dueling scar and a monocle hung from a ribbon around his neck. Next to him was a glum-looking young sailor. Gottlieb's mouth fell open. Who were these men? He glanced at Sophie with awe. She had managed to arrange for the doctor's murder without his even knowing it. He could tell from the doctor's slumped posture and the purposeful look of the two men with him that they were taking him somewhere to be shot.

Fraulein Von Gluck was even more remarkable than he had supposed. She must have known he would never be able to carry it out. She must have sensed the weakness in him and arranged for the work to be done herself.

He glanced at her, but she either hadn't seen Dr. Arbor being hustled off or she pretended not to notice. She was struggling to open a parasol.

"Allow me," Carlos said, seizing it from her and opening it at such an angle as to obscure the poor doctor being taken away by that fearsome Prussian and his burly assistant.

The sweat had broken out over Gustav's forehead. If it hadn't been for that ridiculous black lace parasol she might have seen him. But the man had seen him and looked terrified.

"My God," muttered Tommy. "It was Blue Eyes. And he didn't recognize me. It must be the uniform."

"Maybe it's the shave," said Gustav. "My God, that was incredible. Let's get moving."

"He recognized *me*," said Dr. Arbor, "and he looked ashamed."

Carlos, Sophie, and Señora Gottlieb had gone a few more paces when Carlos stopped in his tracks. All of a sudden he realized that that sailor was the American flyer. He was so frightened he was trembling. Mama was watching him, and her expression indicated she realized he'd finally recognized the man. How could he have been so stupid? It was the man who'd taken the girl away. And now he had her father. Carlos had been so overwhelmed by the fierce Prussian with his sinister scar he'd barely noticed the other man. He must sound the alarm! But what would Fraulein Von Gluck think?

Perhaps, he thought, his mind racing, she'd sent the flyer to kill the girl. She knew how weak he really was. He looked at her, his smoky blue eyes wide. She had such a wise, cunning face. What should he do? He decided to do nothing. The zeppelins would fly. Then he'd decide what to do. Nothing must mar this perfect moment. Perhaps she had taken the killing out of his hands. If she had, it would be a blessing. But if she hadn't?

"What is it?" demanded Sophie.

"The heat," said Gottlieb. "I'm sorry. It's my German blood. I'm not used to this heat."

I'll have time to think, he thought to himself, during the ceremony. Thank God Mama was so calm.

They were at the open space outside the hangar, now. They mounted the rickety wooden steps and stood there. In front of them rows of troops stood at attention. An officer gave an order and the two men ran to the hangar.

Over where the car was parked, Gustav thumped on the side of the car where Louise and Maude were crouched.

Maude suppressed a little scream and looked up. "Oh," she said, smiling at Gustav. "It's you."

"Daddy," said Louise, clambering inelegantly out of the car and embracing her father.

"Get in this car," said Tommy to Louise, "and drive like hell."

Gustav touched Maude's hair lightly. "Godspeed," he said.

"Be careful," she replied, pulling the revolver from her belt.

"No more careful than I have to be to get the job done," he said grimly.

Tommy helped Dr. Arbor into the back seat and Louise slid behind the wheel.

"Here," said Gustav, handing the professor his revolver. "We've got rifles now. You can use this." He clapped Tommy on the shoulder. "Come on. Let's go."

"Remember," said Dr. Arbor, "stay away from the gondola. Go for the rudder first."

"I got it," said Tommy. He gave Dr. Arbor a thumbs-up sign and winked at Louise. "I'll see *you* later."

"Wait a few minutes," Gustav instructed Louise. "When you hear applause or cheering or something of the sort, the ceremony will probably be under way. It's your best moment. I suggest Dr. Arbor keep down."

"I'm going to shoot," said Dr. Arbor with dignity.

"Well, shoot from a crouching position," said Tommy.

\*    \*    \*

Sophie stood on the creaky platform watching the men open the three massive doors. It was a little silly, she realized, for Herr Gottlieb to have arranged for all three to be unveiled at once like this, but she also admired the drama of the gesture. Herr Gottlieb had a Wagnerian sense of theatre. He could have been a great opera director.

Her brief moment of cynicism, however, subsided as she saw the blunt, silvery tips of the three ships emerge from the hangars. She had seen the drawings, but she was still overwhelmed. The size of the ships was enormous.

Hundreds of men with lines pulled against the buoyancy of the ships as they loomed towards her from the dark recesses of the cavernous buildings that contained them. As the gleaming zeppelins were eased out into the sunlight, silver canvas painted to look like metal, Sophie thought of the acres of opera sets all that canvas could provide. She also thought, as the shapes became visible, that the erotic implications of these giant, phallic objects gliding out, straining against gravity, were inescapable. Sophie put her hand to her breast as if to ward off a moment of faintness. The sight before her was absolutely glorious.

# CHAPTER
# 26

TOMMY took off at a run, but Gustav put a restraining hand on his shoulder. "No," he said. "We've plenty of time. Take it easy or you'll look suspicious."

"There's no one around," said Tommy.

"All the more reason for us to look as if we're on some purposeful errand," said Gustav. "Do you remember his directions?"

"Yes. I can find the place."

They walked over to a small tin shed, not unlike the one where Tommy had been kept prisoner. It was padlocked.

"Damn," said Gustav. Suddenly they heard the sound of cheering, hundreds of male voices together in a frightening war cry. Gustav seized the moment, pointed his rifle at the lock and shot it off.

Tommy ran over and tore the metal lock, still hot from the shot, off the door. They rushed inside. There were neat stacks of wooden crates there. Stenciled black letters said "Metal Mine Struts." Gustav thrust the butt of his rifle against one of the crates and was rewarded with the sound of splintering wood.

He and Tommy pried open the wooden planks and saw black metal guns inside.

"We're in luck," said Gustav. "The bullets are here."

"You know," said Tommy, "George was going on about a diversion. I wish we'd had time to plan one. As it is, the best diversion we've got is Louise and Maude and Dr. Arbor escaping in that car."

"All right," said Louise. "I hear cheering. Let's go." She depressed the accelerator.

On the mesa above the campground, George watched in awe. Three huge zeppelins hung in the air, held in place by a swarm of men. Now, he thought to himself, was as good a time as any. He doused the cloth around the shaft of the arrow with disinfectant. It was mostly alcohol, but there was another medium in the mixture, he thought, enough to keep it going. He lit the sodden mass of cloth, fitted the arrow in the bow, and let her fly.

He watched the flaming arc as it went toward the ship nearest him. This was bigger than any target he'd ever shot at. If only the arrow would pierce the skin of the ship deeply enough to open one of the hydrogen bags. And if only the flame would stay lit. It worked in that Bronco Billy movie against a covered wagon. It should work better with a load of hydrogen.

George didn't figure he had enough time to wait and see. Either his plan worked or it didn't. He arranged for the next arrow immediately.

On the platform below, Sophie blinked. Had it been her imagination? She thought she had seen a bright spot of light make its way to the zeppelin closest to the cliffs. The crew in the gondola was signaling the ground crew to let go the ropes, completely unaware of the light. Perhaps the desert sun had played tricks with her eyes.

But a moment later she saw another. The arrow pierced the canvas and there were two smoldering spots on the side of the craft.

Gottlieb had noticed, too. *"Feuer, fuego, feuer,"* he screamed in two languages.

One of the smoldering spots was now a patch of flame. Sophie began to scream, and a moment later the explosion came. A great crack echoed through the desert, and all but a few of the startled ground crew let go of their ropes. The zeppelin, listing and in flame on one side, nevertheless rose into the air, charred bits of canvas falling to the ground. One man clung to the rope as it rose, apparently in panic. He was lofted upwards, then he let go as the heat of the blast reached him. His scream was heard all the way to the ground. The whole ship was in flames now, and some of the crew leapt out of the gondola, fiery human shapes plunging to earth.

The men handling the lines of the other two ships let go of their ropes, and those zeppelins rose into the air. Their crews managed to maneuver them out of range of the flames.

Señora Gottlieb, ever impassive, crossed herself slowly, while Carlos Gottlieb grabbed Sophie and rushed her down the steps away from the scene. "Mama, Mama," he screamed, and his mother followed them down the steps.

"Jesus," said Tommy, standing outside the metal shed with the heavy Lewis gun in his arms, looking up at the sky.

"There are two more," shouted Gustav. "Let's go."

They ran to the hangars. Tommy's plane was tied up on the hangar farthest from the flames. Through screaming hordes of men they made their way to the bottom of the ladder. The two other zeppelins were now above them, hovering crazily in the air, their big wooden propellers revolving at top speed.

"My God," said Maude, looking up at the sky as Louise raced down the dirt road to the gate that led to the northern rail spur.

"They did it," shrieked Dr. Arbor.

"But are they alive?" said Maude.

"Tommy will die in bed with his grandchildren around him," said Louise. "He told me so. It's a while to the gate. Get your guns ready, anyway."

George stood up smiling. It had worked. This had to be a good enough diversion. Much as he wanted to stand there on the mesa watching the fabulous spectacle before him, he thought he'd better get down the hill and see to the horses.

The Lewis gun propped on Tommy's shoulder, the cartridges draped around Gustav, they began to climb the ladder to the roof of the hangar where Tommy's plane was tied. All around them, men were screaming. Gustav's leg began to give way as he climbed. He looked down and saw a man staring up at him and fingering a sidearm.

"Hurry," he shouted to Tommy. He'd dropped the rifle at the base of the ladder.

Sophie's dress was scorched. Her parasol and Señora Gottlieb's fan lay trampled in the dust.

The zeppelin had fallen back on the ground and lay on its side, blazing away with a white-hot heat. Charred bodies hung from the gondola.

Tommy and Gustav made it to the roof of the hangar. The man who'd watched Gustav ascend was following him up the ladder. Gustav was waiting for him at the top. As his hands reached the top rung, Gustav stomped on them and kicked the man in the face. He fell backwards off the ladder, screaming. Gustav ran over to the plane and threw the carbine in the rear seat.

"All right," said Tommy, tossing his gun into the passenger seat. "You'll have to spin the propeller till the engine catches. Clockwise. And remember to duck so it doesn't hit you in the head. When you hear the engine catch, jump in the rear seat. There's still two of those bastards up there and we have a chance to bring them down." Tommy was struggling with the line that held down the plane. "But first," said Tommy, "we've got to get her back to the other end of the roof. I need some room to take off."

Gustav, limping, helped Tommy push the plane backwards. His first fear was that the two zeppelins overhead would observe them and strafe them with bullets, but a glance skyward convinced him the pilots were mostly concerned with keeping their craft away from the inferno on the ground that could send their own ships to the same fate.

The two men, groaning at the strain, pushed the plane on its four wheels nearer to the edge of the hangar.

"Can you take off here?" asked Gustav.

"I guess so," said Tommy. "I landed here, didn't I?"

"Why did that zep blow up, that's what I'm wondering," said Tommy, putting his shoulder lovingly to the plane as he pushed it.

"I'm wondering the same thing," said Gustav. "You don't think our friend George had anything to do with it, do you?"

But Tommy was giving all his attention to the plane.

"Okay," he said, "that's good. Now spin her and jump in as soon as you hear her catch. Then let's go blast those sons of bitches out of the sky."

Tommy wriggled into the pilot's seat, and Gustav seized one of the blades of the propeller and gave it a shove.

"Contact," screamed Tommy. "Oh, this is a hell of a plane."

Gustav ran around the fuselage and dove headfirst into the rear seat, then he threaded ammunition into the drum of the Lewis gun.

"My God," he said, as Tommy tacked down the length of the roof, "flying isn't dangerous, is it?"

"Not with me at the controls, it isn't," shouted Tommy as the plane's wheels left the security of the roof and headed into the air.

The plane dipped for a few seconds as it left the roof, and Gustav feared they were heading down into the flame-filled space beneath. The fire was white hot now, and the complete skeletal structure of the disabled zeppelin lay exposed below them. Then Tommy pulled on the throttle and the plane leapt upward, leaving Gustav with a wrenching feeling in his stomach. Many feet above them hung the two long, silver, cigar-shaped zeppelins. "I gotta get up fast," said Tommy. "Those things can fly higher than this plane, and I bet those fellows want to get up as far away from the fire as they can."

The plane climbed up towards the sea of silver canvas hanging above them. The scale of the zeppelins was so large that the sky was completely obscured. It was as if their plane were flying in a silver-painted world. Tommy lost all sense of where he was in relation to the rudders—his target.

"Remember," said Gustav, shouting over the plane's engine, "stay away from the gondolas. Dr. Arbor says they're armed to the teeth." He was examining the heavy gun in his lap. "I hope this works," he said to himself.

Tommy was underneath one of the big ships now, flying level, his plane looking, he imagined, like a gnat hovering around a watermelon. Suddenly he saw the small gondola hanging from the belly of the ship in front of him. He even saw the men's faces.

He swooped and dove, but not before there was a hail of bullets from above the plane and Tommy and Gustav saw the zeppelin's heavy mounted guns turned in their direction. "They're American sailors!" exclaimed Tommy.

"They're *dressed* like American sailors," said Gustav.

Tommy took the plane back up and flew along the airship's length. They were so close they could almost touch its sides. They flew past a huge painted American flag on the side of the ship, and then Tommy dipped his wings and swooped under it. Now they were in the zeppelin's shadow. It was making slow progress away from the area—Tommy imagined the engines weren't properly warmed up. He sighted one of the engine pods attached like a wart to the bottom of the zeppelin. The wooden propeller was spinning frantically. "Ready?" Tommy shouted behind him to Gustav in the passenger seat.

"Ready," answered Gustav. He knew now why aviators wore goggles—his eyes were smarting from the wind. He squinted in the direction of the propeller and pulled down hard on the trigger of the Lewis gun. The recoil hit him in the chest. Firing one of these while propping the weapon against the fuselage was a far cry from testing them on mounts in the factory. But the gun behaved as he expected. He and Tommy both ducked as splinters of the airship's rudder flew through the air.

Tommy dropped down and swooped away from the ship, and prepared to approach another of the engine pods. Already, he noted with satisfaction, the huge ship had lost power and it even seemed to be listing slightly.

He decided climbing up over the ship this time would be safer. The zeppelin's guns were mounted in such a way as to be able to return ground fire. He climbed up fast, the way he did in his stunt flying, the nose of the plane heading practically straight up into the sky, following the huge curve of the zeppelin.

Gustav scrambled in the rear seat to brace himself with his knees and elbows while still holding the unwieldy automatic gun.

There were four engines in all on this ship. They had shot up one rear engine and now they went to its twin on the other side. This time Gustav managed to shoot out the propeller and get a few bullets into the metal housing of the engine as well. The propeller spun wildly then began to break up. When the final burst of bullets penetrated the engine itself, the shaft spun to a halt, the wooden propeller fragments looking like something a giant animal had gnawed on and crushed with its teeth.

Tommy pulled away and flew back to the rear of the zeppelin, and Gustav let loose a volley at the huge rear fins—the ship's rudder. Tommy didn't want to be too near if it fell to the ground. He could imagine his frail plane crushed under the lolling weight of the giant ship.

The zeppelin was dangling in the air at a crazy angle. The two remaining engines were straining to keep it moving forward, but it was careening out of control, threatening its sister ship a few hundred feet away.

"Let's get the other one," said Tommy as Gustav frantically fed a new round of bullets into the drum-like chamber at the back of his gun.

"All right," said Gustav, "but give those gondolas a wide berth. I don't want to shoot at anything that shoots back."

"Okay. Thank God those things can't turn on a dime." He turned around for a second and grinned. "Pretty fancy shooting."

"Keep your eyes on what you're doing," said Gustav, looking rather pale. "I don't think I like flying."

Tommy took the plane in a wide arc around the ailing zeppelin's huge rear fins. The painted American flags, so prominently displayed, were ripped to shreds where Gustav's bullets had torn them up.

The first ship's gondola was now alongside the second zeppelin's rear engines, pulling toward it. Tommy decided it would be too dangerous to approach them. He and Gustav would be in a line of fire from the first ship's gondola. The second zeppelin seemed to be trying to turn sharply away, although, Tommy reckoned, it would be quite a feat of maneuverability if such a huge object could be turned so quickly. A load of water ballast was released from the second ship. It was trying to get higher. Tommy flew under the second craft, towards the front engine pods.

"No," shouted Gustav. "We'll be in range of their guns."

"We gotta do it this way," yelled Tommy. "The gondolas from the first ship are alongside the rear engines."

Cursing, Gustav kept his head low as they made their way towards the targets. Gustav aimed and let forth a round straight into the approximate center of the revolving propeller. Tommy swooped away from it before Gustav had a chance to see if he had done any real damage, and flew under the zeppelin, his wingtips even grazed the canvas at one point, over to the other front engine. The crew in the gondola could barely see the engines, but the noise had obviously alerted them. Now, from the vague half-moon of metal and glass over the belly of the zeppelin, machine-gun fire burst out. Tommy flew out of range, but Gustav saw a rip in the plane's body near him. A bullet had apparently flown past his head.

"This is crazy," screamed Gustav, but he prepared to fire on the engine pod, even as he waited for more fire.

"They can hardly see us," said Tommy.

Gustav shot again, tracing a line of holes along the airship's engine housing. He heard metallic pinging. Then he went to work on the prop, letting the Lewis gun spew out its full complement of bullets around the whirling blades. Mercifully, Tommy finally swept away, the plane rushing through the corridor created by the two zeppelins, and circled around so Gustav could shoot out the second ship's rudders.

One zeppelin was now being pulled to the left, and the other to the right, and the two ships were on a collision course.

"Let's get the hell out of here," said Tommy. "I don't know what's going to happen when they come together."

Gustav was wiping sweat from his brow, his stomach was lurching from the aerial acrobatics he'd just been through, and his chest felt like a mass of bruises from the recoil of the heavy Lewis gun. His arms and shoulders ached. He flexed his hands, cramped from shooting.

The ships loomed towards each other like big, ungainly, brainless creatures. They met at an angle, and the two sides rubbed against each other. The remaining propellers were revolving frantically, but they weren't able to summon up enough power to move the big ships away from each other. The rear rudders' flaps with their American flags in shiny new paint, twisted back and forth in a futile effort at steering, nothing more now than strips of fabric on a framework. The zeppelins scraped against each other as if they were in some sort of a shoving match.

"Sparks!" said Gustav.

The friction of the two huge objects rubbing against each other had indeed created sparks. Tommy flew up and away as the sparks lit the canvas. Then one of the ships burst into spectacular flames, followed immediately by its twin.

The flash was so sudden that in what seemed like one moment the two silver cylinders were black skeletons barely visible in the center of an orange ball of flame.

Pieces of the craft began to fall to the ground in powdery showers of flame.

# CHAPTER
# 27

WHEN the two ships careened into each other and hung in the air above the compound, every man on the ground looked skyward. Sophie, who had been running away from the scene of the fire, stood still, threw off Carlos Gottlieb's arm, and ignored his urging her onwards. The airplane, a speck against the two ships, was looping around the scene, almost taunting the two giants lolling together.

Maude, Louise, and Dr. Arbor were making their way through the compound at breakneck speed in the Model T. Maude couldn't help but look up herself at the amazing scene above them, but Dr. Arbor, pale but steady, kept his hand on the trigger of his gun and his eye out for anyone who would try to stop them. All around them, men stood with their heads bent back, hands shielding their eyes from the sun. Others seemed to be rushing around in some attempt to put out the fire on the ground, dragging hoses and even carrying buckets. Louise, her mouth set in a determined line, kept on driving.

When they got to the gate, Maude cocked her own gun.

"I'm going to try to drive out," said Louise. "Like I did before. But straight through."

She approached slowly, hoping that the men would be

too bemused at the activity in the compound, and in the air above, to act. When they turned their attention to the car and its occupants, she would gun the engine and smash through.

They were alongside the little shack at the gate now. Three men stood there. Like everyone else in the area, they were looking up at the struggle going on directly above them.

One of the men suddenly saw the car and ran towards it. He cried out, "Stop!" and leveled his rifle.

Dr. Arbor shot him. A crimson wound spread out over his chest and he fell to the ground. His companions ran over to him, and Louise gunned the car and drove through the gate, shouting "Get down" just before they collided with barbed wire.

The car crashed into the gate, and then its wheels spun in the sand below. It wasn't going through the way Louise had so blithely promised.

The two men were running to the car, now. Maude crouched low in the front seat and poked her head out long enough to fire. She didn't know if she'd hit anything. Dr. Arbor got off a few more rounds. Maude looked up again and saw the two men running away, screaming and pointing upwards. Louise kept urging the car forward, but it didn't move.

Maude looked up. Straight above their heads, the two zeppelins were in flames.

"Tommy!" shrieked Louise.

"He's all right," said Maude, pointing to the plane a distance away from the fiery ships.

"Let's get through this gate," said Dr. Arbor.

They climbed out of the car. "I'll keep these men off. You get the car free," he continued, his voice tense.

The two women clambered around the car and began to attempt to free it. Dr. Arbor crouched behind one of the open doors with his revolver.

"I don't see how we can do this," said Louise. She was pulling with bleeding hands at the barbed wire that had become twisted in the car's grill.

Maude looked up at the flaming spectacle above them. "Louise," she screamed, "we're right beneath it." The zeppelins had drifted directly overhead. "Run!"

Dr. Arbor didn't look up. He shot one of the two men. The other, looking up at the zeppelins in flames above them, threw down his rifle and ran out of the area.

"Run!" cried Maude again. A huge chunk of flaming debris was coming down toward them.

They all ran, alongside the fence and behind the little adobe gatehouse, and then they ran some more, until they saw a flaming sheet of canvas descending. It fell onto the car, wrapping itself around the vehicle like a blanket, smoldering and glowing there for a minute until the whole car exploded into flames of its own.

"Quick," said Maude. "Through the gate. Onto the road. We'll have to walk out of here."

Tommy took the plane closer to the flames.

"What are you doing?" shouted Gustav.

"Looking for a Model T," Tommy yelled over his shoulder. He swung wide of the flames and found the road that led north out of the compound. There was nothing on it.

"Maybe they're already out," said Tommy.

"No," said Gustav. "Look." He pointed down below them at the flaming little car entangled in the gates of the compound.

"Oh, my God," said Tommy.

*It's all my fault,* thought Gustav to himself with revulsion. *I killed her.* But then Tommy said, "Look!"

Three little figures were making their way down the road, half running, half staggering.

"They made it," said Gustav. "So far, anyway. We've got to help them."

"Maybe we can do just that," said Tommy. "Let's see how small a space I can bring this thing down in."

He took the plane down, barely clearing falling debris from the zeppelins, and skipping the plane over the gate of the compound. Then, with Cousin Will's brakes screaming into the tires, he executed a bumpy landing on the dirt road. The plane strained against the flaps and the brakes, seeming to want to hurtle itself down the road, but Tommy, his teeth grinding and his face twisted in concentration, managed to control her and bring her to a careening halt.

When the dust settled from the landing, Maude, Louise, and Dr. Arbor were rushing towards the craft.

"Can we all get in?" said Louise.

"Not *in*," said Tommy, standing up in the cockpit. "*On*. Hang onto the struts and I'll taxi down the road. We'll be too heavy to fly. But it beats walking."

Gustav helped Dr. Arbor, now pale and trembling, all his earlier steadfastness dissolved, into the passenger seat. Tommy put his arm around Louise and pulled her into his lap. "I've flown like this before," he said to her. "It'll work."

Gustav and Maude sat on the two wings, clinging to the struts, and Tommy taxied the plane slowly down the winding road to the rail spur ahead.

"We got everyone?" said Tommy, looking around. "I don't want to go back in there a third time, I'll tell you that."

Maude thought of George. Was he safe?

"Daddy, you were so brave," said Louise.

"So were you, my dear," said her father.

"Got yourself quite a story, didn't you?" said Gustav, smiling his crooked smile at Maude.

"Got yourself three German zeppelins," said Maude.

"Just two. I think George may have got the first."

"Now what?" said Louise. "Do we drive this thing into town?"

"Look," said Gustav.

Coming along the side of the tracks was George on horseback. He was leading the other horses behind him. Maude jumped off the wing of the plane and ran to meet him.

"Golly, Maude," he said as he slid off the saddle, "did you see those zeps? Wasn't that something?"

\* \* \*

The following day Maude, Gustav, George, Louise, and Dr. Arbor sat around a table in the cavernous saloon bar of the Aztec Hotel. With them was Lawrence Ames, a portly man in a dark blue suit, with pointy, precise little features and a small moustache. His dark hair, parted meticulously, was glossy and close to his egg-shaped head so that he looked like a wooden doll with painted hair. He wore a blue and white polka-dotted silk tie.

Lawrence Ames was an agent of the United States Secret Service, and he'd been dispatched to Aztec from Salt Lake City after the service had received word from Mr. Voska at the Pneumograph Company in New York about the contents of a telegram sent in secret code by one Joaquin Cruz.

"The government is grateful," Mr. Ames said now, "beyond anything I can convey. I've received word from President Wilson to express to all of you our sincere thanks."

"It was only what any citizen would do, given the chance," said George modestly. He took off his glasses and polished them on the tablecloth.

"I suppose this means war with Germany," said Gustav.

Mr. Ames was silent a moment and looked at Gustav thoughtfully. "That's not my affair," he said. "I just do my own work and leave those decisions to others. But I can tell you, Baron, that even this affair, flagrant as it is, might not bring us into the European war. The president's views on neutrality are well-known."

"It's preposterous," said Gustav. "When the American public learns that they tried to drag us—that is, America—into a war with Mexico—that they were going to bomb innocent civilians? They kidnapped Dr. Arbor's daughter and forced him to do their dirty work. They tried to kill Maude—Mrs. Cavendish."

Mr. Ames cleared his throat. "The American public will never know," he said calmly. "And we're asking you to keep it that way."

"But my story! I wired the whole story to the *Globe*," began Maude, leaning over the table, her eyes blazing.

"Your story will not appear," said Mr. Ames. He sighed. "That's already been seen to. We've appealed to the patriotism of the publisher and he's assured us the story will not be run."

Maude waved her arms excitedly. "You can't do this. The public has a right to know. And I have a right to tell my story."

"It is felt in certain quarters," said Mr. Ames, looking slightly uncomfortable, "that the morale of the American people would be severely tried if they knew our government allowed such a thing to happen. And morale," he continued gravely, "is important if we are to go to war."

Gustav smiled. "We will go to war. We will stop the Kaiser."

"Of course we will," said George. "I imagine it's only a matter of time."

"Just because the government is embarrassed," began Maude, "is no reason to keep me on the society beat."

"A division of the cavalry at Fort Huachuca is already clearing out that nest of spies up on the mesa," said Mr. Ames. "When they're finished, the entire incident will be forgotten."

"I can't believe," said Maude firmly, "that Mr. McLaren at the *Globe* will sit on this story."

The only time Mr. McLaren removed his hat in the office was when he was going up to the fifth floor to meet with the *Globe*'s owner and publisher, Abner Farnum. His hat was off now. The publisher's office was eerily still after the noise and hollering down in the city room. McLaren wore his jacket, too, although Mr. Farnum was always in shirtsleeves, his arm garters hitching them up to the correct length.

Abner Farnum was a brown, wrinkled, bald wraith of a man. He had learned the newspaper business from his father, who had started publishing in San Francisco when duels were often the result of a fiery editorial. Now, Farnum sat behind his desk while McLaren eased himself into a chair opposite.

"The president says we've got to kill that story" he said. "In the country's best interest. He doesn't want the folks to know that he was asleep at the switch up there in Washington."

"We can't kill that story," said McLaren. "It's the story of a lifetime. Why, I've been waiting all my life for a story like this," he added redundantly.

"We're killing it," said Mr. Farnum.

"But Cavendish risked her life for that story," said McLaren. "She's the best man I've got. She'll cry bloody murder."

"I'm a patriotic man," said Abner Farnum. "Kill the story. I don't go along with this business that the president is always right, with one exception. Times of war. And that's what we're heading to. I want this country to think it's capable of beating the Germans. I don't think the story's good for the country right now."

"Well, you own the *Globe*," said McLaren.

"That's right."

"Cavendish won't like it," said McLaren gloomily.

"Well, do something nice for her. Give her some candy or flowers or something. Christ, McLaren, you aren't afraid of your own reporters, are you?"

"No, sir. Maybe I should offer her the police beat."

"If that's what she wants, do it."

"All right. And maybe a raise? Say five dollars a week?"

"Is that really necessary? You think I'm made of money here? You should know better than that, McLaren."

In El Paso, Texas, Tommy signed the contract on the lieutenant's desk and stood up. "You won't be sorry," he said. "This bird's already proved itself."

"We want to use it right away, and a few more like it, too, of course," said the army officer as he blotted Tommy's signature. "Can you get back to San Diego on the train?"

"Sure, if I can get off at Aztec, Arizona. There's a girl I want to see home."

The lieutenant yawned. "Oh, the one in that yarn you told me. The debutante?"

"That's right."

"Cutter, I like your plane. It's just what we need. But you don't think for one moment I believe that tale of yours about zeppelins, do you? Stick to flying, son. Let someone steadier and less imaginative handle the salesmanship."

Sophie Von Gluck, Carlos Gottlieb and his mother had been traveling for almost a day now. Sophie's white-hot fury hadn't subsided in all that time. The ridiculous little man at the wheel next to her had been silent for most of the journey. She hated the fact that she needed him to escape. As soon as they reached the wretched little Mexican town he'd promised, she would be able to shed him. And his horrible mother, too.

He turned to her. "It's not far now. We were lucky to have escaped. I don't know what would have happened to you if I hadn't got you out of there."

"Idiot!" she shrieked at him. "How can you even talk of our escape after your colossal failure."

"I am as devastated as you are," he said. "I had hoped that I would be able to prove my abilities to the Fatherland."

"You won't get another chance after this, I assure you."

"Well," he said testily, "you have failed, too, haven't you? What will happen to you?"

"What will happen to me?" She turned to him and laughed. "You silly little man, nothing will happen to me that I don't choose to have happen to me. If you think I'll take the blame for this, you're sadly mistaken. It was a coup I'd hoped to pull off, but it failed. There will be others, however. They haven't heard the last of me. But you—you are finished. I'll see to it."

Maude had rushed out of the saloon bar into the dusty main street of Aztec. She'd walked the length of the town and back again, and then she'd sat on a bench outside the hardware store and watched a red dog sleeping in the dust.

It was dusk now, and the surrounding hills cast a rosy glow over the place.

She heard footsteps on the wooden boardwalk and turned to see Gustav coming towards her. She moved over on the bench and he sat down.

"I'm sorry," he said, "about your story."

She shrugged. "Maybe it's not as important as I thought it was . . . not that I'm not furious anyway. After all, we'll probably be going to war. A while ago, in my attic, you told me that our lives aren't so important, in the grand scheme of things."

"Did I say that? I'm not so sure that's entirely true. I'm beginning to think our lives are extremely important." He took her hands between his. There was emotion in his voice. "For a long time my deepest feelings were for a cause, for principles, for a struggle. Now I . . . feel different." He wrapped his arms around her and pulled her to him.

George sipped his sarsparilla and looked up at his companion, Mr. Ames, who was nursing a beer and fiddling with his bow tie.

"When the war starts, are you going in?" asked George.

"I'm already in," said Ames. "There'll be plenty of work for the Secret Service."

"I don't think," said George thoughtfully, "I'll be old enough in time. But who knows, we might fight the Germans again. I'll be ready."

"I imagine you will," said Mr. Ames.

# About the Author

K.K. Beck has given us two previous period novels about that charming flapper, Iris Cooper, in DEATH IN A DECK CHAIR and MURDER IN A MUMMY CASE. Her three very young children are not keeping her from her work on a new book. She lives with those children and her husband, Ernest, in Seattle, Washington.